THERE'S ALWAYS A CATCH

CHRISTMAS KEY BOOK ONE

STEPHANIE TAYLOR

DON'T MISS OUT ON NEW RELEASES...

Want to find out what happens next in the Christmas Key series? Love romance novels? Sign up for new release alerts from Stephanie Taylor so you don't miss a thing!

Sign me up!

"We are each other's harvest; we are each other's business; we are each other's magnitude and bond."
—*Gwendolyn Brooks*

1

HOLLY PULLS SKIRTS AND TANK TOPS FROM HER CLOSET, TOSSING THEM onto the floral print duvet. The air-conditioning is cranked up high inside the tidy beach bungalow, the curtains drawn against the stagnant outdoor heat. The rooms feel crystallized with an iciness that cuts right through the humidity of summer on Christmas Key. A black and white wedding picture of Holly's late grandparents looks on from the nightstand, the closed-mouth smiles on their smooth, young faces both innocent and knowing. She holds a stretchy pink dress up to the front of her body in contemplation. It's short and looks good against her tanned skin, but it's the dress of a woman whose heels click on the pavement during a night out in the big city. It's the dress of a woman who eats tapas on South Beach and dances until dawn. It is a dress her mother would wear. It is *not* the dress of a woman about to present a plan for civic and economic development to a group of white-haired senior citizens who survived the Great Depression and WWII.

She tosses it on top of the discard pile and keeps searching.

A small mesh bag full of seashells sits on the nightstand, and a crumpled up speeding ticket rests on the floor next to Holly's sweaty shorts and t-shirt. Her golden retriever, Pucci, is hiding his big, shaggy body beneath the bed, huddling next to a forgotten page of the *Miami Herald* from 2011 and a chewed up rubber flip-flop.

Holly's bare feet slap across the cold tile floors as she mutters aloud to herself. The speeding ticket is ridiculous, nothing but another power struggle between her and Jake. She grabs a white sundress from a hanger; it's more dressy than her usual island attire, but not so much that she'll feel like she's in costume as she stands before her friends and neighbors at the village council meeting. Holly puts Jake out of her mind and instead ransacks her armoire in search of her favorite bikini, opening and closing drawers as she hunts for it. It's been her lifelong habit to substitute swimwear for underwear (just in case she feels like taking a swim in the tropical waters of the Gulf of Mexico in the middle of the day, which she occasionally does), and now she needs the right bikini top to wear as a bra under her dress.

Holly stands in front of the window over her dresser, yanking at a bikini string in a futile attempt to free one top from a pair of mismatched bottoms in the tangle of bathing suits that she holds in her hand. The clothesline she's strung between two palm trees in her backyard catches her eye; sure enough, dangling from the line in a neat, colorful row like the flags of so many tropical countries, are all of her favorite suits.

She closes her dresser drawer and cups her full, bare breasts in the crook of one arm before walking out to the yard to grab the swimsuit from its clip on the line. After almost thirty years on a partially-uninhabited island, Holly is of the mind that extreme modesty is mostly unnecessary—much like having any sort of formal rules about undergarments—so she strides barefoot across the wide blades of the St. Augustine grass in her backyard. Her long legs and unkempt hair give her the appearance of an Amazon gliding through a tropical garden.

Sunlight filters through the lush jungle of trees in her yard, the sounds of the ocean crashing onto the shore in the very near distance. The air smells of citrus. Holly stops to admire the deep tangerine-hued skins of the pineapple oranges growing on the tree near her back door, dangling from the branches like so many juicy Christmas ornaments.

"Mornin', Governor," a voice calls out. Leo Buckhunter sits on his porch just beyond the low bushes that divide their two yards.

"Buckhunter." Holly flushes immediately when she realizes that she's not alone. She tightens her grip on her bare chest and turns her back to him. "I didn't see you there. And for the record, I'm not the governor," she says, though she knows he's only trying to annoy her. In the few years that they've been neighbors, Buckhunter has taken every opportunity to get her goat. Holly is usually in the mood to dish it right back to him, but something about being topless in her front yard in broad daylight leaves her feeling too exposed to come up with a suitably snappy comeback.

"Of course you're not. No self-respecting governor would run around in front of her constituents with her coconuts in her hands."

Holly rolls her eyes, turning her attention to the string of bikinis on the line. "Well, this is Florida, so I wouldn't rule anything out when it comes to politics, Buckhunter. Will I see you at the meeting this afternoon?"

"Yes, ma'am. Though hopefully we won't be seeing quite so much of *you*," he tosses back, raising his dented tin cup to her. He sips his coffee, the gray-blonde mustache above his goatee twitching with amusement.

Buckhunter sits comfortably in the rocking chair he's crafted from the driftwood that washes up on Christmas Key's shores. Leo Buckhunter—though almost everyone on the island refers to him by last name only—is something of a mysterious character. He always wears the same half-smile on his face, lines etched into his rugged skin by years of laughter and sun. His eyes are the clear blue of a chlorinated pool, but with the depth and gravity of the ocean.

If pressed, Holly would *almost* call him sexy, but the fact that he's nearly twenty years older than she (her mother's age!) puts an end to that discussion. Not to mention that there's absolutely zero attraction between them. Buckhunter is sharp and funny, but even after three years on the island and countless nights of drinking and conversation, no one really knows where he's from or what his real story is.

With her sun-dried bikini in one hand and her chest still covered by the other arm, Holly tries to look as composed as possible. Because, really: why should she care what Buckhunter thinks? He might be out there minding his own business on his front porch while she galavants around topless, but, technically speaking, it is *her* island. She walks back to her own house as casually as a woman strolling the aisles at the grocery store.

Putting aside the aggravation over the speeding ticket and the embarrassing accidental peep show she's just given Buckhunter, the morning has actually gone quite well: tasks have fallen away from her to-do list with ease, and last minute details are sorting themselves out as if in the hands of some benevolent, unseen force. It's been a flawless operation from the moment she swung her feet off the bed and set them on the cold tile floor at dawn. Well, flawless until she saw the flashing lights of the island's only police cruiser behind her on Main Street. In actuality it's less of a police cruiser and more of a souped-up golf cart with red and blue flashing lights, but because it clips along the sandy streets five miles an hour faster than any other golf cart on the island, it does carry some authority.

Even now, thinking about Jake pulling her over fills her with irritation. Holly had watched the grimacing face of her ex-boyfriend as he stepped out of his police vehicle and approached her own hot pink golf cart, strutting up to the driver's side of the cart, eyes shielded by his reflective aviator-style sunglasses. What Holly couldn't see—what was blocked from her view, but what she knew was there—was the hurt in Jake's eyes that burned through her like a beam of sunlight focused on an ant through a magnifying glass.

"License and registration," Officer Zavaroni said, his tone void of emotion.

"Jake," Holly said. "You have *got* to be kidding me." Without thinking, she'd placed one sandaled foot on the pavement, ready to stand face-to-face with her ex and talk like adults.

"Ah, ah, ah—you stay put." Jake held out a hand, his big palm blocking her. He arranged his body so that his imposing stature was evident, one hand straightening his holster as he stared her down.

Why Jake even wore a holster was beyond her, but he'd told the islanders (with much bravado) that carrying a Smith & Wesson on his hip was necessary to make visitors aware that the island was being protected, and to keep them safe in the event that a stray alligator reared its ugly head. It had always made Holly nervous, that gun, and whenever he stayed at her place, she'd forced him to put it away in a pink Victoria's Secret box that she kept on the top shelf of the linen closet. Something about stashing a gun in a box that looked like it should be filled with cupcakes or panties just made it feel less dangerous to her.

As a boyfriend, Jake had always humored her and tolerated her quirks; Holly loved that about him. He'd laughed about her single-minded passion for Christmas Key, and admired the way she stubbornly devoted herself to the things she loved. Theirs had been an easy and satisfying relationship, and she'd never wanted things to change.

Holly waited in her golf cart, hoping he'd crack. The muggy Florida heat pulsed all around them with a heartbeat of its own as she sat on the seat that she'd covered in a pink and green Lilly Pulitzer print fabric. Perspiration formed on her upper lip, and a bead of sweat wound its way down her cleavage like a snake. She could feel the adventurous drop of sweat leaving a trail of wetness in its wake.

"License and registration." Jake stood over her. The memory of him on one knee on the beach came back to her.

Holly waited as long as she could afford to, given her busy schedule that day, but Jake's stance was unyielding. She shook her head and reached for her purse.

"This is ridiculous, Jake, and you know it." Holly shoved her license at him and flipped down the sun visor of the golf cart to find the registration she'd clipped there.

"I'm going to need you to get out of the vehicle." Jake stepped back, pointing at a spot on the pavement. Heat rose from the blacktop in visible waves, and Holly knew he was punishing her for her hesitation that night on the beach, for her wide-eyed stare as the moon glinted off of the diamond ring that he'd held between his thumb and forefinger.

"Morning, Jake. Holly." A white-haired woman in a housecoat and bedroom slippers approached with a tiny white dog on a leash. "Eight a.m. and it's already hotter than a billy goat's ass in a pepper patch, isn't it?" The older woman pursed her lips.

"Morning, Mrs. Agnelli." Jake stepped back, tipping his black baseball cap in her direction.

Holly smiled at Mrs. Agnelli as she passed, but remained in the cart defiantly. She stared hard at Jake. Was this sort of passive-aggressive confrontation what it had come to between them? The break-up itself had been far easier than working out all of the kinks that came with sharing space (and *not* sharing space) on what was turning out to be a relatively small island.

"I said *out*, Holly," Jake demanded. There were deep rings of sweat under the arms of his crisply ironed uniform. At the end of the day Jake had always come over to her place and showered, walking around shirtless for as long as possible and nursing a beer as he cooled off in Holly's air-conditioned house. She'd seen him do it a hundred times, and had always admired his broad, muscled chest as he threw his uniform into the clothes washer in her laundry room, running a hand over his flat, hard stomach while he chose a spin cycle.

"Jake, I'm sorry, but I'm really busy. I've got a lot to do this morning." Holly pushed the sweaty hair across her forehead with her palm. "And if you want to get technical, there really is no *out* when it comes to a golf cart. I am essentially already *out* by virtue of the fact that there is no *in*. In fact, I'm basically sitting on a bench with wheels." Holly kept her bare thighs firmly planted on the seat.

Jake glanced around Main Street, sliding his sunglasses off with one hand so that he could look her in the eye. "Listen, I just want to talk to you, and you haven't been returning my calls."

"Is that against the law? Not calling you back?" she snapped, regretting her tone instantly.

Jake recoiled. "No. Of course not. But we have this...*thing* going on between us, and I want to talk about it."

Holly reached down to release the parking brake, the desire to escape flooding her body. "I really don't think we have a 'thing' going on, Jake."

He lowered his voice. "Did you or did you not let me stay the night at your house last month?"

"We both had too much to drink that night. That doesn't mean we're getting back together."

"Well maybe it should mean that." Jake lifted his chin an inch.

She tapped her thumbs against the steering wheel, waiting for him to move out of her way. "Okay, maybe it should mean that, but it doesn't. What it means is that you and I shouldn't be drinking rum together on a hot summer night while we listen to the Eagles."

Jake inhaled deeply, nodding like he agreed with her. "Holly Baxter," he said, disappointment in his voice. "I have no option but to ticket you for failing to obey the traffic laws of the island." Jake flipped back the cover of his ticket book and began scribbling, copying down her license number as he slowly chewed the piece of gum that he'd held lodged between his back molars. Jake's square, defined jaw worked visibly as he wrote, moving rhythmically like a cow chewing its cud.

"Look, Jake, if you want to ticket me for saving us both from making a huge mistake, then go for it. But I'm pretty sure it won't hold up in court. We both know I didn't break any traffic laws here. You're just punishing me for not being the woman you wanted me to be."

Jake scrawled his signature at the bottom of the ticket with a flourish, tore off Holly's copy, and handed it to her. "You blew through the stop sign."

When he acted like this it was hard to remember the Jake she'd loved. *That* Jake had stayed up late into the night with her, feeding her cold pasta in bed, listening to her talk about all of the things she wanted to do with the B&B, and all of her hopes for the island. She'd been charmed into thinking that a man who'd chased her around the yard with a garden hose under a starry summer sky, hosing her down with laughter as he drunkenly called her his *little spumoni*, his *tasty cannoli*, his *dolcezza*, was the kind of man who'd support her need for independence, but she'd been wrong.

It wasn't long after her grandfather—her beloved grandpa, the man who'd pruned and coaxed a slithering, swampy island into a holiday-themed village for his family and friends—had passed that Jake started talking about her selling the B&B and moving to Miami. He'd complained about the jungle-feel of the island, about how the average age on Christmas Key had to be at least seventy-eight (in fact, it was seventy-three), and he'd lamented the fact that he'd never see "real action" as a cop on an island full of old people and box turtles. It was then that Holly realized that, while Jake loved her, he didn't really love her island. And that had been the deal breaker.

"I expect that in the future, Holly," Jake pushed his sunglasses back up the bridge of his nose slowly, "you'll consider the laws of our streets important enough to obey. That stop sign you drove through was placed there for a reason." He pointed down the street with two fingers like a flight attendant giving the emergency exit speech before takeoff.

Holly waited for him to soften again so that she could be nicer— she knew she needed to be nicer. After all, this was the guy who'd rubbed her feet as they watched *The Bachelor* together; the one who had cried when his grandma passed away in New Jersey before he got the chance to say good-bye; the man who'd given her a bouquet of hand-picked flowers every month on the 17th because that was the day they'd had their first date—and as she watched his handsome face, she felt the familiar heat of attraction seeping through her core. There was no question that she was attracted to him: at six-foot-one, Jake was a hundred and ninety pounds of dark, tanned, Italian testosterone. His voice was deep, and his eyes burned with desire.

Jake said nothing, but for a brief instant Holly knew that their interaction could have gone either way: she could have easily gotten out of the cart and thrown her arms around him, or she could have driven away.

She put the golf cart in gear and pulled back into the street.

Without slowing down, she pushed the accelerator to the floor, rounding the bend in the road.

2

HOLLY RUSHES THROUGH THE DOOR OF THE B&B, KEYS JANGLING IN HER hand, hair still wet from her lightning-fast shower. Instead of blowdrying it, she has her damp locks tucked under her New York Yankees baseball hat. Her clean bikini peeks out from under the shoulder of her white linen summer dress.

"Hey, doll." Bonnie Lane is behind the desk in the B&B's back office, licking envelopes as she watches her boss breeze in. "We got almost everything done this morning, and I think I successfully sold those fishermen on the package deal with my irresistible Southern charm."

Holly drops her bag on the desk and sets her baseball cap on top of it. "Are you serious?"

"I most certainly am. And I promised them that I will *personally* make sure they have a fabulous time here—especially the single ones."

Holly glances up from the pile of mail she's sorting through. "Well, I hope your sass doesn't confuse them about what's actually included in their package deal." She shoots Bonnie a look that is full of mock-disapproval. Their friendship—though unlikely—runs deep and strong, full of maternal undertones from Bonnie and daughterly teasing from Holly. Without ever saying so, they both know that Holly is the daughter Bonnie never had, and Bonnie is the mother Holly always wanted.

"Oh, lordy, girl. In my vast experience, men *always* assume that the whole nine yards are included in the package deal." Bonnie tosses a sealed envelope onto the pile she's making, then picks up another.

"Did they go for the price we pitched for the whole week? Do they want to do everything we offered?" Holly walks over to a cork board on one wall and stands in front of it, resting her hands on her narrow hips. On the board, she's pinned a hand-drawn map of the island as well as lists of ideas and various angles she wants to explore as she plans for the future of Christmas Key. She reaches out and runs a finger over a list of possible business ideas.

"Yes, sugar, they want to take you up on everything we talked about," Bonnie says, looking her boss up and down. "Cute dress, by the way."

"Thanks," Holly says absentmindedly, taking a business card off the cork board and putting the pin back in.

"You ready for your big meeting?"

"I think so." She turns to Bonnie. "I mean, I'm nervous about what sort of reaction I'll get, but I'm ready." Holly shakes her oversized silver tank watch until it flips over on her wrist. The village council meeting starts in her B&B's dining room in less than an hour.

"Well, hon, I know people on this island are of two very different minds when it comes to progress, but you've got your grandpa Frank behind you, and pretty much everyone here loved Frank—he charmed the dickens out of all of us."

"I know." Holly sinks into the chair across from Bonnie, leaning forward onto her elbows. "I just never imagined doing all of this without him, but I know I have to." Frank Baxter's gregarious personality and big dreams for his little island were what drew people to Christmas Key in the first place, and Holly has every intention of carrying on as if he's still at her side. For her, there is no other option.

Bonnie picks up a pamphlet and fans her ample cleavage. She narrows her eyes, changing the subject. "I'm sorry, honey, but before you go into that meeting, I think you should know that there's been talk."

"What kind of talk?"

"Keep in mind that people like to chatter, okay? And we mean no harm by it, but—"

"I'm ready," Holly interrupts, making a *get on with it* motion with one hand.

Bonnie takes a deep breath. "The word around town is that you had a little run in with the Po-Po out on Main Street this morning."

"Oh, my God," Holly sighs, letting her forehead fall against the desk. "Really? Already?"

"Yes, already. These are the perils of living with old people, I'm afraid. We have nothing better to do than observe younger people, and then offer our unsolicited opinions and advice on how they should be doing things. So here's mine: invite him over for dinner, make him a nice chicken parm, fill him up with red wine, and then beg him to take you back, sugar. You need him."

Holly closes her eyes and pounds her forehead lightly but theatrically against the edge of her desk.

"I don't need him, Bon. I don't need any man. All I need is my island."

"Sweetie..." Bonnie says gently, reaching across the desk to touch the crown of Holly's head. "Everybody needs somebody. Trust me."

Holly makes a *humph* sound, her face still touching the desk.

"And just because your mother left, and Frank and Jeanie are gone, it doesn't mean you need to pay some sort of penance by living alone forever. You deserve happiness."

Holly lifts her head from the desk and peeks at Bonnie.

"Okay, what I really want to know, sugar, is did he get rough with you? Maybe take out the handcuffs?" Bonnie starts breathing heavily on purpose, her slightly plump arm outstretched, manicured hand splayed on the desktop. "Honey, did he *take you in and frisk you*?" She kicks her accent up a notch, her drawl as thick as buttercream frosting.

"*Whooooaaaa* there, lady! Jake just wanted to ticket me for nothing so he could show me who's boss."

"Who's boss around here is *you*, darlin'," Bonnie says. "But clearly he's forgotten that you're the *mayor* of this island. What an adorable jackass that man is," she says under her breath, leaning back into her chair and dropping the pamphlet she's been using as a fan. She picks up another envelope and licks it carefully so that she won't get any of her red lipstick on the edges.

Holly lets out a breath that she hasn't even realized she's holding. "Yeah, *mayor-shmayor*," she says. She sets her chin in her hand. "I'm mostly just the head of the village council. It's not like I can wield my massive power to overthrow law enforcement in my spare time. And he didn't really mean it—he's just being pissy with me because I won't take his calls."

"Maybe it would clear the air between you two if you just called him over to your place and asked him to use his baton on you. No— I've got it!" Bonnie holds one glossy, red-tipped finger in the air. "Pin him to the sidewalk and tell him you're making a citizen's arrest because he's carrying a giant, concealed weapon of *love!*" Bonnie nearly falls over in her chair with laughter as she wipes at her eyes.

"Bonnie," Holly says, lowering her chin and looking at her friend from under her eyebrows.

"Honey, a roll in the hay wouldn't hurt either of you, and who better to take a tumble with than someone who already knows just what you like?"

There is a certain logic to the argument.

Holly covers her face with both hands. "I already made that mistake once when I let him follow me home from the Ho Ho last month—now he won't leave me alone!"

Bonnie whoops loudly, slapping the desk with her palm. "Girl, no wonder he's sniffing around you like a dog nosing under the table during Thanksgiving dinner. You threw him a scrap, and now he wants more!"

This particular analogy leaves Holly shaking her head with amazement. "Not to change topics and give you whiplash," she finally says, pushing her chair back from the desk, "but do you have the proposal printed and stapled for me to hand out at the meeting?"

"Right here, sugar." Bonnie pulls a thick folder out of the wire box on the corner of her organized desk and hands it over. "I also asked the kitchen to set out coffee and water, and we're doing a spread of pastries and muffins, just like you asked."

"Thanks, Bon. I'm going to go make sure the chairs are set up so we can get the meeting started on time." Holly sets her Yankees cap back on her head, pulling down the brim until it hits her where she likes it.

"I'm sure you'll get started on time, as long as Mrs. Agnelli doesn't take the floor and cuss out Joe Sacamano like she did at the last council meeting." Bonnie opens her laptop and shoos Holly out with the wave of a hand. "Now go on, and don't you worry about a thing around here. I've got everything covered." Bonnie smiles up at her boss.

"Okay, I'll see you in there." Holly scoops up her packets and heads for the door.

"Hey, sugar? You might want to leave your baseball cap here so that you look less like a teenager headed to the beach, and more like the mayor of a soon-to-be major travel destination."

Holly gazes out at Main Street from inside her cozy office, her eyes dreamy. "A major travel destination...but only if things go my way."

"Just keep your eyes on the prize, love. Your grandparents wouldn't have left you in charge here if they didn't think you could handle it."

Holly believes her—she wants desperately to believe her—but she shoves her blue baseball hat into her purse, pulls her damp, auburn hair into a bun, and gives the desk two sharp taps with her knuckles for luck on her way out the door, just in case.

3

FRANK BAXTER ALWAYS HELD THE VILLAGE COUNCIL MEETINGS ON THE third Wednesday of the month at ten o'clock in the morning. It was his thinking that Wednesday was right smack in the middle of the week, so any potential visitors who'd taken a long weekend to visit the island would have cleared out after the previous weekend, or would not have arrived yet for the upcoming one. That meant they weren't losing business at any of the island shops by shutting things down for an hour or two, assuming, of course, that all of the locals *wanted* to shut things down to attend. Most of the time they did, since it was really the only occasion each month that saw everyone gathered in the same place at the same time, and to be perfectly honest, they'd never had a mad rush of visitors to keep them away from village council meetings anyway. But Frank had always hoped that one day they would.

Today's meeting has an unusually full turnout. One hundred percent of the island's residents have hung signs in their shop windows and set their DVRs (or VCRs, for those refusing to budge on technology) to record their midday shows. They've come to the village council meeting dragging oxygen tanks, liver-spotted spouses, and baskets of baked goods to share with neighbors. Mrs. Agnelli is making the rounds, hugging everyone as if she hasn't seen them in years. Joe Sacamano is leaning back in his chair casually, chewing on a toothpick. People are filing into the B&B's carpeted dining room through both doors, and there is interested chatter as they choose seats.

Holly looks out at the crowd from behind the podium and sips her water. There is a slight anticipatory tremor in her hand as she tries to recap her water bottle. "If I could have your attention, please," she says in a loud voice. It's a challenge sometimes, trying to project an air of authority to people two or three times her age, but she musters as much confidence as she can and smiles at everyone as they turn their attention to the podium.

The sound in the room dulls to a low buzz as people sit. It's working. Holly forces herself to look her neighbors in the eyes with a steady gaze; she breathes deeply to calm her jangled nerves.

"I'd like to call to order the village council meeting for July sixteenth," Holly says, turning to Heddie Lang-Mueller on her right. Heddie sits with her back so straight that it looks as if she's been strapped to a board from the waist up. Her pale gray-blonde hair is knotted in a tight bun at the nape of her neck, a silk scarf tied just so around her slim throat. She holds her pen over a notepad, giving Holly one firm nod to let her know that she's ready.

Holly turns back to the crowd. "May I have a show of hands of the registered voters in attendance, please?"

Hands shoot up all over the room. Heddie counts them silently, her lips moving. She writes a number on the notepad.

"Excellent. First of all, as always, I want to thank you for coming. Our fair island is well on the way to becoming everything my grandfather hoped it would be when he bought it and moved his family here almost thirty years ago." Silence falls over the crowd. Holly can feel all eyes in the room trained on her, and she suddenly wonders if her purple bikini is visible through the white fabric of her sundress. She glances down at her torso as casually as possible, trying to assess the situation, but she can't tell.

Just then, she spots Jake standing at the back of the room, arms folded, sunglasses on top of his head as he watches her intently.

She forges on. "As most of you know, my grandparents wanted to share this island paradise with people who had the same dreams of freedom and happiness that they did."

Gwen and Gen slip in through a side door and join their sister, Glen, (and all three of their husbands) in the second row. Heddie changes her tally of registered voters by two.

"For those of you who knew my grandma, I'm sure you can attest to the fact that no one—and I mean *no one*—loved Christmas more than Jeanie Baxter." Chuckles pepper the room, gray and white heads nodding in agreement. "As she fought cancer like the champion she was, it brought her great pleasure to ride around this island in their golf cart, Christmas lights blinking from the roof, tinsel blowing in the wind all year long. My grandma loved every view of the water from December Drive, and it always tickled her when Grandpa Frank took her 'parking' on Candy Cane Beach." Joe Sacamano gives a low wolf whistle. "And she loved having lunch at the Jingle Bell Bistro, where Iris and Jimmy taught her all of the dirty holiday limericks they know."

The crowd erupts in laughter, and Iris Cafferkey turns to her husband Jimmy, wiping tears from her eyes.

"Anyway," Holly says, pausing to let the laughter die down. "What I'm trying to say here is that my grandparents had a dream. They imagined a secluded paradise in the Gulf of Mexico, far away from the crime and pollution of Miami. They wanted a place where people could retire happily, fish from sunup to sundown, and meander around the island on golf carts instead of in cars. In order to secure the autonomy of this island and to make sure that we weren't annexed by any other city or town—"

"Well, it's not like anybody is lined up to take us over," Joe Sacamano bellows from the center of the room with a hard laugh. A few people nod in agreement.

"Yes, but like I said," Holly continues, "in order to make sure that *didn't* happen, Frank and Jeanie went through the process of making

Christmas Key a municipality. We've officially been our own village since 1987, and with that privilege comes the responsibility of controlling our zoning and building laws, as well as governing our island and ourselves."

"Be nice if Mr. Sacamano did a little *self-governing* of his own," Jimmy Cafferkey teases, sun-browned arms folded across his chest, a twinkle in his eye. Iris gives him a light whack on the shoulder. "Learn how to keep his bloody paws off of all the lasses as they roll into town."

"I'm about to deny you a tab at the bar, Jimmy Cafferkey!" Joe shoots back jovially. "Though the lovely Iris is always welcome at the Ho Ho Hideaway. Come to think of it, maybe I'll make all of *her* pints on the house from now on," he says, winking at Jimmy's wife. "And I'll charge *you* double." The crowd roars with laughter.

Holly laughs and takes another sip of her water as everyone settles down. "So, to that end, as mayor of Christmas Key, I want to always bring to you—my neighbors and friends—any ideas for development and expansion that might affect our village and our lives."

"Now, Holly," Darwin Miller says, standing up next to his wife Gen. "If I may."

"You may," she concedes.

"Some of us have much to gain from any sort of development or expansion—or, dare I say it, *progress*—but others have much to lose."

"That's right." Maria Agnelli gets to her feet in the front row, but because Mrs. Agnelli isn't more than a hair over four foot eleven, standing up doesn't make her look much taller than sitting down. Everyone braces themselves for a blue streak of fiery Italian opinion and conjecture from a woman who's known for speaking her mind. "Some of us retired here with the notion that we'd be living out our golden years on an island that time had forgotten. I don't need any progress around here, young lady. I don't give a goat's arse about attracting visitors and all that. I'm just as happy as a clam bumping around this island with the same old folks I see everyday. I don't want a damn thing to do with your progress."

"And see," Gen Miller stands up next to her husband, "I don't mind the visitors. As you can imagine, my sisters," she nods at her mirror images, Gwen and Glen, "and our husbands and I all benefit greatly from the tourists. We stay afloat by selling groceries and supplies to all of you, but what good is a gift shop on the main street of a perfectly lovely village if nobody visits?"

"Very true. And, if I may bring us back to my main point," Holly says, holding a finger up in the air, "I'd like to continue on in the spirit of what my grandpa set out to create. At the end of his life, we spent a fair amount of time talking about his dreams and visions for Christmas Key, and being the forward-thinker that he was, Frank encouraged me to always keep an eye towards controlled expansion."

"Now, Holly Baxter." Mrs. Agnelli is still standing. "We all know your grandfather bought this island because your mother was a single teenager who was in a *family way*." A few of the men chuckle behind their hands, and several of the women *tsk-tsk* (whether out of amusement or because they possess a modicum of decorum, it's unclear). "And he and your grandmother wanted to raise the both of you around a bunch of old codgers so that she wouldn't find herself up the duff again."

Jimmy Cafferkey cackles loudly; Iris swats him again.

Holly is briefly stunned into silence. Her mouth opens and closes like a fish on land, and she blinks several times before recovering. "Thank you for pointing that out, Mrs. Agnelli." She nods, warming to the topic. "Yes, my mother *was* seventeen and pregnant when they bought this island, and yes, my grandparents wanted to keep her out of trouble. But I think that desire right there is at the very heart of what Christmas Key is *all about*. I mean, is there a single one of you who moved here hoping for big city life? For crime?" She looks at each of them, locking eyes with every person in the front row. "Did anyone come to the island praying for a corporate career in a high rise? For traffic? For unfriendly neighbors?" Holly pauses, letting her eyes graze the rest of the crowd. "No. You moved here—we all live here together—because we want freedom from those things. We crave the natural beauty of the tropics, and we love supporting one another in our dreams, and sharing in our successes as a group."

The room is silent.

"But in order to keep moving forward, we need to at least *entertain* the idea of progress. In the future I think it's entirely unlikely that we'll be able to survive off of pensions and Social Security alone, and it's my goal to purposefully—and I did say *purposefully*—guide us towards an increase in tourism and development. We have to find some way to sustain ourselves."

A few heads nod in the crowd, though Maria Agnelli is still standing just below the podium, hands on her small hips, looking up at Holly sternly.

"I got the good news today that a group of fishermen wants to book a weeklong trip to Christmas Key, and they'll be here in a couple of weeks. That means we'll have ample opportunity to provide our goods and services to them." She stops to let this news sink in. "I know we're accustomed to weekenders and little gatherings of people here and there, but the fact that we're as far out into the Gulf as we are means that even a trip from Key West is a trek out into the great unknown."

"That's right, lass. If somebody wants to get here, then they damn well better *want to get here!*" Jimmy Cafferkey says in his Iris-tinged lilt.

"That's true, Jimmy. A trip to Christmas Key should be an adventure. And that desire to get here should be met by our eagerness to please those willing to make the trip. Because ultimately," Holly says, pausing for effect, "they bring us not just money and a more robust economy for the island, but for those of us who don't make it onto the mainland very often, they also bring with them human connectivity, and a taste of the outside world."

Holly stops here, hoping she's made her case. The room is silent for a moment, and then a loud, slow clap starts in the back of the room. It's just one person at first, and when Holly scans the room, she sees that it's Buckhunter. Her initial fear is that he's being sarcastic after their encounter that morning near her clothesline, but he gives her a crooked, sincere grin to let her know that he really means it.

Then, like wildfire, the applause spreads. Not to everyone, but to enough of the crowd that Holly realizes how much support she actually has. Tears prick at the back of her eyes. Without meaning to, she gives a laugh that turns into a sob of joy, and her hand comes up to cover her mouth, the light brown freckles that dot the bridge of her nose still visible beneath her shining eyes.

"Thank you," she says softly. "Thank you for hearing me out." Holly takes a moment to compose herself, then turns to Heddie next to her. "I'd also like to hand out a packet of information that I worked up on potential progress and growth for the island. I extended it out a few years so that—hopefully—what I'm proposing will make sense."

Heddie stands up from her spot next to Holly's podium with the stack of packets in her hands. She splits them, handing half to Holly. They pass them down the rows on each side of the room as quickly as possible. The hands of the islanders—weathered, arthritic, plump—flip through the pages of the document curiously, brows furrowed as they begin to scan the packets.

"Now," Holly rushes back to the podium, "when we talk about progress, I'd like you to consider the benefit to *all* of us here on the island. And please keep in mind that in order to both positively impact our economy, and yet still retain control over the changes that might come our way, we need to be really intentional with our advertisements and plans."

"I still don't agree with all of this, Holly," Maria Agnelli says, sinking down into her chair; she's holding a balled-up Kleenex in one shaky hand. "But if your grandpa Frank wanted it, then...I guess maybe," she trails off. "Frank always did take care of us."

In proposing that the island throw itself into the fray of advertising, promoting, growing, and catering to change, Holly is well aware that she's asking many of her neighbors to step outside of their comfort zones. She's even factored a certain amount of pushback into the equation, and she expects it; she'd be disappointed if everyone rolled over quietly and acquiesced to her proposal without question. Part of the excitement and the challenge for her is convincing everyone else that it's possible to slowly open the drawbridge and let people in without totally blowing up the walls that surround the village. It's going to take work, but she's ready.

Holly steps down from the podium and stands next to Mrs. Agnelli. She takes Maria's cool, wrinkled hand into her own.

"I hope you all trust me when I tell you that eco-tourism is the wave of the future. The natural beauty of our island, combined with our proximity to the Dry Tortugas, means we can advertise our little piece of paradise as the ultimate destination for fishing, snorkeling, hiking, camping, biking, etcetera."

"And drinking," Joe Sacamano pipes up. "Don't forget that we're a premiere drinking destination!"

"Here, here!" Jimmy Cafferkey seconds.

"Yes, with two bars and only a hundred and thirteen full-time residents, we probably have more bars per capita than any other city in the country," Holly laughs. "But, if you look over the information I've given you, you'll see that I've included an advertising plan as well as a budget, and I'd like to call for a vote to approve the plan."

"I'll vote right now, Mayor," Joe Sacamano says, holding the side of his reading glasses as he skims the packet. "This looks like a solid plan to me."

"Thanks, Joe—I appreciate that. Ballots are due by five o'clock this afternoon. If you have any questions, I'll be in my office at the B&B. Meeting adjourned."

Holly wraps things up, nodding at her neighbors as she gathers the leftover packets to take back to her office. "Thanks, Heddie," she says to the tall, striking woman.

"Yes, love, you are very welcome," Heddie says in her German accent. "I will type everything up and get it to you." Heddie's movements are slow and graceful—it's clear to see her as the German film star she once was, though she always brushes that particular topic away with feigned irritation if anyone brings it up.

"You're a gem, Heddie," Holly says. "Old Blue Eyes was a dummy to let you go."

"*Oje, stoppen necken,*" Heddie says in her native tongue, smoothing her already perfect hair across her scalp as she tucks her handbag under one arm. "Don't be ridiculous." The rumor on the island is that Heddie counts Frank Sinatra among her many former beaux, but it's a piece of gossip that remains unconfirmed by Heddie herself.

"Nice plan," Jake says, interrupting Holly's thoughts as she watches the islanders interact around her. In his hands he's holding the black baseball cap with POLICE embroidered across the front in white thread. His holster dangles from his hip. "By the way," he whispers, leaning in confidentially, "the purple bikini was a good choice. It was always one of my favorites."

Holly feels the blood rushing to her head, spreading across her face and leaving two pink stains on her cheeks.

With a winning smile, Jake tugs his hat on over his short-cropped black hair and gives her a parting nod.

It's just like Jake to antagonize her with a speeding ticket and then, a few hours later, flirt with her about her bikini. She feels that familiar heat between them as it spreads through her body, and her eyes trail over his strong back and tanned neck as he walks out of the dining room.

Memories of Jake kicking her feet out from under her in her bedroom and knocking her backwards onto the bed with a shriek of surprise spring to mind. He's always been one for the sneak attack, landing on top of her like a tiger pouncing on its prey, ready to tangle as she laughs happily beneath him. It had been fun, their island romance, and a part of her wants to fall back into their easy relationship and the way things were before he ruined everything with the proposal. If only she could forget all of his talk about leaving the island, then they could smooth things over and go back to the way it used to be.

The memory of Jake's frosty attitude as he handed her the traffic ticket is already fading from her mind as she assesses his firm backside and weighs it against the cost of rekindling their flame. It might be worth it, and she can probably forgive him for saying that living on the island with so many retirees is as dull as dishwater. Besides, who cares about their ridiculous showdown on Main Street that morning? It isn't like she was ever going to pay that damn ticket anyway.

4

"MAYBE WE SHOULD WALK A LITTLE SLOWER?" MARIA AGNELLI PLEADS. Mrs. Agnelli pumps her arms furiously alongside Glen, Gwen, Gen, and Holly, trying to keep up with the younger women. Every Thursday, they take an early morning stroll along the beach that wraps around the west side of the island. Up ahead, it connects with a wooden-planked boardwalk called Pinecone Path. The islanders refer to this stretch of white sand and palm trees as Snowflake Banks, and the ladies meet there bright and early each week to get their walk in before the summer humidity ratchets the temperature up to unbearable levels.

"Sure, Maria," says Gen. "We can slow down."

This morning Pucci leads the pack, bounding ahead of them and digging his nose into the cool sand every thirty or forty yards before coming up with a snout that looks as if it's covered in powdered sugar.

Glen, Gwen, and Gen—better known as "the triplets" to everyone on the island—have their hair pulled back in identical sun-bleached blonde French braids. As is their lifelong habit, they each wear a particular color scheme that they follow closely in all matters concerning fashion. As juvenile as it sounds, it helps everyone else to tell them apart. Without knowing that Glen wears primary colors,

Gwen favors black, white, and pastels, and Gen almost always wears tropical colors like pink, turquoise, or orange, it's nearly impossible to know who you're talking to. All three of the triplets smile and laugh like life is one huge party, lighting up like human sun flares the minute someone engages them in conversation, and not a single one of them has ever met a stranger. Without fail, they entertain all of the island's visitors with stories and chitchat, their identical voices and laughter weaving together in a pleasing tapestry.

The sisters are all lean and robust at the age of sixty-seven, with strong, tanned limbs, and wicked senses of humor. It's hard to believe that they're only twenty years younger than Maria Agnelli, and that Holly is almost forty years younger than the triplets.

"I saw that sexy police officer ex-husband of yours undressing you with his eyes at the meeting yesterday," Mrs. Agnelli says, poking Holly in the side.

"We were never actually married, Mrs. Agnelli." She's pointed this out to Mrs. Agnelli at least a hundred times.

"Oh, right," Mrs. Agnelli says with a frown. "You were just shacking up. I can't believe you were dumb enough to let that gorgeous man go. Remind me again what the hell you did that for?" She pulls a wadded ball of Kleenex out of the pocket of her walking shorts, wiping at her wrinkled brow.

The triplets all turn to Holly with expectation. They're walking five abreast on the broad expanse of firm white sand. The sun flicks hotly through the palm trees, dropping hints of the scorching heat it will bring once it rises high enough in the sky to crest the trees.

"Ahhh, well." Holly chews on her lower lip. "I guess we just didn't see eye-to-eye on some of the bigger issues in our relationship." The triplets nod in understanding. Gen pulls a small bottle of water from her fuchsia fanny pack.

"Oh, right. The sex." Mrs. Agnelli nods knowingly. "But honey, you don't have to always *enjoy* it, sometimes you just have to *do* it."

Gen Miller chokes on her water.

"Oh, I think you should enjoy it," Gwen says dreamily. "It can be *really* lovely."

"We never really had any problems in that area of our relationship," Holly admits. There is a moment of hesitation when she realizes that she's about to have a sex talk with Mrs. Agnelli and the triplets, but she pushes it aside. (After all, there's no doubt that a group of women who've lived for a combined total of two hundred and eighty-seven years have a thing or two to share with her about life, love, and sex.) "But he wanted me to marry him, and I can't do that."

The women stare at her wordlessly. They're of a generation that believes in marriage and family above all else; a woman who sees a handsome husband as a hindrance rather than an end game is a foreign thing to them. Maria Agnelli shakes her head with disapproval, clicking her tongue as she does.

"I can't see why I have to give up everything I want—everything I've worked for—just to please him," Holly says. "I know he doesn't love this island the way that I do, and if I marry him, next thing I know I'll be pregnant and distracted. Or he'll rope me into moving somewhere else for *his career*," she says, throwing air quotes around the last words.

"You told him all of this?" Gwen asks, re-tucking her mint green tank top into her white shorts.

"Yeah, I told him. He swears it wouldn't be like that, but I can't afford to lose sight of my vision for this island." Holly shrugs.

The group slows their power-walk, holding onto one another for support as they catch their collective breath and admire the silhouettes of the tall palm trees against the pink and blue morning sky.

Holly bends forward to touch her toes, leaning into the stretch. It feels good to just pause and breathe. She gets so busy running the B&B and dreaming about the future that she sometimes forgets to slow down. It's a daily challenge for her to stop thinking about the outside world (Do they have any upcoming bookings at the B&B? Has she remembered to post the previous night's stunning sunset on Instagram with just the right hashtags?) and simply enjoy the coming and going of the tides.

Pucci runs back with a stick in his mouth for his mistress, dropping it at her feet and looking up at her with hopeful brown eyes; Holly grabs the stick and winds up, hurling it as far and as fast as she can toward the water. Pucci takes off like he's been shot from a cannon, cutting through the surf as he wades out to find his prize.

"Jake swears I can run things on Christmas Key no matter what, but I know that when you get married, the baby talk starts, and before you know it: *boom*—all you're doing is changing diapers and fighting about money."

"Oh, being pregnant is wonderful, Holly! And motherhood changes you in all the right ways," Gwen says, reaching down to take the dripping wet stick that Holly's dog has retrieved from the water. Gwen throws it for him, though not as far as Holly had. "I was completely done having babies by twenty-eight; I had all four boys by then," Gwen says.

"That could be because you and Edgar were so busy having such a *lovely* time in the bedroom," Glen teases her sister.

"Well, Holly, you could have given him as much as he wanted anyway," Mrs. Agnelli says, "and then just washed out your na-na with vinegar until you were ready for babies."

"Maria! That doesn't work!" Glen protests. "That's just an old wive's tale."

"It worked for me—I never got pregnant when I didn't want to," Mrs. Agnelli says indignantly. "And I never told Alfie no when he asked for it."

"But Maria," says Gen, "you have *nine* kids. Who needed vinegar? You didn't have to worry about getting pregnant, because you were *already* pregnant!"

"Oh. Right." Mrs. Agnelli looks out at the water. "Well, then maybe it was my sister Theresa who did the old vinegar trick..." she trails off, staring at the silvery waves that lap the shore in the morning sunlight.

"Honey, your sister Theresa is an eighty-year-old nun. The only thing she used vinegar for was to scrub the pews after mass." Glen puts her arm around Mrs. Agnelli's shoulders, giving her a squeeze.

"Listen, Holly, if you're not ready for babies, then you're not ready," Gen says, looping her freckled arm through Holly's smooth, tan one. "But," she says gently, "don't let the fact that your own mother didn't get it right determine whether or not *you* become a mother yourself."

"You're right—I know you're right—but I can't picture it. Any of it. At least not right now." Holly pauses. "Breaking up with Jake felt like the right thing to do; I just wish I didn't feel like throwing myself into his arms every time I see him. We have a good time together, and he's so sweet and patient. He puts up with me, and he's really sexy—"

"Yep, you got that one right," Maria Agnelli chimes in.

"I know...so what do you think? Was I out of my mind to break it off?"

The triplets exchange looks before Gwen speaks. "Honey, you probably made the right choice in the long run, no matter how much it hurts now."

"You shouldn't have to postpone your dreams for any man, no matter *how* handsome he is," Glen adds.

Mrs. Agnelli walks over to Holly and puts both hands on her arms to pull her closer. "Holly Jean Baxter," she says, her voice firm and her eyes serious. "You go ahead and wait on babies until whenever you're ready." Holly looks down at Mrs. Agnelli, expecting some sort of Yoda-like proclamation from the woman who has something to say about everything. "But in the meantime, honey," she says, "use the vinegar trick."

5

When Holly's grandparents moved her over to Christmas Key as a toddler, it was still a wild and untamed piece of land. They brought a wilderness guide along with them to pull their boat up to shore and keep it there as they explored their newly-purchased island. It was nothing but a figment of Frank Baxter's imagination at that point—just a humid, teeming pile of flora and fauna anchored to the ocean floor, holding fast as the endless currents of turquoise ebbed and flowed around it. In that, he'd seen infinite potential.

Holly pauses now in front of the refrigerator in her tidy white kitchen, staring at a photograph that's stuck to the door with a magnet. In it, a two-year-old Holly—wearing nothing but diapers, tennis shoes, and sunscreen—stands in a patch of sunlight on the damp, recently-plowed earth that would soon become the start of what is now Main Street. Every time she opens her refrigerator, it reminds her what kind of magic is borne of love and imagination. It reminds her that having big dreams reaps big rewards. With a wistful feeling, she runs her fingers across the faded photo as she holds two lemons and two limes in a basket she's made from the front of her t-shirt.

Holly walks to the counter and lets the citrus fall from its makeshift holder; the lemons and limes drop from her shirt onto the butcher block, where they roll to a lumpy stop next to the backsplash.

The blender chews up ice as Holly moves around barefoot, pulling a shot glass and two mismatched margarita glasses from her cupboard. Her favorite U2 CD is cranked up high, and Bono tears through the songs on *The Joshua Tree* as she sings along.

Holly looks out the window over her sink, watching the late afternoon sun work its magic. As it does nearly every day during the summer, a gray, roiling storm had covered the island like a heavy blanket after lunch, whipping palm fronds to and fro and dumping rain like heaven's roof had sprung a downspout. The hot sun returned just behind it to dry up the swampy puddles, and the amphibians croaked and skittered out of their hiding places. Now Holly watches the drips of water sparkling like gems on the tips of the palm fronds as she rinses off the fruit under her faucet.

She's living on the parcel of land that Frank and Jeanie Baxter had cleared nearly thirty years ago. It still feels like a jungle on that part of the island, with the tall trees and thick foliage that her grandparents had left all around the property. The Baxter land now holds a main house and a second home—built in the traditional Conch style—both single-story houses with louvered shutters and sloping metal roofs to reflect the hot tropical sun and to allow clean rain water to run off into metal cisterns. The outside of the houses are made of a mortar of sand, water, and lime, and the insides are constructed with tongue and groove wood on the floors, walls, and ceilings so that they'll stand strong against Mother Nature should a hurricane tear across the island.

Holly sets the washed lemons and limes back on the cutting board. She loves her property. She'd lived at the B&B full-time in her twenties until her grandparents' passing, only moving back into Frank and Jeanie's main house when she felt certain that it was the right thing to do. By then, Frank had rented out the guest house next door to Leo Buckhunter, so Holly's only real option was to move back into the home she was raised in, and she'd immediately set about painting and decorating so that she could make it her own.

Holly pours two thick, strong frozen margaritas into the glasses. It's four o'clock, so Fiona is due to show up any minute, and Holly wants to greet her best friend at the door with a cocktail in hand.

"Knock knock," Dr. Fiona Potts calls out, pushing the front door open without waiting for an answer.

"She has arrived," Holly says dramatically, tipping her head in the direction of the lanai so that Fiona will follow. "And the drinks are served."

"Damn, you're good." Fiona tosses her straw purse onto the couch in Holly's front room and kicks off her sandals. She takes the drink gratefully and follows Holly toward the back of the house.

"Your wall is coming along nicely," Fiona says, nodding at the half-done project on Holly's lanai.

"Yeah, I've had a couple of sleepless nights. It keeps me busy." Holly flops into the chair across from her friend, admiring the wall that she's been working on for the past year.

After years of gathering unbroken shells from around the island, Holly decided to turn one side of her house into a mosaic of sorts. Now, whenever inspiration strikes, she holds the shells up to the wall of her house that's covered by the lanai, piecing the husks of sea creatures together so that they fit like a puzzle. Sleepless nights often find her listening to CDs and mixing up small batches of mortar to glue the shells to her wall. When she's totally done, the back of her house will look like a stretch of sand where the tide has washed out, leaving a bounty of shells behind.

The women prop their bare feet up on footstools and sip their margaritas, watching the sunlight dance through the trees as Holly recounts her conversation with Mrs. Agnelli and the triplets.

"She said *what*?" Fiona pulls her feet from the chair and sits up, laughing. She has both hands wrapped around her drink, and the spaghetti strap of her summer dress slides off one shoulder, revealing a constellation of freckles that spill down into the front of her décolletage like falling stars.

"I know, right? VINEGAR!" Holly tips her drink back and lets the frozen margarita slide down her throat, brain-freeze be damned.

"That woman kills me. I swear she's the only elderly patient I've ever had who can out-curse a whole biker gang. And it's not just your average four-letter words she's dropping. She's *creative*, and she usually hits her mark." Fiona is the island's only full-time physician and, as Holly's closest friend, she occasionally shares the non-confidential information about things that happen in her office with their neighbors.

"It was a hoot. The stuff she says is totally outrageous. I hope I'm half as funny when I'm her age."

"We should all be so lucky." Fiona tips her margarita toward Holly before bringing the glass to her lips again. "Hey," she says, shifting topics. "What's going on with you and Jake? I've heard rumors."

"Such as?" Holly's face is a mask of innocence; she knows that tongues wag all over the island where she and Jake are concerned.

"Like he pulled you over on Main Street and the passion between you was as thick as molasses. I heard that there was so much steam that it was almost pornographic."

"Oh my God—stop!" Holly wails, waving a hand at her and grimacing. "Please tell me it was Bonnie who told you that and not someone else."

"Really. It's the word around town." Fiona smiles devilishly. "And I also heard that he came up to you at the village council meeting and you two were making bedroom eyes while he checked out your see-through dress."

"Oh, lord."

"So it's not true?"

"That I wore a see-through dress? Yeah, unfortunately that happened—but not intentionally."

"Ha. Who cares about the dress. It probably earned you a couple of extra votes, you calculating little minx. But I meant the eye-smoldering between you and Officer Studly—is that part true?"

"Well, hopefully the dress thing got me a few votes—at least that would make the embarrassment worth it. As for Jake, I don't know...

he thinks we have a thing, and I think we don't. At this point, all I know for sure is that we're still broken up—"

"In spite of the fact that you basically clubbed him over the head and dragged him back here the night that Joe Sacamano burned through his entire repertoire of Eagles hits at the Ho Ho?"

"That was bad, wasn't it?" Holly admits reluctantly.

"I don't know if it was *bad*. I'm not judging that."

"Mixed messages, though?"

"Well, yeah. A little."

Holly sighs. "It's just...it's *hard* sometimes. It's not like I can rebound with someone else and be done with him, you know?"

"I hear that. Your options are certainly not plentiful here." Fiona traces rings on the table from the condensation left by her margarita glass. "But you know what I admire about you?"

"What?" Holly chuckles.

"You're this weird combination of a planner and a doer."

"A doer?"

"You know—you have long-term plans and goals, but you always do what feels right in the moment."

"Like sleeping with my ex because I drank too much rum and because I love 'Hotel California'?"

"I guess, yeah, but that's not a bad thing." Fiona shakes her head. "It's really not."

Holly considers this. "I think it's probably the only way to survive out here. The planning is for survival, and the doing is because you're able to really live in the moment in an environment like this."

"God," Fiona says, looking out into the late afternoon sunlight beyond the lanai. "I love it here. It's changed my life, Hol. Completely."

"Damn straight. Christmas Key is the cat's pajamas," Holly says with a wink. Going to college on the mainland with antiquated terms in her pocket like *cat's pajamas, tizzy, nincompoop,* and *hoodwinked* had made Holly a bit of a novelty act at frat parties, and the first time one of her sorority sisters got drunk and Holly accused her of having an "attack of the collywobbles" they'd all laughed and tossed pillows at her in the dorm room. Silly Holly and her old people talk. But the college boys had quickly realized that a girl who'd grown up on an island—running around in nothing but a bathing suit; a girl with a working knowledge of beer and rum, and a far more interesting life than the rest of her sorority sisters—was someone worth having around. And yet she'd returned to Christmas Key as single as the day she left.

Fiona watches a gecko scurry up the wall of the lanai. "What would I do without you, Hol? How would I ever survive here if there was no Holly Baxter to make me margaritas and keep me company?"

Holly shrugs at her, smiling.

A drop of water falls from the eave of the lanai and lands on Fiona's foot. They sit quietly for a moment, listening to the summer sounds of tree frogs and insects. The cicadas buzz from their hiding spots, their ever-present chatter like rotating sprinkler heads in the distance.

"You'd probably drink alone at night and take up pinochle so that you could join the ladies who play on Sundays."

Fiona reaches over and gives Holly's bare thigh a light slap. "You know what I mean."

Over their first drink together, shortly after Fiona's arrival, she'd admitted to Holly that when she arrived on Christmas Key and saw nothing but a handful of gray-haired Baby Boomers and septuagenarians driving golf carts up and down Main Street, her gut reaction was to get back on the boat, tell the program director that there'd been a mistake, and go directly back to civilization. But the lure of having a chunk of her student loans paid off by the government for putting in two years as the only doctor in an underserved location forced her to put one gladiator-sandaled foot in front of the other and move down the dock. The deckhand from the small ferry finished unloading her bags from the boat's hold and deposited them at her feet unceremoniously.

"Good luck," he'd said with a salute, jumping back onto the boat and unhooking the rope from the dock.

Fiona wheeled her suitcases along the sidewalk, sweating

profusely and smiling at the friendly people who waved and stared. A trio of cheerful identical faces greeted her almost instantly, and each of the triplets hugged her warmly before walking her the rest of the way down Main Street, gold bracelets clinking in the sunlight as they'd pointed out people and businesses and shared all of the important island gossip. This kindness, she told Holly over that first drink, had been the only reason that she'd allowed the boat to disappear towards the horizon without her on it.

And then, standing in front of a two-story building with turquoise-painted Key West shutters shading its long rectangular windows, was Holly, waiting to greet the island's new doctor. She waited there in front of the matching turquoise front door of Poinsettia Plaza, eager to show Fiona into her office and help her get settled. They took to one another instantly, and the following year was a blur of laughter, white sand, margaritas, and friendship.

"For the record, I'm glad *you're* here," Holly says, "or I wouldn't have anyone to invite over for cocktail hour. It would just be me and Buckhunter out here in the back forty together." Holly raises her empty glass at shirtless, leather-skinned Leo Buckhunter as he drags a hose across the grass of his own backyard. "Hey, Buckhunter, you do know it just rained, right?" she shouts, leaning towards the lanai's screen. "You don't need to water the grass."

He stops short, gives her a sarcastic look, and goes on dragging his hose.

"You're welcome!" Holly calls after him.

"You're such a smartass," Fiona hisses, smiling at Buckhunter and waving. "He's so *mysterious*. And he knows how to mix a mean mojito," she adds, watching his upper-body muscles ripple as he yanks at the hose.

"Well, he does own a bar," Holly points out, tipping her head to one side and assessing him through her friend's eyes. She honestly doesn't see it: Buckhunter is just Buckhunter to her, no matter how she slices and dices him. He's rangy and sun-burnished, a tad long in the tooth for her taste, and dangerous in the way that bartenders who can take home a different woman from a bar each night are. To Holly, he comes across as an outlaw with a past. She likes him well enough as a neighbor and as a friend, but she prefers her men a little younger and a lot less enigmatic.

Buckhunter takes the cigar from between his lips and stops to look at Holly, eyes narrowed. "I'm not watering my grass, darlin'. I'm using my hose to wash off your golf cart—Marco just dropped by and left you a present." He tugs at the hose again.

"What?" Holly stands up and sets her empty margarita glass on the table next to Fiona's. The women hurry through the house and out the front door, feet still bare as they step onto the dirt driveway in front of the house. Sure enough, the hot pink hood of Holly's cart is streaked with white bird droppings.

"Damn it!" Holly fumes, fists on her hips as she scans the palm trees around her house for signs of Marco.

"Such is the price of having a parrot as a pet," Buckhunter says, squeezing the trigger on the hose nozzle. A hard stream of water shoots out and he aims it at the golf cart. The water rinses off the Marco droppings with a few flicks of his hard, tattooed wrist. "There you go, milady." Buckhunter lets go of the hose handle and the flow of water halts abruptly. "Just like new."

"Yeah, thanks for catching that, Buckhunter. I hate it when Marco nails my cart and then it dries up in the sun and I have to scrape it off later."

"No problem." His clear blue eyes cut away from Holly and land on Fiona. "Hey, Doc," he says, finally greeting her. "You done giving enemas and taking blood pressure for the day?"

"Yep. I've survived another day of Preparation H and angina, and now I'm just having a drink with the mayor here." Fiona flips her loose, strawberry-blonde hair over one round, freckled shoulder.

Even if she doesn't personally see the allure, Holly knows that Fiona is just a tiny bit smitten by her aloof, weather-worn neighbor. And she gets it. After all, one woman's dangerous and undesirable is another woman's cryptic and complicated.

"Want to join us?" Fiona offers.

Holly sighs inwardly. She doesn't mind sharing her margaritas with Buckhunter, it's more that she has mixed, unresolved feelings about him living right next to her, on *family* property. She doesn't mean to feel that way, but his proximity sometimes gets under her skin. She's never really understood why her grandpa rented the guest house adjacent to the main one to Buckhunter. Frank Baxter never gave any real explanation as to why he was sharing the family property with this stranger, and now there was no way for her to find out.

But Buckhunter is handy enough as a neighbor—washing bird droppings off of her cart, taking Pucci for long walks on the beach—and he even came over with lanterns and flashlights when a tropical storm knocked their power out for three days last summer. Her grandpa's only proclamation on Buckhunter had been that he was someone she could trust in his absence, but what on earth made him think that Leo Buckhunter was any sort of replacement for the grandfather she'd loved and counted on her whole life? Why should she trust a total stranger? Holly had to admit that Buckhunter *had* been good to her, and she'd never once caught him checking her out; she never felt like he was interested in her at all, even when she ran around her yard with her melons in her hands. And in a weird way, her grandpa was right: while she loves pestering Buckhunter in a good-natured, eye-rolling way, she *does* trust him, and she trusts that he'll be there if she needs anything.

"I'd love to join this little powwow of the island's biggest movers and shakers, but my work starts when the sun hits about this spot in the sky," he says, pointing at the horizon. Buckhunter chews on the tip of his fat cigar, moving it to the other side of his mouth. "I need to be over to the bar around five-thirty to make sure that happy hour is in full swing, and then I pull my shift until the wee hours. So no drinking for this guy—at least not before work." He starts gathering the hose in big loops that wind around his sharp elbow as he walks back across the yard. "But feel free to drop by this evening if you ladies are hungry or in need of a beer," Buckhunter calls over one shoulder, leaving the sweet smell of cigar smoke in his wake.

Holly searches the trees above for signs of Marco. "Where is that damn bird? I'm about to turn him into a feather pillow." She whistles up into the trees.

"I doubt you'll make much headway there; that bird runs this island." Fiona trails her around the property, arms folded as they look through the foliage for the aging parrot. "It's like he's the King of Christmas Key or something."

"He kind of is," Holly agrees, spotting Marco's rainbow of feathers in her purple orchid tree. "Marco!" She holds out her arm. The bird glances at her suspiciously with one eye, obviously trying to decide whether or not he wants to bother with human interaction. Marco has rightly earned the reputation of a bird who thinks he's a cat. He drifts around Christmas Key as he sees fit, finding companionship wherever and whenever it strikes his fancy, but his true loyalty to humans extends to just one person.

"Should we take him back to Cap?" Fiona asks, watching her friend as she summons the bird out of the tree.

"Definitely. He ends up on this side of the island all the time, but for some reason, if he's here after dark then he won't take the initiative to fly home. He just sits outside my bedroom window all night, whistling and talking. It drives me bananas."

Fiona laughs. "So he's basically like a man, whistling outside your bedroom window at night to get your attention?"

"Exactly like a man! I don't know how bird years translate into human years, but he's about twenty-seven, I think, so yeah, essentially he *is* like a man howling at me in the middle of the night. It's ridiculous."

Marco surveys his surroundings then, soars down from the uppermost branch of the orchid tree and lands on her bare shoulder.

"Hey, buddy," she coos, letting him get settled. "Okay, Dr. Potts. Let's roll. Wanna follow me in your cart? We can have an appetizer at Jack Frosty's if you need to drool over Buckhunter again this evening."

"I don't know that I *need* to drool over him," Fiona says, "but I'm definitely not done checking him out."

"I can support that. I fully understand the need to feast the eyes upon any man on the island who doesn't already qualify for Medicare."

"Well, I've already feasted my eyes on most of the men on this island while they're in hospital gowns, and—believe me—it ain't pretty." Fiona ducks back into the house to grab her purse and sandals. She flips on Holly's porch light on her way out so that her friend won't return home to total darkness.

Marco perches on the cupholder of Holly's dash, holding on confidently with his talons as she backs her cart out onto the unpaved road. Fiona backs up after her, and they both flick on their carts' headlamps; the late afternoon light is already dusky on the shady side of the island.

It only takes about five minutes to zip down Cinnamon Lane and merge onto Main Street. The women parallel park their carts against the curb outside of North Star Cigar, Co., and Marco hops back onto Holly's shoulder for the short walk into Cap's shop.

"Ladies," Cap Duncan says, spreading his arms wide as Holly and Fiona walk through the open door. "Can I sell you a fine Cuban? A thick Culebra? Or maybe a more glamorous Petit Corona?" The distinct sweet and woody aroma of tobacco fills their nostrils. "Ah, I see you've rescued my main man and brought him back to me. Here, you little *bastardo*," Cap says lovingly, cocking his head at Marco in invitation. "Come to me, you devil." Marco makes the leap from Holly's narrow shoulder to Cap's meatier one with a single flap of his wings.

"He was out at my place again, terrorizing my golf cart with his excretions, and preparing for a night of lovesick catcalling outside my bedroom window."

"Much like your ex-boyfriend, no?" Cap gives a mirthful twitch of his eyebrow, walking behind the dark mahogany counter with Marco next to his ear.

Holly rolls her eyes at him.

"Are you two lovebirds back to feathering your nest yet?" The skin next to Cap's eyes folds and creases like tissue paper from the years he's spent on the ocean, and his teeth are like the jangled ivory keys of a broken piano. A tiny gold hoop glints in his left earlobe.

"Seriously—does everyone on this island know everything about everybody else?" Holly rests her hip against the glass case at the front of the store, eyeing Marco as he flutters his wing on Cap's shoulder.

"Yes, dear," Fiona says, throwing an arm around her friend's shoulders. "By nature of our close proximity, we all know when someone else on the island flushes their toilet or lets their ex sleep over. These are the perils of living on an island the size of a dollar bill."

"Oh good. That's awesome." Holly adjusts the shoulder of her tank top, sliding her polka dotted bikini strap beneath the fabric. "Hey, how's business, Cap?" she asks, turning her attention from gossip to commerce.

"Doing okay. There are enough gentlemen on this fair isle who enjoy a good stogie to keep me in the black."

"That's excellent news. I like to hear that."

"Of course you do, boss." Cap chuckles. He's known Holly since she was knee-high to a grasshopper, just like the majority of the people on Christmas Key.

"Come on, Hol, let's go get something to eat at Jack Frosty's," Fiona says. "See ya later, Marco. You too, Cap."

"Have a wonderful evening, young ladies." Cap pulls his loose white hair into a ponytail with one hand, eyeballing Marco on his shoulder. Cap's hair is thinning and wispy, but he refuses to cut off the last remnants of what he refers to as his "pirate hair," or to take out the gold hoop in his ear. He winks at Fiona. "And when you get to the bar, make sure you give Mr. Buckhunter my best, Doc."

"Oh my God!" She steers Holly toward the door. "Is he seriously giving me a hard time about *Buckhunter?*"

"Hey, Doc," Cap calls after them as they reach the door. There is laughter in his voice. "I've got this thing on my backside I want you to check out—it's been killing me," he says. "Should I make an appointment to see you during office hours?"

Because Fiona still has her arm around Holly's shoulders, the women come to a sharp stop at the same time. "I don't even need to see it to diagnose it, Cap. It's called *pain-in-the-butt-itis,* and I'm afraid it's incurable."

Holly snorts.

"You two are both lovely gems, you are." Cap smiles under his white goatee. "Makes me wish I was half the age I am, Doc. I love me a lady with some fire in her belly!"

"He's incorrigible," Fiona says, dragging Holly along as she blows Cap a kiss through the large front window of his shop.

"I know. Cap's always been one of my favorites." Holly waves at him, remembering how Cap taught her to sail when she was ten. His sense of humor is spot-on, and the only things in life Cap takes seriously are his cigars and his friendship with Marco. Cap reads voraciously and eclectically, and he's been almost everywhere on the planet. His stories about sailing around the world are great bonfire fodder, and his personality is made up of just enough salt and vinegar to entertain everyone on the island.

Holly and Fiona look both ways as they cross Main Street arm-in-arm.

"Be good tonight, girls!" Bonnie calls out as she passes them in her golf cart. "Or be really, really bad and then make sure you show up at church to say a Hail Mary or two on Sunday!" She cackles, her eyes twinkling. The Christmas lights that Bonnie has wrapped around the cart blink on and off as she disappears down Main, her slightly-pudgy arm sticking out the side of the cart as she gives a theatrical pageant wave.

Fiona pulls Holly in the direction of Jack Frosty's. "Do you think everyone knows I have a thing for Buckhunter?" she laments. They walk into the open bar and Holly chooses a rough-hewn wooden barstool at the counter. She takes off her Yankees cap, setting it by her elbow.

"Yes, dear," Holly says with a smile, throwing an arm around her friend's shoulders and giving her a friendly shake. "Everybody knows. And keep in mind that we all know everything about each other on an island the size of a dollar bill."

"Damn. I get my own words get thrown right back in my face. I guess I deserve that."

"Indeed," Holly laughs, getting Buckhunter's attention with a nod and a raised finger.

They order a heaping pile of nachos and two iced teas, then munch on chips while they watch Buckhunter toss bottles in the air and pour shots under the clear fairy lights that dangle over his bar. All around them, their neighbors come and go, greeting one another and stopping by to chat with Holly and Fiona as another summer night wraps its arms around the little island in the sea, engulfing it in a sultry, starlit darkness.

6

"So, the vote's in," Bonnie says the next morning, peering at Holly over the pink and yellow striped frames of her reading glasses.

"And?" Holly rushes into the office of the B&B, Pucci trotting right behind her like a trusty assistant. He immediately retreats to his lime green dog bed in the corner of the office, turning in a circle once, twice, and then settling down to listen. Holly kicks off her sandals and sits down at her white wicker desk. She opens the cover of her laptop and pushes the power button.

"We're at a sixty-three percent approval rate for the advertising plan and budget you proposed," Bonnie says, passing a printed page across their shared desk space.

Holly had found the matching wicker desks in Key West on a weekend trip with Jake. They'd waited eagerly at the dock as the delivery boat pulled up, then strapped the desks to the roofs of their golf carts, lugging them back to the B&B as they laughed hysterically. Holly said she felt like they were two ants carrying giant sugar cubes on their backs, and Jake leaned forward in his golf cart comically, pretending that the roof was about to cave in on him. She'd immediately set the desks up in the office so that they faced one another, pushing them together to form one big table.

"That's more than half. I guess that's all we needed." Holly takes off her Yankees cap and pulls her light brown hair into a loose bun on top of her head. She jabs a pencil through the shiny pile to hold it all in place. She and Bonnie have their laptops running, and their matching iced lattes from Mistletoe Morning Brew are on the coasters at their elbows. "So let's put the advertising piece in motion by placing the ads with the *Sun-Sentinel* and the *Miami Herald*. We can look at placing something full-color in *Florida Travel + Life* or *Islands* when we get a feel for how much impact these first ads have." Holly yanks open the large drawer under her desk and flips through the hanging files. "I've got the mock-up we did right here."

"Got it, boss." Bonnie reaches over to take the sheet they'd drawn up. "I'll call the *Herald* first and see if we can run it before Labor Day weekend." Her long nails tap against her phone screen as she makes the call.

The morning passes like minutes. Holly sips her cold coffee and makes plans for the various ways they can showcase Christmas Key to potential visitors. She's been keeping up a healthy stream of photos and interesting tidbits about the island on Instagram, Facebook, and Twitter over the past two years, but in the back of her mind she's always known that she was laying the groundwork for something bigger—it's not just fans she wants, it's visitors. It's commerce and revenue. It's progress.

Now, with the majority of the islanders on board to support her long-term vision, social media posts need to be regular, engaging, and enticing. Holly already has a plan to tailor her upcoming posts around the seasons and the events she's dreamed up for Christmas Key: she'll post destination wedding ideas after the new year, hoping to attract spring and summer brides. Midsummer will be the time to start encouraging winter travel and family holiday trips to paradise. And—with luck—she'll be able to get some of her bigger ideas off the ground, like a food and wine festival in the fall, and an annual Christmas bazaar.

Bonnie fields calls as they come in, sending Holly the one from the *Sun-Sentinel's* advertising department. Right on the tail of that call comes one from Joe Sacamano to let her know that he's putting together a jam session for that night at the Ho Ho Hideaway, just a stone's throw down the beach from Holly's house. He's really sorry, but she'll probably hear some of the music, so she might as well just come on down and join them. Plus Buckhunter will be there, so she really ought to bring the good doctor along for a beer. (Holly can't wait to tell Fiona that along with Cap, Joe Sacamano is now also helping to orchestrate her love life.)

Holly is ready to take a break and go foraging for lunch when the phone rings again. Bonnie's out of the office for a second, so Holly picks up the line herself, pulling the pencil from her bun and letting her hair fall loose around her shoulders.

"Christmas Key B&B. This is Holly," she says, standing up so that she can toss her empty coffee cup into the wastebasket.

"Hi, baby. It's your mother."

Completely involuntarily, Holly's digestive tract forces stomach acid up through her esophagus. Of course it's her mother. She glances at the desk calendar beneath her notepad and cup of pencils: yep, it's about time for a check-in to see what's going on financially with the island, and it's high time for Coco Baxter to remind her only child that thirty is a ridiculous age for a girl to still be single and childless.

"Coco. How are you?" Holly sits back down, leaning her head against the hard wicker back of her desk chair.

"Why don't you ever just call me 'Mom'?"

"I don't know. I guess Coco suits you better."

As a leggy sixteen-year-old, Coco had been a sleek, wild horse with a taste for Jack and Coke, a fickle heart, and a love of older boys. Within months of convincing Frank and Jeanie Baxter that she should be allowed to leave parochial school and finish out her education at Coral Gables High, Coco managed to get arrested once for public intoxication, total her father's convertible Saab, and get pregnant. Holly was born at the start of Coco's senior year of high school, and Coco had immediately handed the infant over to her parents to raise. For as long as Holly could remember, her mother had treated her more like a pesky younger sister than like her own child.

"Let's not fight, Holly. I want to spend time with you. You're thirty now—we're practically the same age!—I'd love for us to get along more like friends than like mother and daughter. Can we do that?"

Holly taps the eraser of her pencil against her desk manically, her eyes unblinking. Just hearing Coco's voice at the other end of the line messes with her head.

"Anyway, I was looking at my calendar, and I'd really like to pop down for a visit sometime in the next month. Does that work for you? Would this be a good time to come to the island?"

Holly snaps out of her trance, tossing the pencil onto her desk with a clatter. "Yes, Coco, summer is a fabulous time for you to visit. The breeze is cool, the skies are clear, and all of the bugs have gone into hibernation for fall and winter," she says.

"Really?"

"No, *Mother*. Summer on this island feels like being tucked inside of Satan's jockstrap next to a few hot coals. It rains every afternoon like the sky is trying to piss us all into oblivion, and the mosquitos will eat you alive if you don't shower in bug repellant. But you should come. It'll be fun." Her voice has gone screechy, and Holly inhales through her nose deeply to calm herself.

"I guess I've forgotten how unlivable that place is in the summer."

"It must have also been unlivable for you during the spring, fall, and winter...because I don't think you've ever spent more than a few months here at a time." Holly hates the way one phone call from Coco can unhinge her, transforming her from a capable, grown woman into a hurt little girl in sixty seconds flat.

"Holly," Coco says tiredly, "if you don't want me to come, you can just say it."

Holly pauses, wishing in hindsight that she'd let this call go to voice mail instead of answering it. "Nah, it's fine. Are you bringing Alan?" If her stepfather comes along, then that gives her mom something to do while she's on the island so she's not just skulking around the B&B, poking her nose into everyone's business. And Alan is all right; aside from the fact that he clearly adores his high-maintenance wife and doesn't seem to begrudge her touch-and-go mothering style, he and Holly actually get along pretty well.

"Yes, I'm bringing Alan. That man needs a vacation!" Coco laughs, clearly happy that the conversation has gone her way.

"Okay, well, just send me your details, and I'll get you a room here at the B&B for however long you stay."

"Can't we just stay in the house next door to you?"

"Leo Buckhunter is still renting that house. So no, you can't stay there."

"Ha," Coco says, but there is no laughter in her voice. "Isn't that just like your grandfather."

"Isn't what just like him?"

"Oh, nothing, just that he would rent out that house to a raga-muffin who'll probably never vacate. Anyhow, I'll email you our travel info as soon as I have it all worked out, okay?"

Holly sits there for a while after hanging up, doodling spirals all around the edges of a notepad that has *Christmas Key B&B* printed across the top in a bright turquoise font. Knowing that more than half of her neighbors agree with her vision has infused Holly with a renewed sense of purpose. She pushes the thought of Coco visiting Christmas Key out of her mind and goes back to thinking about dreamy Instagram photos, full-page ads in bridal magazines, and vineyards that might want to book spots at her food and wine festival. She'll need a full-time wedding planner with a storefront on the island, obviously, and possibly catered boat cruises with a gourmet chef headquartered on Main Street. Daydreams of foot traffic, cosmopolitan travelers, and an uptick in cash flow fill her head.

Nervous excitement rushes through Holly's veins the same way it did when she and her grandpa sat in their lounge chairs on Candy Cane Beach, projecting ten, twenty, thirty years into the future. When he'd gotten sick, they'd talked at length about his dreams for Christmas Key, of what he would do if only he'd bought the island as a younger man. Holly remembers his frail arms as he gestured out at the horizon above the water. She'd noticed the slack skin on his jaw as he turned his profile to her. Her grandmother had already been gone for three years at that point, and Grandpa knew that his heart was giving out when he decided to start handing Holly all of the bits and pieces of his vision.

One day, as he'd sat wrapped in a giant striped beach towel, his white hair like a dusting of snow across his balding pate, he'd pointed at the sun setting over the Gulf in a somber, prophetic gesture. "You know how you can always count on the sun to rise in the east over by the dock on Main Street? And how, without fail, it crawls across the sky all day long before it finally falls into the water on the west side of the island?"

Holly nodded, her arms wrapped around her bare shins as she sat forward on her lounge chair. A cool burst of air off the water raised goosebumps on her skin.

"No matter what else happens, that sun does its job, day in and day out. You can count on that ball of fire in the sky to be strong and true no matter what. Do you know what I'm saying?"

"I think so," Holly answered, hoping that she did.

"You're like my sun, Holly. I know you've always been my shining star, my girl who hung the moon," he said wistfully, his gnarled fingers and crooked knuckles trailing a shaky path across the dusky sky. "But in reality, you're more like my sun." He took her young hand in his weathered one. "Because no matter what, I know I can count on you to rise and set like clockwork. To light up my world and to do what needs to be done around here."

The tears in her eyes and the tightness in her throat stopped her from actually speaking, so instead she'd just nodded again, squeezing his hand.

She meant everything she'd said at the village council meeting: in order to survive and prosper, they desperately need to be forward-thinking, to consider relying on revenue sources other than electric company pensions, Social Security checks, and nest eggs from years of frugal living. She doesn't want to come right out and say that they won't all live together on the island forever, that she plans on outliving them all and wants a back-up plan for herself and her beloved home, but it's true—those are the cold, hard facts. Holly needs to know that her own future is secure, and that her island can sustain itself—maybe well into a future that even she won't be around to see.

"We've got an ad placed in *The Herald*," Bonnie says, returning from her errand. She sits back down on her side of the desk. "And I made sure to have them add a footnote in teeny-tiny print to remind visitors of the bounty of beautiful, single ladies on Christmas Key."

"Fabulous. I can't wait to have a bunch of old guys show up here, hoping to buy island brides and drag them back to civilization." Holly rolls her eyes and balls up a Post-it note. She tosses it in Bonnie's direction playfully like she's lobbing a snowball at a friend. It misses and lands on the floor.

"I was hoping more for lonely, wealthy retirees with sailboats—and preferably all of their own teeth," Bonnie says, resting her chin on her hand as she gazes out the window.

"Keep dreaming, woman. I'm just looking for visitors with some disposable income and a hankering for paradise."

"That would work, too. Hey, listen, sugar. We've been at it here for more than two hours. Why don't you take Pucci-pooch-pooch for his walk before his eyes get any sadder. I'll go check with the kitchen to see if they have the menus drawn up for the fishermen's visit."

"Yeah, that sounds good," Holly says, distracted. "My mother just called, and now I feel like I'm short a few pints of blood. I should probably get some air." She saves the calendar of island events she's working on to a folder on her desktop and stands up, stretching her arms overhead.

"Oh, sweet molasses, child. Is it already time for a visit from Coco?"

"So she says." Holly sets her Yankees cap back on her head. "But she's bringing Alan, so at least she'll be occupied while she's here."

"Hmph," Bonnie says, looking at Holly over the frames of her reading glasses.

"Okay, I'll walk this old mutt while you figure out the menu situation. And then we need to map out the fishermen's visit in more detail."

"Meet you back here in twenty?" Bonnie gets up and bends to scratch the retriever between his ears.

"Yep. Want me to get you a sandwich?"

"The usual, please. Just have Iris and Jimmy put it on my tab."

Holly clips the leash to her dog's collar.

"Oh, and a root beer!" Bonnie shouts at Holly, who is already in the hallway.

She pops her head back into the office. "Got it. Tuna on wheat with extra onions. And a root beer."

"You're an angel, Holly Jean."

Out on the street, Holly puts on her clear-framed sunglasses. The lenses are a reflective polar blue that turn the world into a cool, icy wonderland.

Big band music pours from a speaker outside Tinsel & Tidings on Main Street as Heddie Lang-Mueller walks through the door, a paper bag in her arms. Tinsel & Tidings serves as the island gift shop for visitors, but it's also the general store for the island. The triplets always stock essentials and treats on the shelves in the back of the store, from the fresh produce and frozen chicken breasts shipped in twice a week, to little luxuries like imported chocolates and wines. In spite of the fact that they live in the middle of nowhere, the triplets make it possible for a person to easily get their hands on a bottle of extra virgin olive oil or a knotty sweet potato in a pinch.

"Hello," Heddie says, coming down the walkway that leads from the door of Tinsel & Tidings and runs directly into the sidewalk. She's waving one thin hand, a smile on her face. "How are you, Holly?"

"I'm great—the vote went our way!" She and Heddie pause where their paths meet.

"That is excellent news. Just wonderful. Your grandfather would be proud." Heddie gives a small smile, which—given her efficient German countenance—Holly knows is the equivalent of a grin.

"Thank you. I think it would make him happy," she says. Pucci's pink tongue lolls across his sharp incisors as he sits on his haunches next to her feet.

"Indeed," Heddie agrees in her crisp accent. "Well, I've got ice cream in my bag, so I should get it home." She raises the paper bag with a smile. "It's too hot today for anything else but frozen treats and air conditioning."

"True story." Holly tugs at Pucci's leash gently. "I'll see you later, Heddie."

Even with the heat of the midday sun on his golden fur and the warm pavement under his paws, Pucci looks happy to be out of the office. Holly crosses Main Street and walks past Poinsettia Plaza, turning south to where the road merges onto Holly Lane at the Christmas Key chapel. The rustic, weathered, white wood of the church peeks out from beneath a cover of tall sand pine trees. Each side of the small building is inlaid with an intricate stained glass window, and the front door has a simple Oxford gate latch made of hand carved wood. Holly stops to look up at the modest steeple while Pucci sniffs around the fallen pine needles.

"Do I need to ticket you for not picking up after your dog?" a voice says from behind her.

Holly turns, though she doesn't need to look to know it's Jake. "Sure. That's H-O-L-L-Y B-A-X-T-E-R. Just give me that ticket, and I'll put it right next to the one you gave me the other day." She holds out a hand, palm up, waiting.

"On your fridge?"

"Crumpled up on the floor somewhere. Probably under my bed." Pucci runs back to Holly and folds his hind legs so that he can sit next to her feet obediently, looking back and forth from his mistress to his former master with curiosity.

"Incidentally, I'm sorry about that. You can tear that ticket up if you want to." Jake bends down to grab Pucci's furry face between his hands, scratching him behind both ears. "She's going to be feisty and impudent to the end, huh, buddy?" he asks Pucci.

"Feisty, yes. I'm not sure about impudent." She takes her sunglasses off and looks up at him. "But I do accept your apology."

"Listen, I promise I'll try not to give in to my emotions so much—good or bad." Jake puts his hands in the pockets of his shorts. They stand there for a moment, Pucci panting heavily between them.

Holly nods and wraps the end of Pucci's leather leash around her hand absentmindedly.

"Hey, I've gotta run," Jake says, taking a step back. "But congrats on the vote going your way."

"How did you hear about that?"

"It's already all over Main Street," he says. "Just like everything else that happens on this island."

"Like us?"

"Right—like every single detail about us." Jake takes a moment, weighing his next words. "You never get tired of that? Really? You never just want to live in peace without people bird-dogging your every move?"

She relents, her face softening. "*Jake.*" In the lilt of that one word is every thought and feeling she wants to convey to him. In his one-syllable name, Holly breathes sympathy, sadness, both wariness *and* weariness, and more than a little disappointment. She understands what it means to long for things—sometimes things that can't coexist —and she also knows what it means to stubbornly refuse to back down. "Listen, I get it if you want to leave here, and I don't blame you...it's not non-stop excitement, and sometimes it feels like we're roughing it or living in another century, but I'm happy with my life just the way it is."

"And what about the idea of us getting married makes you so *un*happy?"

She can't answer him. Ingrained deep within her is the knowledge that, ultimately, she's on her own, and the only person she can truly count on is herself. That stubborn self-reliance is as much a part of the fabric of her being as the need to be both a planner and a doer, as Fiona said. Pucci and Jake both stare at her, waiting for a revelation that isn't coming.

"Alright. I know. We're not talking about this," Jake says, holding up a palm in surrender. "Will I see you tonight at the Ho Ho?"

"I'll be there."

"Good. First beer's on me." He slides easily into his official police golf cart and drives away.

Holly watches him go, then makes a double kissing noise at her dog to let him know she's ready to move again.

Iris and Jimmy Cafferkey's Jingle Bell Bistro sits on a stretch of white sand beach. It has a wraparound porch that looks out onto the water, and huge windows that face the ocean. Iris and Jimmy serve the best food on the island. Their seafood chowders are to die for—lobster, grouper, cobia, pink shrimp—no matter what's available or in season, Jimmy whips up a creamy, delicious soup to go with his sweet Irish soda bread. Because the food is so good, and because most people want to mingle with their neighbors at least a few times a week, the Jingle Bell Bistro has a steady stream of customers most days, just like Mistletoe Morning Brew.

Holly leaves Pucci in the shade on the porch, his head lowered onto his front paws. He pants to cool down, his big brown eyes following his mistress as she walks in the front door.

Inside the bistro, Iris is busy rushing from table to table, her light, graying hair clipped up into a neat twist as she clears plates and takes orders. There are about ten people scattered around the small dining room, talking at tables for two, or reading newspapers and sipping coffee by the windows that look out at the sea. Jimmy is working in the kitchen, a yellow bandana knotted over his hair and a clean apron over his gray t-shirt, his stocky frame visible through the window where Iris drops off and picks up her orders. Their daughter Emily makes her way around the restaurant, pouring water into glasses and making conversation as people eat their lunches. Every so often, she gathers up the empty plates and soup bowls to carry back to the kitchen.

"Hi, Em," Holly says, giving her a tight hug. "How are you?"

"Good," she says. "Is Jake here?"

"No, he's not. But I just saw him on the way over."

"Did he ask about me?" Two metal barrettes pin Emily's straight blonde hair back above her ears.

"I told him I was coming over here, and he said to tell you hi," Holly fibs easily, knowing how much a hello from Jake means to Emily.

"Oh. Is Pucci here?"

"He's on the porch—you can go see him if you want."

Emily sets her pitcher of water on an empty table and goes outside to pet the dog, the bell over the door tinkling behind her. Emily was diagnosed with Down's Syndrome at birth, when Iris and Jimmy were already in their mid-forties. By her eighth birthday, with their two older kids in college, they'd both quit their jobs at law firms in Dublin and moved to Christmas Key to raise their young daughter.

Because she's just two years younger than Holly, Emily had joined her in being tutored by the two retired schoolteachers on the island, and they'd gotten their high school diplomas without ever setting foot in a brick and mortar schoolhouse. It had been an ideal education, filled with real life science experiments in the island's tide pools, reading classics like *Robinson Crusoe* beneath swaying palm trees on the beach, and learning the different ways to prepare and eat the island's natural bounty of tropical fruits and plants.

For much of Holly's childhood and adolescence, Emily had been her closest friend. They celebrated their birthdays together, had sleepovers, and played endless games of mermaids or dolphins on all of the island's beaches. When they got too old for mermaids, the girls shimmied up the trunks of the palm trees to watch the open seas for pirates, and cracked coconuts on the craggy rocks at Snowflake Banks to drink the sweet water and eat the coconut meat with their bare hands. Emily was the first person to congratulate Holly when she got engaged to Jake, though it was no secret to anyone that Emily would have preferred to be the one wearing an engagement ring from Officer Zavaroni.

For his part, Jake loves having his own fan club, and he has a great time ferrying Emily around Christmas Key in his police golf cart, pointing out birds and wildlife and listening to her stories. The sweet things Jake does for other people always make Holly question her own stubborn need for independence.

"Hey, stranger!" Iris says, wiping her hands on her apron as she breaks into Holly's thoughts. "Lunch to go?"

"If it's not too much trouble. The usual for Bonnie, plus a root beer, and I'll have a cup of chowder, a side of soda bread, and a sweet tea, please."

"We can do that," Iris says. She steps behind the counter to ring it all up. "And I wanted to tell you that we thought your plan was really impressive, lass. The advertising, the budget you drew up, it all made sense to us." The cash register dings with the total charge. "So don't you pay any mind to the naysayers."

Holly hands over her credit card for Iris to swipe. "Thank you. I'm glad you guys are on board."

"We want this island to grow and prosper. If we were all independently wealthy then it might be nice to keep it a secret so that we could have it to ourselves, but we're not. We need to plan long-term here, and we need to think about the younger people."

"Thank you for saying that, Iris. I know we're a little underrepresented right now in terms of our numbers, but I'm just trying to be realistic. We need younger people around here to keep things moving forward."

"Agreed," Iris says, pulling a pen from behind her ear and passing it to Holly.

"I'm hoping to slowly attract some full-time and part-time residents—ideally some younger families with kids who appreciate living just a hair off the grid. It's my worst nightmare to imagine Christmas Key as a ghost town someday," Holly says.

"And that's why Jimmy and I fully support you boosting our visibility a lot and our population a little. It has to be done, lass."

"I'm glad you guys see it that way."

"We do. And whether we live here for thirty more years or drop dead tomorrow, we owe a lot of our happiness to this island. Jimmy and I'll do whatever we can to make sure things move forward." Iris slides the receipt across the counter for Holly to sign.

"That means a lot." Holly drags her pen across the signature line with a flourish. "I can't tell you how much I appreciate how progressive you and Jimmy are when it comes to thinking about the future."

"Well, as you can imagine," Iris raises her chin in the direction of the front window with its wide view of the porch and the beach beyond, "sometimes thinking about the future is *all* I do." Outside on the porch, Emily is on her knees, petting Pucci and talking sweetly to him.

The two women lock eyes, the front counter still between them. "Iris," Holly says meaningfully, grabbing Iris's warm hand in hers. "We're all family here; we need each other. And Emily is the only sister I've ever had." Iris gives Holly's hand a squeeze, her eyes shining with unshed tears. Nothing more needs to be said.

Holly walks back to the B&B slowly, juggling Pucci's leash, the bags of lunch, and the drinks. Holly Lane is unpaved where it branches off of Main Street, the road really just a wide, sandy path. As she passes the chapel again, Holly thinks about the conversation that she and Jake *almost* had there not twenty minutes earlier, and about what Iris said: with all the money in the world at her disposal, would she really want things to stay exactly the way they are? Maybe, maybe not. She loves Christmas Key wholeheartedly, but she's equally in love with its potential. Even subtracting the need for it to financially sustain itself, the desire to mold it into her own vision of paradise remains.

Holly's loyalty to Christmas Key runs deep, and admitting that the island has faults—even ones that have nothing to do with the place itself—means acknowledging that something is lacking. At one point, when she'd grown tired of playing mermaids and dolphins but realized that Emily never would, Holly lamented the lack of friends and romantic prospects to the point that her grandparents actually considered sending her to a boarding school off the island. In the end, she'd chickened out at the thought of being away from them and from Christmas Key, but she'd been more than ready to leave for college—and more than ready to return to the island after graduation.

Even now Holly sometimes fantasizes that she'll walk into the coffee shop or the bistro, and that standing there will be a man she's never seen. A handsome stranger who smiles at her crookedly through a rakish five o'clock shadow, holds the door for her, and says something incredibly witty. But most of the people who come to the island are honeymooners, families, or retired married couples, and their visitors are almost always friends-of-friends or relatives of the island's residents. The few adventurous souls who set out to explore the Florida Straits and the uninhabited keys are usually interesting characters, but so far none of them have ever been single, attractive, available men in their thirties.

Holly pauses for a moment before she rounds the bend, still holding everything in her hands as Pucci sniffs around. She takes another long look at the beach and the water, thinking about Jake while the dog does his business. Jake had come to the island fresh out of the police academy, and it hadn't taken more than a week for them to realize that they were a pretty decent match—actually that they were the *only* possible match for one another on the island.

They'd kayaked around Christmas Key in their spare time, joked flirtatiously, and made dinner together. The sex has always been great, and it all made sense. And right there is the heart of the issue for Holly: the whole thing has always felt too *easy*, like the fact that they're both young, attractive, and single is enough to cement their relationship for life. And it's not. But if not Jake, then who? Or does there even have to be a man in her life at all? Maybe Pucci and Marco are enough for her right now.

With a last look at the water, she tugs at Pucci's leash gently to get him moving again.

Bonnie is still out when Holly gets back to the air-conditioned office with lunch. She sets the bags and the drinks on her desk and gives Pucci a dog bone from the jar on top of her filing cabinet, which he takes back to his dog bed and hides protectively under one paw.

"I'm not going to steal it back from you, boy," she says to him. "It's all yours."

She opens the styrofoam container of soup from the bistro, stirring it with a plastic spoon while she stands in front of the white-framed windows that look directly out onto Main Street. Holly has a great view of all the action from her office, so she eats her soup right there, watching her neighbors as they putter around in golf carts, moving in and out of the coffee shop and the gift store in their knee-length Bermuda shorts and sandals.

Clinging to the edges of the blue sky are dark, angry clouds. On her walk back from the Jingle Bell Bistro, Holly could feel the humidity hanging in the air as the storm approached. When the temperature and the humidity both climb as high as they do in the summer, being outside in the heat feels like swimming through hot syrup. She looks at her watch in between spoonfuls of soup. It won't be long now before the violent rains and cracks of lightning rip through the trees on the island, sending sheets of water flying side-ways at the windows, and temporarily filling the gutters with what seems like three feet of water. When it's over and the skies have cleared, she'll go home and sit on her lanai again, listening to the cicadas and looking at her guava and lemon trees in the yard. It's a pretty good life, being the mayor of paradise.

Holly tosses her empty soup container and spoon into the trash and gets back to work.

7

THE UNTAMED FEELING OF THE ISLAND AT NIGHT IS ONE OF HOLLY'S favorite things about Christmas Key. Nightfall on the island brings out the nocturnal animals. Twigs snap in the trees as they move around, their eyes like lasers pointed at the humans who congregate merrily in a wood shack on the water. The moon casts a long, luminous reflection across the Gulf, and iguanas and geckos crawl up the trunks of palm trees and skitter under fallen logs. Because she knows every one of her neighbors and doesn't fear pirates or boogeymen, Holly loves being out in the pitch-black darkness of the slithering, pulsating jungle at night, looking up at the unfettered sky of stars above.

Fiona bowed out of a night at the Ho Ho Hideaway at the last minute by claiming a summer cold, but Bonnie is more than happy to join Holly at Joe Sacamano's beachside bar. She pulls into an unmarked parking spot in the sandy lot at the Ho Ho next to Holly's golf cart, shuts off her headlight, and touches up her lipstick in the rearview mirror by the light of the moon.

The women link arms as they trudge up the steps of the bar. "Ready, sugar?" Bonnie asks, clutching Holly's elbow.

"Ready for a beer? Absolutely." Holly takes a deep breath and steps up to the bar, her small, orange purse tucked under one arm.

The Ho Ho Hideaway opens directly onto the sand and the ocean, and because of its proximity to Holly's property, she can easily walk along the beach between her house and the bar if she wants to. She and Jake have walked that very bar-to-house route many times after imbibing a little too much of Joe Sacamano's homemade rum, or over-indulging in Arnold Palmers spiked with Cap's potent moonshine.

"Can I interest you in a shot of my special Christmas Key rum?" Joe Sacamano asks, flipping over a wet shot glass and slamming it on the counter like a dare. "Made from 100% Florida sugarcane and aged in oak. It came out really sweet and rich this time. First shot's on the house."

"Hit me," Holly says, flipping her loose hair over one shoulder and setting her purse on the counter. Joe pours a shot and slides it across the bar. She tosses it back, feeling the warmth of the liquor slide down her throat and work its way through her. "Mmm, butterscotch," she says appreciatively.

"You think?" Joe beams with pride. "I wasn't sure if I was tasting caramel or butterscotch. Damn good though, huh?"

"Really good. You ought to bottle that and sell it, Joe. Maybe make a few extra bucks."

Joe laughs and pours her another shot. "An old geezer like me? I got no need for a storefront and all that headache. I just want to make my booze and pour it, then play my guitar for all of my rabid fans." He spreads his hands expansively, laughing because the bar crowd is essentially the antithesis of a group of rabid rock fans. With his cropped, snowy curls and lazy grin, Joe is widely considered the best looking older man on Christmas Key, a distinction that barely fazes him after the years he spent on the road playing guitar with some of the biggest acts of the sixties and seventies.

"Did you bring your lady friends with you?" Joe asks casually, capping the bottle of rum and setting it on the counter in front of him.

"Just Bonnie..." Holly spins around, searching the crowd of islanders gathered near the railing that overlooks the beach. The sound of the ocean in the darkness beyond the bar is a roaring, soothing repetition of crashing waves. "Well, we came in together, but it looks like I already lost her."

"I'm sure she'll turn up. Social butterfly, that one, eh?"

"The most social butterfly I've ever met," Holly agrees, knocking back the second shot of rum. "And I noticed you two sitting together at Candy Cane Beach on the 4th of July. Very cozy." She winks and sets the glass down, putting her hand over its open mouth as Joe reaches to uncap the bottle and pour her a third drink.

"Let's talk more about this idea of yours to sell my rum," Joe says, eyes twinkling.

"Nice change of topic, Sacamano. Very deft."

Joe laughs, caught. "Ah, well. Worth a shot. But in my vast experience, I do know that distracting a woman once she's got her teeth sunk into something is like trying to whistle at a tiger to stop it from charging a deer."

"So I'm the tiger, and you're the deer here?"

"I am a deer in headlights here, milady. Admittedly." Joe sets her empty shot glass in his copper sink behind the bar.

"So?"

"Nothin' to it, Mayor. I love all women, and all women love me." Joe backs up, smiling benevolently as he looks around his bar. "I am a man of the people."

"Oh, jeez."

"I'm just not interested in settling down with anyone—probably ever." Joe leans forward on the bar, placing his elbows on the shiny burgundy tile that covers the bar top.

"I know what you mean," Holly says drily, unsnapping her purse and searching for a tube of lipgloss. "I'm not too keen on settling down myself."

"Really? Ever?" Joe stands up again, assessing Holly with as serious a face. "A woman as young and beautiful as you shouldn't rule out love, doll."

"Well," Holly says, dropping the lipgloss into her purse and snapping it shut. "I just shot down what was probably my only chance at love and marriage because he had the nerve to propose, so..." She shrugs.

"Eh, don't beat yourself up over that one, kid. If it's not there, you can't force it." Joe runs a hand through his white curls from his forehead straight over the crown. His gold pinky ring glints under the low lights of the bar.

"It's not him—it's me. It has to be," Holly says. "He's a great guy, but I don't think I'm the marrying type."

"You never know." Joe grabs a rag and wipes the bar top. "I didn't think I was the marrying type either, but that didn't stop me from doing it a time or two."

"Or three," Holly teases.

"Ouch. Yeah, I guess there are a few ex-Mrs. Sacamanos roaming around out there," Joe says, chuckling, "but I think I'll stop at three." His eyes scan the crowd, landing on Bonnie just as her gales of laughter rise above the commotion of the bar and the crash of the waves. "I've had some fun with a lady or two in my day, and at this point I'm just as content to keep Louise as my main squeeze until the end." Everyone on Christmas Key knows that Louise is Joe's Fender, his favorite guitar and the apple of his eye.

UB40's "Red, Red Wine" comes on over the speakers and Holly gets up. She pushes her stool in and rubs her lips together, spreading the lipgloss around. "Well, I defer to you in all matters of marriage and relationships, Sacamano. I clearly have no idea what the hell I'm doing, and I've made a bit of a mess for myself by breaking up with a guy I still have to share a tiny island with." She tucks her purse under one arm. "But if you ever want to talk about selling that hooch, stop by and see me at the B&B sometime. I've got some ideas to advertise and market it."

"Will do, Miss Baxter. And just in case you feel like mucking things up a bit more, our favorite officer of the law is here tonight."

Holly shoots him a look. "It wasn't that bad, was it?"

"Eh," Joe tips his hand from side-to-side, weighing the damage.

"You two were pretty hot and heavy on the dance floor, and if memory serves, it was my Don Henley impression that set things off. So I'd say it was either pretty bad, or really, really good." He wiggles his eyebrows at her suggestively.

"Jesus, Joe." Holly puts one hand over her eyes so that she won't have to look at him.

"Aww, I'm just messin' with you, Mayor. Jake's out there wandering the beach with a bottle of beer," he says, nodding past the railing at the dark shoreline beyond. "Probably stargazing or drowning his sorrows. Or both. You should go find him."

"Thanks for the shots, Joe." She pats the bar before walking away.

Holly winds through the small crowd, smiling at the Cafferkeys. Iris and Jimmy toast her wordlessly with bottles of beer. Maria Agnelli has carved out a corner of the room as her own personal dance floor and she's swaying to UB40 with her eyes closed, one hand holding her loose skirt up above her wrinkled knees, the other balancing a tequila on the rocks as she dances.

"You like reggae, Mrs. Agnelli?" Holly leans in, holding onto Maria's elbow so that she won't startle and spill her drink.

"I love all kinds of music!" Mrs. Agnelli says loudly, opening her eyes and smiling up at Holly. "All of my children were conceived to different music."

"No—stop it, Mrs. Agnelli!" Holly shifts her clutch purse from one armpit to the other.

"It's true: little Frankie was born nine months after Alfie and I got our first Sinatra album," she says, her eyes merry from the drink. "Our Doris came about because Alfie and I couldn't get enough of that Doris Day song 'Choo Choo Train.' And then our surprise baby, Paulie, joined us after the British Invasion. I just loved those cute Beatles," she says, sipping her drink.

"That's...a *lot* of information." Holly pats Mrs. Agnelli on the shoulder. "I need to find Bonnie now; I think she got away from me again."

Mrs. Agnelli nods and keeps dancing, giving Holly a wave.

Holly glances around the bar. No Bonnie. A smart woman would take herself home after two shots of rum and call it a night, but knowing that Jake is just down on the beach pulls her in that direction, as much as she wishes it didn't. She salutes Cap across the bar and makes her way down the steps in the dark. With her flip-flops in one hand and her purse in the other, she stands on the cool sand, listening to the sound of the music from the bar as it merges with the rolling of the waves.

Sitting by the water in the moonlight, legs pulled up and elbows resting on both knees, is Jake. He's got a bottle of Corona in his left hand; it dangles between his legs as he holds it by the mouth loosely.

"I thought you were buying me my first beer." She strolls over to where he's sitting.

Jake turns his head and glances up at her. "So go put one on my tab." He takes a swig of his beer, then digs a hole in the sand with the bottom of the bottle. He lets the beer rest there.

"I'm just teasing. Joe bought me a couple of shots of his new rum." She tosses her flip-flops on the sand and sets her purse on top of them.

"Wanna watch the waves with me?"

"Might as well." The memory of waking up in Jake's arms the night he stayed over is still fresh. Holly drops to the sand next to him, intentionally leaving about a foot and a half between them. They sit there quietly for a couple of minutes, enjoying the water and listening to the clink of bottles and the laughter of their neighbors coming from the bar behind them.

"Sounds like things have been pretty busy around the old B&B."

"Yeah?" Holly wraps her arms around her bare legs, chin resting on her knees. "More gossip on the street?"

"Not really, I just asked Bonnie how things were going while we were in line for coffee this morning. And every time I drive by the B&B, I see you at your desk working like a madwoman."

"Things have been busy. It's good." Holly doesn't really feel like engaging in work-talk on a Friday night, so she lets the amicable silence engulf them again.

Jake takes a long pull on his bottle of beer, and Holly admires his strong profile. The navy blue night sky looks like a blanket that's been hole-punched a million times so that pinpoints of bright light can flood through.

"Jake," she says, leaning over and nudging him with her shoulder. He grunts and takes another drink of beer. A relationship discussion might be as much of a mood-killer as work-talk, but it can't make things much more awkward than they already are. "I feel like I don't know...how to *be* with you yet. I'm really struggling here."

Jake nods, still not looking at her. "It's only been a couple of months, Hol. We're figuring things out."

"I know. But I thought it would be easier."

"Us living on this island and just sleeping together when the mood strikes is never going to make things easier." Jake turns to her, smirking. "But I am willing to keep trying that if it's working for you."

Holly leans into him, bumping his shoulder with hers again. "You know what I mean."

"Yeah, I do." He stares out at the water, still holding the bottle of beer between his knees.

Joe Sacamano cuts the music and plugs in his electric guitar on the small stage he's created inside the Ho Ho Hideaway. Holly and Jake listen as he taps the microphone and asks the crowd if they're ready for some rock and roll. Everyone claps and hoots.

"Remember what happened when Joe did his Eagles set?" Jake says. "Are you willing to take that risk again?"

Holly looks him in the eye and holds his gaze. "I think I can handle it."

"Okay, well, proceed at your own risk, Baxter," he says, taking another swig from his bottle of beer. "The combination of moonlight and music seems to be your undoing, and I'm not sure if I feel like putting out tonight."

Holly throws her head back and laughs. "Oh, please. You *always* feel like putting out!"

Jake swirls the beer around in the bottle. "It's good to hear you laugh again," he says.

"This is how I want it to be all the time, Jake."

"I'm not sure that we're going to be able to swing that, Holly. At least not without the rum and beer." He holds up the bottle. "And I'm pretty sure that the mayor and the only cop on the island can't just be drunk 24/7."

Holly leans back into the sand and rests on her elbows. The thin tank top she's wearing rides up, leaving a couple of inches of bare skin between her shirt and the waist of her denim skirt. "Probably not. But if you're really going to stay here, then we have to figure out how to be friends again."

"Just friends? You know that's not what I want." He looks her in the eye, holding her gaze with intensity.

Joe launchs into a cover of "Let's Stay Together" in the bar.

"Did you pay Joe to play this one?" she asks, shaking out her wavy, air-dried hair behind her.

Jake tips back his beer bottle, drains it, and sets it on the sand. "I only wish I was that smooth." He stands up and brushes off the back of his shorts. "Wanna dance?" She looks at him skeptically. "Just as a peace offering," he assures her.

Holly stares at the hand he's holding out to her. Does she want to dance? Does she want to do more than dance? Does she want to wake up in Jake's arms? Does she want to get back together and pretend that she'd never had second thoughts? It could all be so easy...in that moment she's not sure what she wants, so she reaches out and takes his strong hand. "Sure. But just as a peace offering."

They move into position slowly, each fumbling for the other as Jake takes her in his arms. They let the notes of the song wrap around them as they sway in the sand, Holly's head coming to rest on Jake's chest while Joe croons in the distance.

"You're right—this is hard," he admits, pulling her closer. "I'm still totally confused every time I see you. We're supposed to live together on this island, but not *together*. And when you show up at a village council meeting in a see-through dress and wet hair, I can't decide if I want to yell at you for tormenting me, or throw you over my shoulder and take you to bed."

Holly snorts. "You're such a caveman."

"You turn me into one." Jake pulls back from her to look down into her eyes. "For some reason I just want to protect you—to keep you safe—but then you turn around and throw it in my face. You're maddening, woman."

Holly smiles. Her heart rate kicks up a notch or two. They're dancing so close that she can feel the whole length of Jake's hard body pressed up against hers.

"Come on, Hol," Jake pleads, pulling her closer. His lips are just inches away from hers. "Let me take you home," he whispers. "Let me remind you how good things can be."

"Maybe," she says into his shoulder, pressing her lips against the cotton of his shirt. She can feel his warm skin under the fabric; she can smell that familiar Jake smell—part soap, part musk, part beer. The two shots of rum are scrambling her best intentions, and Holly feels the world spin around them. It's just her and Jake in a puddle of moonlight—just the two of them standing on their own private island in the middle of a bigger island—and she wants to believe his words. It's been more than a month since their night together, and she does a quick mental bargain with herself, weighing the cost of one more night with Jake against the confusion it might create between them.

Jake's hand cups her cheek; her face and ear fit in his large palm, his fingers between her gold hoop earrings and her jawline. Fifty feet away, all of their neighbors and friends are dancing and drinking in the bar as Joe starts a slowed down, meandering version of "God Only Knows" by the Beach Boys.

"What do you say? Can I take you back to your place?" Jake asks, bringing his lips to meet hers. She tastes beer. "I know what you want, and I know how you like it." He probes her mouth with his warm, familiar tongue.

In under ten seconds, Holly runs through the whole scenario in her mind: the sheet-scorching night they'll spend in her bed; the sultry feel of waking up in the darkness under the ceiling fan with Jake breathing softly next to her; the inevitability that she'll realize tomorrow what a huge mistake she's just made.

"Jake," she whispers hoarsely, separating her lips from his. "Wait."

He pulls back sharply, the softness draining from his eyes. It's obvious that he's already moved further into the evening in his mind, and he's assuming that she has too. Her hesitation is a bucket of cold water to the face.

"I'm sorry. We shouldn't," she says.

"Who makes the rules here, Holly? Isn't there some loophole that says you can have a drunken night with your ex occasionally, and it doesn't really mean anything in the light of day?" His voice is raspy with desire.

"I don't know, Jake..."

"Or maybe it does mean something. Maybe we can just skip over that whole part where I asked you to marry me. I mean, things between us weren't bad, were they?" He's looking down into her eyes.

"Jake, things were never bad—never. I know you don't believe me, but it's honest to God not you. This is all me; these are my issues."

"That's what you say, but I feel like part of this must be my fault. Things were great between us and then suddenly...I don't know. It's like when I asked you to marry me, it totally pushed you away."

Even though they've completely stopped dancing, Holly keeps her hands on Jake's waist, her gaze focused on his shoulder. "I've gone over this in my mind a million times. Believe me," she says in a near-whisper. "We had almost everything going for us—"

"Except what, Holly? What did we not have going for us?" he interrupts.

Joe's song ends and everyone in the bar breaks into applause as he launches into the next one. Holly tucks her hair behind her ears and pulls away.

"Almost isn't enough for me, Jake. I'm sorry, but it's just not." She folds her arms across her chest. "I need to know that I'm not just marrying someone because..."

"Because what? Say it," Jake says, his voice hard and demanding. "Just say it."

"Because I don't have any other options."

Jake steps back, starts to say something, then stops. He puts his hands on his hips. His face is hurt, though he's obviously trying to mask it with nonchalance. "Okay." He nods. "Okay, I get it."

"Jake," she says, her body language as defensive as her tone. "I have so much work to do on the island. I made a promise to my grandpa that I'd pour my heart and soul into this place, and that's what I have to do. I need to stay focused."

Jake backs away, both palms facing her as he shakes his head. "I give up, Holly. I'm finally ready to accept it."

"Accept what?"

"You. Your stuff. This *place.* " He gestures wildly at the darkened beach and the palm trees. "It feels kind of crazy to even say this, but has it ever occurred to you that maybe you don't actually own this island?"

Holly stands, arms dangling at her sides, fingertips brushing against the skin of her thighs below the hem of her jean skirt. "How do you mean?" She frowns at him.

"I mean," Jake says, running both hands through his short hair, "maybe you don't own this island—maybe *it* owns *you*. It's food for thought, Holly. Seriously."

Before she can say anything, he turns and walks back to the bar, taking the wooden steps two at a time. She stares at his back as he moves through the crowd on the well-lit dance floor and disappears from view.

It feels like a million years since she arrived at the B&B that morning, and Holly is more than ready to go home—alone. She wrestles with the idea of jumping into her golf cart and driving away from the bar without going back in, but it would only be polite to track Bonnie down and let her know that she's leaving. She walks back towards the bar, stopping to pick up her flip-flops and purse where she left them in the sand.

"It's not fair," a female voice says from the shadows.

Holly stops in her tracks. "Who is it?" she asks, moving closer.

Emily Cafferkey stands up from the spot where she's been sitting Indian-style on the sand, her back to the bar in the shadows.

"Em—you scared me! Do your parents know you're out here?"

Emily ignores her question, instead lightly crushing the half-full can of Coke she holds in her hands. "It's not fair, Holly. You don't even want him, so why can't I have him?"

"Oh. Em." Holly's heart clenches; she knows how much Emily loves Jake.

"You don't have to answer that," Emily says, a touch of anger in her voice. "I know why I can't have him. I'm not stupid. I'm different, and I'm not pretty." She turns her back on Holly, letting her chin drop to her chest.

"Emily, no." Holly reaches for her friend. There are people you can lie to out of kindness, and there are people who know you too well for that. Sometimes you cushion your words to spare feelings, and other times you know a person well enough to know that any lie you tell would ring hollow. Instead of grasping for words, Holly wraps her arms around Emily from behind, pressing her cheek against her friend's silky blonde hair. "I'm so sorry, Em." And she is sorry—sorry that she doesn't have the right words, sorry that life is unfair, sorry for the pain of unrequited love. She's been in Emily's position before and it hurts like hell—maybe more than anything else on earth besides losing the people you love.

Emily straightens up, sniffling. She raises her head proudly, patting the arm that Holly's wrapped around her shoulders. "It's okay, Holly. It's okay. I love you."

Holly loosens her grip and lets Emily go, watching her old friend as she walks to the steps of the building, her short body swaying slightly as she takes each wooden step one at a time.

The strains of Joe's guitar wail into the night as he jams, letting the chords take him on an uncharted journey; the music floats all around her. But Holly isn't going back in there. Bonnie is a sharp enough lady to deduce for herself at the end of the night that she's taken off, and it won't be a big deal.

Under the watchful eyes of the night animals and the diamond-sharp stars, Holly drives back to her house, shoes and purse on the seat next to her. Buckhunter's kitchen light is on next door as she pulls into her driveway. For just a minute she's tempted to knock on his door and see if he wants to have a nightcap with her. Holly sits on the bench of her golf cart, looking at his porch. Would that be weird? To pass a few minutes in the company of a neighbor? Something about going home alone after the way she and Jake just left things feels off. Sort of lonely.

She makes up her mind to be spontaneous and neighborly. She parks her cart and walks up to his porch. Standing there, poised to tap on his door, Holly spies two beach towels slung over the back of his rocking chair. And sitting right by the front door are two pairs of shoes: a man-sized pair of flip-flops, and a pair of sandals with rhinestones that Holly immediately recognizes as Fiona's.

She smiles, looking down at the shoes, hand still closed in the fist that was about to knock on the door. In a weird way it pleases her to think that Fiona faked a cold to steal an evening with Buckhunter, because why not? It wouldn't hurt Fiona to be less of a planner and more of a doer, and if what she wants to do is Buckhunter, well, then more power to her. Holly backs away from the door, tiptoeing across the grass to her own darkened house.

At least someone's going to have a good night, and with no strings or dangerous emotions attached. Holly's happy for them. She changes into a stained t-shirt and a pair of cut-off shorts, pulling her sweaty hair into a pile on the crown of her head. She mixes up a small batch of thinset mortar in her kitchen and grabs her bucket of shells. With Pearl Jam on the stereo, and the ceiling fan spinning overhead on her lanai, Holly spends the next two hours fixing conch and lucine shells onto her outside wall, her mind drifting as she fits them together carefully before she sets them.

It might have been nice to talk to Buckhunter about the stuff with Jake. Maybe. She glances at his house, wiping the sweat from her forehead with the back of her wrist. Her hands are covered in dried thinset, the white moons of her nails darkened with mortar. It's probably just that he's a bartender and used to listening to people's problems, but Holly wouldn't have minded downing a whisky with him and unloading a little.

Across the way, a figure walks through Buckhunter's kitchen, pausing in front of the window. From a distance, Holly can't tell if it's Buckhunter or Fiona, but she's suddenly glad that he has company. It's better to leave things the way they are, and to keep her business to herself. She doesn't need Jake, she doesn't need her mother, and she's managing just fine without her grandparents, so why on earth should she need Buckhunter?

The sound of the cicadas hiding in the darkness beyond the screened-in lanai nearly drowns out the crashing waves in the distance, and she has to go into the house to turn up her music.

When she comes back, humming along to the song on her stereo, she holds another shell up to the wall with her grimy hands, fitting it in between two others. It's a perfect match.

8

AFTER TWO WEEKS OF PREPPING MENUS, PLANNING ACTIVITIES, AND organizing rooms, the fishermen finally arrive on the last day of July. Holly and Bonnie watch as nineteen rugged men of all ages spill from the ferry, looking overheated and jet-lagged. They're a motley crew of males: some potbellied and balding, others grizzled and covered with hair. Most are wearing wedding bands. Holly greets them all with a smile, shaking hands and welcoming each guest.

She's stopped just short of arranging a ticker-tape parade for the island's first large group of visitors, but Bonnie would be more than happy to bounce up and down, cheering and tossing confetti at all nineteen of them, giggling as colored bits of paper get caught in their beards. She even offered to hand out business cards with her home phone number to each of them—just in case of emergency, of course. Holly nixed this idea immediately.

"Welcome to Christmas Key," Holly says, shielding her eyes with one hand as she watches the boat swaying in the sparkling water next to the dock. "Looks like you all got here in one piece."

"That depends on what you consider one piece," says a man whose face she can't see, even with the brim of her baseball hat casting a shadow over her eyes in the bright light. He steps off the trawler, the last of the men to climb from boat to dock. With his back to the sun, he's nothing but a tall, lean, muscular silhouette to Holly, his voice somehow both rocky and smooth, as if his vocal chords are paved with gravel and melted caramel. He moves to the other side of her, lifting his bags in both hands easily. "I think Dave left a good chunk of his stomach back there somewhere around Key West," he jokes, nodding at a middle-aged man who is wiping his forehead with a red bandanna.

As Holly's eyes adjust to the light, she sees that the last man off the boat is rather handsome. And young—at least in comparison to the rest of the group. "Well, I'm glad you're all here," she says to the good-looking stranger.

"So are we. River O'Leary." He puts his hand out to shake hers.

"Holly Baxter," she says, shaking firmly.

"Nice place you have here." He casts a glance around the dock, admiring the tall, weather-worn wooden navigational post that greets visitors. It's peppered with handmade plaques from top to bottom, each plaque held in place with two fat, rusty nails.

The villagers started the post the year that Frank paved Main Street. Everyone picked a location that meant something to them, then calculated its distance from Christmas Key. They each decorated a small piece of painted wood with that information and an arrow that pointed in the direction of the destination. At the bottom of the post is a sign that reads, "Portland, Maine—1,478 miles," and at the top is one that simply says "Heaven," and has an arrow pointing to the sky. The signs in between say things like "Santa Barbara, CA—2,352 miles" and "Chicago—1,240 miles."

"You don't have one for Oregon." River nods at the signs.

"Not yet, but the island is still growing. Who knows, maybe someone with ties to Oregon will wash up on our shores someday." Holly smiles up at him. He's tall, and she has to tip her head back to really look at him. "Hey, how about we get you boys to the B&B so you can unpack and start this vacation?"

Several of the men second that idea, but their faces are tired, and the guy who reportedly left part of his small intestine in the Gulf of Mexico still looks pretty green.

"Sounds good." River shifts his bags in his hands.

Holly and as many villagers as she could round up are parked in the sandy lot right by the dock. They're using their golf carts to haul luggage and fishermen up Main Street. Holly watches everyone load up, clipboard in her hands, Yankees cap on her head. She directs traffic and answers questions as everyone finds a cart, islanders shaking hands with fishermen as they quickly get acquainted. As the group works to sort the fishermen and their luggage out, there's a moment where Holly pauses and realizes that this is what her island could look like. If twenty more people move to Christmas Key, the talking, the bodies, the activity —everything jumps up. Twenty more people would be that many more bodies in the mix. It would change the feel of everything.

"Hey, honey!" Bonnie calls out, pulling up next to Holly in her golf cart. Riding shotgun is a white-haired man with a round belly and a white mustache. His eyes are merry, his cheeks pink. "This is Bill Hammond from Oregon. Don't you worry about a thing; I've got this one covered!" Bonnie makes an OK sign with her fingers, laughing to herself as she steps on the gas and tears up Main Street.

In less than ten minutes the rest of the luggage is loaded up and carted off, tires crunching across sandy gravel as the last cart rolls onto the paved road of Main Street.

That leaves River standing, thumbs hooked in the back pockets of his khaki cargo shorts, his bags at his feet. A smile plays at his lips as he watches Holly sitting in the driver's seat of her golf cart, efficiently checking items off of her list on the clipboard.

"Need to call and check on this," she mumbles to herself, holding the lid to the pen between her teeth as she scribbles a reminder for later.

"Got room for one more?" River walks up to the passenger side and nods at the empty seat.

The pen lid falls from Holly's lips. It clatters onto the clipboard and rolls to the floor. "Of course! I'm sorry, you were so quiet there that I thought I had everyone shipped off already." She looks over her shoulder to double-check that everyone else is gone. "Hop on."

River tosses his bags onto the backseat and slides in next to Holly, the clipboard on the bench seat between them. She releases the parking break with a click and pulls out of the lot.

"Sweet ride. What kind of horsepower are we looking at here?" He braces himself against the dash with one flip-flop clad foot. "About 300 or 310? You got a V8 under the hood?"

"Sure. Totally. She's road ready."

"Did you just say 'She's road ready'?" His mouth turns up on one side in an amused grin.

"Why, did that sound like I knew what I was talking about?"

"Kind of," River laughs.

"Yeah, I actually don't. I grew up on this island, and we don't have any cars here."

"You grew up here?" He looks around, taking in the quaint storefronts and the ruggedly-paved road. What feels to Holly like a massive amount of progress and construction must look to an outsider like a barely-populated campsite.

"I did. My grandparents owned this island, and they raised me here." She realizes that her life story is falling from her lips in front of a total stranger, but for some reason she's at a loss to stop it from happening. "I did go to college in Miami, so it's not like I've never left the island. I even learned to drive a car there. It was terrifying."

"What was terrifying—Miami, or driving a car?"

Holly laughs. "Both, to be perfectly honest." She straightens the bill of her hat. "People drive like maniacs on the freeway, and I'm not used to doing more than about twelve miles an hour."

River's right arm is extended overhead; he grips the edge of the cart's roof casually. "So you grew up on a gorgeous island, and big city life freaked you out and sent you running back home? I like it. It sounds like a movie or something."

Holly smiles. "It'd be a pretty boring movie: girl grows up on an island filled with old people and wildlife. The tides come in and go out. The end."

"Oh, come on. There has to be more to it than that."

"Maybe a little," she says, tilting her head thoughtfully.

"You don't say." He gives her that same half-smile that he gave her when she said her golf cart was road ready. "You a Yankee fan?" He nods at her baseball cap.

"Definitely." Holly makes a sharp right into the driveway that wraps around behind the B&B. It ends in a sandy parking lot that'll fit about ten golf carts. "You?"

"Eh. I'm more of a Mets fan," River admits, unfolding his long limbs and climbing out of the cart. He bends down so that he can look at her under the roof of the golf cart. "But that doesn't mean we can't be friends."

"Ha. Says you," Holly shoots back, putting the cart in park. "My grandparents are from Brooklyn, and we're die-hard Yank fans."

River laughs. "Got it, boss."

"I'm teasing," she says. "But if we talk baseball, things might get ugly."

"Noted." River pulls his duffel bag from the back of the cart and slings it over one shoulder. "Hey, you got any showers around this place? I smell bad enough to offend even a fellow Mets fan, not to mention a Yank-lover."

"Absolutely. Right this way." Holly makes a grand sweeping gesture with one hand, leading River in through the back door of the B&B.

"Thanks."

His tall, muscular body fills the narrow back hallway of the B&B as River follows her to the front desk. Holly tosses a backward glance and catches his eye; she feels her skin flush.

"Okay, let's get you all checked in," she says briskly, stepping behind the front desk so that she's shoulder-to-shoulder with Bonnie. Bonnie bumps her with one hip.

"This is some place you have here," River says, leaning forward to look at a framed picture on the wall of the lobby. It's a shot of the original eight islanders, which includes a knee-high Holly and her gorgeous, petulant, unsmiling mother. Coco had been convinced to come along for the first month on Christmas Key, after which she'd unceremoniously bailed.

Holly watches him from the corner of her eye as she pulls up the reservation on her computer. "Yep. I started the B&B when I got back from college. It's mine," she says. Bonnie bumps her again with a hip, giving her a look. "Um. Looks like we have you in the Seashell Suite."

"Sounds beachy." River turns his back on the photo and drops his duffel bag on the floor. "Will you be mad if I get sand in the sheets?"

Bonnie kicks her ankle behind the desk frantically. This sort of banter is right up her alley, and Holly knows it's killing her to just witness it rather than participate.

Holly shoots her a wide-eyed look that's supposed to say "knock it off." Instead, Bonnie takes it as "jump right in."

"Sugar, if you leave Christmas Key without sand in your sheets and a little bit of a sunburn on your unmentionables, then you haven't really visited a tropical island, have you?"

River gives a hearty laugh—straight from the gut. "I'll get started on that right away, ma'am." He takes the card key from Holly that she's swiped for his room and looks her in the eye. "See you at dinner?"

"I'll be serving it." She points him down the hallway toward the Seashell Suite. "See you at six."

"What is *wrong* with you?" Bonnie hisses at her after he's gone.

"What is wrong with *you*?" she hisses back.

"Darlin', this is it," Bonnie says, turning to face her and taking Holly's hands in hers. "The good lord is calling. He's sent you a fine, strapping young man to bring a little excitement into your life, and you need to answer that call." Her face is serious, like a doctor giving a grim prognosis. "I'm dead serious: Answer. That. Call."

Holly laughs lightly. "I need to get ready for dinner."

"Honey, go home and shave your legs and put on something cute." Bonnie waves a hand dismissively. "Dinner is under control."

It's not lost on her that an attractive young man who seems at least mildly interested in her has just landed on her island. But Christmas Key has to be her main focus for the time being, and she needs to keep her head clear while she deals with any lingering feelings between her and Jake.

"I've got a few errands to run. Can you handle things around here?" Holly opens the cash register and takes a twenty and two fives. "I need to buy a few things from the triplets before dinner."

"Sure. Just bring me back receipts for that petty cash so I can have everything squared away before your mother gets here. I know she'll want to see the books and ask a million questions," Bonnie says, rolling her eyes.

"Got it." Holly gives her a salute on her way out the front door.

"And sugar?" Bonnie says sweetly. Holly pauses, hand on the door knob. "You might want to put on some cute knickers and a dab of perfume—I think *you're* dessert."

9

THE DINING ROOM IS SET FOR NINETEEN. KEY WEST PINK SHRIMP WITH grits is on the menu. The B&B staff of five is still scrambling to get everything pulled together after a last minute kerfuffle in the kitchen over whether the fishermen's first dinner should end with key lime *pie* or key lime *tartlets*. Bonnie finally settles it when she convinces Holly that the men won't care a lick what shape their dessert comes in, so long as they're washing it down with cold beer.

Holly stands in the middle of the quiet room by herself for a minute, looking at the five round tables that are set for the fishermen. She and Bonnie carefully ironed and spread brocaded table runners stitched with turquoise starfish over the white linen tablecloths, and they tucked matching napkins in the shape of fans under the lip of each heavy white dinner plate. Holly personally made sure that all of the silverware was polished until she could see her own frazzled reflection on the knives and spoons. It might not be possible to keep up a 5-star restaurant worthy presentation for every meal during the fishermen's stay, but she really wants the first night to be special.

With some coaxing, Buckhunter has agreed to tend bar for the evening, but with the caveat that he can excuse himself during dessert and run over to re-open Jack Frosty's in case the fishermen feel like migrating down Main Street for a nightcap. Emily has also signed on for the same duties she does at the Jingle Bell Bistro for her parents: fill water glasses, bus tables, and make conversation with the guests. Holly's wearing black pants and a white shirt like Emily's, and they both have aquamarine-colored aprons wrapped around their waists.

"We ready in here, chief?" Bonnie asks, one hip jutting out saucily as she consults her notepad. She's holding a pen in one hand to use as a pointer to boss everyone around. Emily is close on her heels with a carafe of water.

Holly stops smoothing and rearranging the tables. "I think we're ready. We just need some men."

"Honey, truer words were never spoken." Bonnie looks up from her notepad, lips pursed.

Emily giggles, still holding the carafe of water.

The first of the fishermen to arrive for dinner poke their heads into the door of the dining room.

"This where you're serving up the goods?" Bill Hammond asks, running his hands over his ample belly. He's showered and put on a clean t-shirt, and as the men trickle in, it becomes apparent that jeans and t-shirts are *de rigueur* dinner attire in Oregon.

"Come on in!" Holly says, picking up a silver pitcher of water. She fills the goblets on the tables, nodding at the fishermen as they amble in.

"Well, I see a bar in the corner, men, so I think we're off to a good start," Bill says, hooking a thumb towards Buckhunter as he lines up bottles behind the portable bar.

"Have you been to Florida before?" Holly asks one of the men. He hands her his empty glass to fill; the ice cubes clink against the metal lip of her carafe as she pours.

"Nope. First time," he says, taking the water glass from her. "Everyone warned me it was humid, but I guess you really don't know what that means until you get here."

"Kind of hits you like a brick wall, doesn't it?" She reaches for another glass to fill. Holly chats amiably with the men as they choose seats at the tables, but she can't stop herself from keeping one eye on the open doorway.

"Am I too late for dinner?" River is suddenly at Holly's elbow, smelling of soap and shaving cream.

She stares at him dumbly.

"No, really—am I too late?" he asks, breaking the awkward silence when she doesn't answer.

"No. I'm sorry, not at all." Holly takes a step back and bumps directly into the wall. The icy water in her pitcher sloshes around, mimicking the unsettled feeling in her own stomach. "You're fine—come on in. It looks like there's an open seat right over there."

"Great, thanks." River smiles and shoves both hands into the pockets of his black linen shorts. He looks at her appraisingly. "So, no Yankees cap tonight?"

"Wrong blue. It clashes with my apron," Holly says. She tucks her hair behind her ears with one hand, averting her gaze. "I hope you like shrimp and grits, and the bar's right over there if you want to start with a drink."

"Hey, buddy," Bill Hammond says, slapping River on the back. He hands him a bottle of beer. "Got you a cold one."

"Thanks, man." River takes the beer and smiles at Holly. "Thanks for feeding us so well--it sounds delicious."

"Sure thing. Enjoy." Holly gives a small nod and hurries out of the room to help run the main course.

"Ooooh, those men look good tonight!" Bonnie says in the hallway, blocking Holly's path. She fans herself with one hand. "I'm glad I went home and freshened up, because I spy a couple of cuties in there I'd like to get to know better."

"I'm shocked," Holly teases.

Bonnie pats her fiery hair, her face nonchalant. "Honey, a girl's gotta have some fun. It can't be all work and no play around this place. And I'm not just talking about myself, you hear?"

"Meaning?" Holly lowers her voice.

"Meaning I think you should take my advice and get to know that tall drink of water a little better." Bonnie wags a finger at her. "The electricity between you two could light up Atlanta for a week!" She puckers her lips and shimmies her shoulders like she's doing a Latin dance.

"Bonnie, get out of town!" Holly laughs, wiping the condensation from the carafe off of her hands by running them down the front of her apron. "I've got enough on my plate right now."

"Listen, honey, I saw you two talking, and I can't see where some good old-fashioned flirtation would hurt you one bit. But I can name one very hot Christmas Key police officer who might be less amused by it than I am."

Holly rolls her eyes. "Jake knows we're not getting back together, Bon."

"I don't care what he does or doesn't know. Officer Zavaroni would love to have your Yankees cap hanging on his bedpost every night, and the thought that it might end up on some other guy's nightstand isn't gonna sit too well. I guess the real question is whether or not you're up for an adventure."

The men's laughter and conversation drifts out into the hallway.

"Bonnie, you're killing me here." Holly shakes her head. "Listen, I need to get rid of this empty pitcher and start running food. If we survive salads, the main course, and dessert, we'll have a drink afterward to celebrate pulling off our first big group of visitors, okay?"

"That's a deal, sugar. I'll be at the front desk if you need me for anything."

In the kitchen, the clatter of dishes and the steam from the giant pot of grits fills the air. Iris and Jimmy shout instructions at one another over the kitchen noise. Holly jumps right into the fray, stacking full plates of food up her arm like an experienced server, and knocking the swinging door open with her rear end on her way in and out of the kitchen. It's time to get her head in the game and deliver the food to the tables. Thoughts of Jake, and daydreams about a handsome stranger who may or may not be flirting with her, need to go on the back burner for the time being.

She has nineteen hungry men to feed, and the sooner she gets that done, the sooner she can shower and have a beer.

And by god, she needs a beer.

10

As Buckhunter had hoped, the men decide to amble down Main Street to Jack Frosty's after dinner. They leave the B&B with toothpicks wedged in their mouths, hands hitching up their shorts and jeans after stuffing themselves with dinner and dessert. Their good-natured banter echoes under the streetlights, leaving a trail of jovial laughter behind them.

With the last of their guests out the door and wandering into a sultry evening, every islander on the B&B's premises converges on the kitchen and dining room to whip things back into shape so they can join the fishermen for a cold beer at the bar. The mood in the kitchen is festive and upbeat. Holly laughs at Bonnie as she cha-chas around the giant stainless steel sink, snapping her dish towel at Jimmy Cafferkey and trying on a wonky Irish accent for size. Holly has been so intent on getting things lined up for their guests that she hasn't even realized how excited her neighbors are about having new faces on the island. It's validating to see that having visitors in their midst is so invigorating to everyone.

In under an hour, they have the two professional-grade dishwashers running in the clean kitchen. The tablecloths and linens are sloshing around in the front-loading washers in the laundry room, and all the lights in the dining room are dimmed. In the bathroom, Holly strips off her server's uniform and pulls on a pair of cut-off 501s and a striped tank top, then she follows everyone else out the front door.

As they walk the few steps down Main Street to the bar, Bonnie pauses and waits, looping her arm through Holly's so they can walk together.

"Let's have some fun tonight, okay, hon? You've done good work getting these guys here and settled in, and now you deserve a break."

"I couldn't have done it without you, Bon," she says gratefully. "I mean it."

Bonnie reaches up and puts her finger on Holly's nose, pressing it lightly like an elevator button. "Anything for you, sugar. You know that."

Arms still linked, they step up the rough wooden stairs and into the open bar on Main Street. The lights are on full bore, ceiling fans whipping the air around at top speed. River is admiring the rainbow of dirty, beat-up license plates from around the country that Buck-hunter has nailed to a weather-worn wall, and strings of miniature Edison bulbs come from every corner of the room, converging over-head in the center of the room. It's got a bright, carnival feel tonight, and the jukebox is blaring a country song.

River stops at the bar, picks up two bottles of beer, and approaches Bonnie and Holly. "Ladies. One for each of you. Sorry if I just assumed on this, but you both looked like you could use a cold one."

"A longneck will always work for this gal," Bonnie says, taking the bottle of beer from River. "Thank you kindly, stranger." She bumps Holly's hip with her own before leaving the two of them standing by the jukebox.

"Excellent dinner." River looks down at her intently. He's standing just a hair closer than he needs to, and his eyes linger on Holly a beat longer than they should.

"Thanks—and thank you for the beer," Holly says, raising the bottle to her lips. Even at night, the humidity is still so intense on the island that the skin on her shoulders and collarbone glisten with a sheen of sweat. "You're not drinking?"

"I'm pacing myself. I feel like it would be bad form to start a fishing trip by emptying all the taps on the island. I'll grab a Coke when the rush at the bar clears out."

"I can probably get you one sooner than that." Holly walks up to the bar and leans across the counter. "Buckhunter!" she calls. "Can I get a Coke, please?"

She takes the ice cold can back to River; he pops the top and sips the foam. "Guess you gotta know the right people, huh?"

"Well, if you live here, you know *all* the people."

"How many live here full-time?"

"Hundred and thirteen. And we have a couple of part-timers who come from October through April."

"So only nut jobs like us visit during the summer?" He peels the fabric of his shirt away from his skin.

Holly nods, the beer bottle poised in front of her lips. "Yeah, that pretty much sums it up. The only people who trek out here in the summer are nut jobs and my mother."

"Your mother?"

"She's coming down for a visit. Long story." Holly takes a pull from her beer and glances around the bar. Jake is in the corner talking to Joe and Cap. She looks away quickly.

"Hey, brother." A guy in plaid shorts practically falls on River's back as he looks at Holly through bleary eyes. The guy is obviously a few beers into his first night on Christmas Key. River slings an arm around the shorter man's shoulders, steadying him on his feet. "You fraternizing with the enemy here?"

"I'm trying to bring her over to our side, Josh," River says to his friend. He claps him on the back. "I just need to work on her a little bit longer."

Holly frowns. "Wait, *I'm* the enemy in this scenario?"

"We all saw you in that Yanks hat," Josh says, swaying on his feet.

"It might be time to get you back to your room, dude," River says.

He looks around the bar for someone to help him out. "Hey, where's your old man?"

"My dad?" Josh looks confused. "I think he's talking to that redhead."

"This is Bill Hammond's son, Josh," River says to Holly. "He doesn't hold his liquor well. Which could be because he's still a teenager—"

"I'm twenty-two, man," Josh protests. "I'm *twenty-two*."

"Yeah, well, you need to learn to pace yourself there, Joshy." River takes the empty bottle from Josh's hand and sets it on the bar. "Give me a sec, okay?" he asks Holly. He drags his buddy across the bar to where Bill and Bonnie are drinking their beers, and unceremoniously hands Josh over to his dad.

Holly sips her beer while she waits, leaning against the jukebox with one hip as she scans the list of songs. She punches a few buttons. Springsteen is always the first thing she chooses at Jack Frosty's. Without fail, she drops a few coins in and chooses "Glory Days" or "I'm on Fire" or another of her favorites before finding a seat, and Buckhunter always stops whatever he's doing and just listens to the music for a minute, paying reverence to The Boss before resuming his pouring. She pushes B31 and "Brilliant Disguise" comes on. Buckhunter pauses behind the bar and raises a finger in the air, his head bobbing in time to the music.

"Nice choice. But you seem kind of young for eighties music," River says as he approaches, picking up his can of Coke from the table where he left it.

"I'm thirty," Holly says. "Not that young."

"Still, I'd peg you as more of a Backstreet Boys enthusiast than a Springsteen fan."

Holly cringes like she's just bit down on a tart lemon. "That's terrible. Really."

River laughs. "Terrible? My kid sister was a huge BB fan. And she loved that Timberlake kid when he was in his boy band." He drinks his Coke, thinking. "Yeah, you're right," he finally laughs. "I'm sorry, that was a really mean thing to say."

"Yeah, I was never into boy bands. One of the men on the island —he's gone now, passed away a few years ago—was big into short-wave radio," she says, taking another drink. "He was always messing around, seeing what kind of signals he could pick up. All we had here on the island when I was a kid was the music that the older people listened to: big band, some jazz, lots of forties and fifties stuff. Anyway, one day when I was about twelve, he picked up a college station from Texas. He invited me over to hear it, and I was hooked. I loved everything they were playing, and when I went away to college on the mainland, I hit every record store I could find. You should see my collection."

"Lots of Springsteen?"

"Sure. And Madonna and Prince, tons of The Smiths, New Order, O.M.D., Depeche Mode—stuff like that."

"What about The Cure? Are you a closet goth girl?"

"Totally closeted!" Holly laughs, thrilled to find someone she can talk about music with. She'd had high hopes for Fiona the first time they met up for happy hour on Holly's lanai, but was sorely disappointed when her new friend browsed through her CD collection quickly and then pronounced herself "more of a classic rock fan."

"So why aren't you wearing all black? And moping around?"

"Too hot." Holly leans back until her elbow rests on the low bar. Her long hair is sticking to the back of her neck, and she tries to catch a breeze from the fans overhead. "All black in this heat is too much for even the most devoted goth girl. And moping is strictly a cold weather activity."

"I see your point," River says.

"Now back to this whole bit about me being the enemy. I need to hear what that's all about."

"Oh, come on. Josh is drunk! He's not in his right mind." River waves the topic away with his hand.

"Whoa-ho-ho," another of the fishermen says, leaning in to River as he passes behind them. He clamps one hand on River's shoulder. "You sharing a drink here with the Yanks girl? Never thought I'd see the day!"

"Okay—spill it!" Holly demands, slamming her nearly empty beer bottle on the bar. "What's the deal?"

"I'm Ed, by the way." He extends a hand to Holly. "And the deal is that you're talking to a man who played triple-A for the Mets farm team from 2001 to 2005. Would've gone to the majors if he hadn't hurt his shoulder at the end of his first season."

"What?" Holly looks back and forth between River and the other man. "Are you kidding me?"

River picks a spot on the floor to look at. He shakes his head. "Guilty as charged."

"What position?"

"Pitcher."

"Well, I'll leave you two kids to hash this out," Ed says, giving River's shoulder another slap. "And thank you for a great dinner," he says to Holly.

"No problem," Holly says, turning back to River. "Wow, I'm impressed."

"Naturally. I mean, in my experience, women are generally pretty bowled over by a gimp who bombed out of the farm league a decade ago."

"I don't know," she says, mildly awed. "I actually am kind of bowled over."

River laughs, looking around the bar. "That must be because you're island-bound and therefore unable to mingle with a broader cross-section of the male species."

"You could be right," Holly says, swallowing the last of her beer. "So what do you do now?"

"Other than fish? I fish some more. Professionally, that is. Mostly in competitions up and down the west coast and in Alaska. And I help to run a non-profit for foster kids in Oregon. We put together sports teams and run tournaments for kids in the system."

"Okay, that sort of impresses me too," Holly admits, frowning.

He shrugs easily. "Now that you know my deep, dark secrets, goth girl, are we going to be able to put our differences aside and make nice?" He runs his hands through his hay-colored blonde hair, leaving it disheveled and sweaty.

"Maybe. As long as you don't tell me that your favorite band is Limp Bizkit."

"A Bizkit reference? Nice. Actually I'm more of a Creed fan. Throw in a little Nickleback and some Buckcherry..."

Holly pretends to gag at all of the nineties bands he's tossing out. As they laugh, Ed drops by with two shots of whisky; he hands one to her and one to River.

"Drink up, young people."

Holly thanks him and clinks her tiny glass against River's, knocking it back without hesitation. The entire bar breaks out in a loud cheer.

River holds his shot glass aloft, toasting the crowd. "You ever played catch at night?" he asks her from the corner of his mouth, his eyes still on the other people in the bar.

"As in baseball?"

"Yeah. Like with a ball and a mitt."

"I used to play with my grandpa sometimes, but never at night."

"Do you think you could still get your hands on a couple of mitts and a ball?"

"You're serious," Holly says, her forehead creasing as she tries to read him.

"Completely. Look at that moon out there—if we played on the beach, it would be like playing on a lit up field at night."

Holly looks over at Bonnie; they exchange a glance across the crowded bar. Holly can tell that she's having a great time talking to Bill. Poor Josh sits at the tiny table between his dad and Bonnie, his forehead pressed against the table top as he sleeps off his jet lag and beer buzz.

Before she gives herself a chance to overthink it, she's saying, "I guess I can look in the storage closet back by my office."

"Great. Should we grab a few more people to play?"

Holly flushes. She isn't sure why she assumed that it would just be the two of them. "Of course. Yeah. Let's get a group."

River closes out his tab with Buckhunter while Holly searches for Fiona to see if she wants to join them. Ten minutes later, they've got Jimmy and Emily Cafferkey, Fiona, Cap, and two of the fishermen, and they're planning a golf cart caravan over to the beach while Holly heads back to the B&B to try and dig up some dusty equipment.

The sound of the fishermen and locals getting to know each other ebbs and flows under the lights. For a moment, Holly feels alone in the center of all the action as she watches everyone gather their things and make plans. Buckhunter expertly tosses bottles and pours drinks, keeping a steady stream of conversation going as he works. Some of the older islanders stayed away this evening, but there's a good crowd at Jack Frosty's mingling with their guests over margaritas and beers. In that instant, it all feels surreal to Holly. She's put all of this together, the men are finally here, and she's about to go and play catch by the light of the moon with a former minor league baseball player. It all feels right. The only thing nagging at her is Jake.

The sounds around her fade into the background as her eyes seek him out—she can't ignore the fact that her ex is standing just feet away as she navigates what is turning into an obvious and completely unexpected flirtation with River. But Jake must be in the men's room, because she doesn't see him anywhere in the small bar.

Holly tells the rest of the late night baseball crew that she'll meet them at Snowflake Banks before hurrying out onto Main Street to go and dig around at the B&B. The smile fades from her face when she notices a golf cart idling next to the curb just outside the bar. As she watches, it pulls away slowly, the reflective lettering that spells out POLICE visible even in the dark.

With a flashlight tucked under her chin as she scours the deep storage closet, Holly lands on three baseball mitts and a bat, but no ball. She searches high and low, muttering to herself as she dumps out boxes of old paperwork and sifts through a hodgepodge of items tossed into the closet over the years. In the end, she takes the mitts and the bat and hops into her cart to meet everyone before they start to think she's changed her mind.

"Any luck?" River calls out as she parks on the sand.

"Three mitts—pretty beat-up, but still in decent shape—and one bat. No ball. Sorry," Holly says, out of breath as she meets the small group.

"We can improvise," River says. He looks around the wide stretch of sand, then points at a palm tree. "Coconuts."

Emily laughs happily. "Baseball with coconuts?"

"Yep. We need a small one, and it'll be bunting and underhand throws only, okay? We don't need to give anyone a concussion."

"It's kind of dark over there," Holly says, hands on hips after passing out the mitts and letting Cap take the bat. He's standing near the water with the scuffed wooden bat on one shoulder, assuming the position of a batter at home plate.

"I've got this covered," River assures her, pulling a cell phone from his pocket. He turns on the bright screen and shines the light onto the sand, scanning around for fallen coconuts.

"Well this is something, isn't it, lassies?" Jimmy Cafferkey says to Emily, Holly, and Fiona. "Who'd have thought we'd be playing baseball on a whim like this?" Jimmy's cheeks are pink in the moonlight. A pleased smile lights up his face.

"Found one!" River shouts from about thirty yards away. "It's just the right size."

One of the other fishermen—a guy named Steve—claps his hands. "Let's play ball!"

It doesn't take long before River has Holly and Emily wearing mitts and standing in a triangular formation with him. And he was right: the moon is so bright that when they stand right next to the water, it reflects off the waves and lights up their stretch of sand. The three of them take turns tossing soft, underhanded throws at one another, the coconut sailing through the air and landing with a firm thud in their mitts.

Holly holds her glove to her nose, inhaling the familiar but long-forgotten scent of leather oil.

"Holly, your turn!" Emily says, lobbing the coconut in her direction. Holly catches it easily. She touches the dry fur on the outside of the fruit, holding it in her palm. Cap is swinging the bat and sharing stories with Steve and Mack, the other fishermen. Jimmy is watching the game of catch with Fiona, and sipping the bottle of beer he brought with him from the bar. Something about the scene—maybe the smell of the old baseball mitt and the memories it conjures, or the way that doing something spontaneous can flood you with joy— brings tears to Holly's eyes.

"Coming your way again, Em," she says, tossing it back to her friend.

"Let me in the game, I think I'm ready," Cap says, shaking out his arms like he's loosening up to come out of the dugout.

"You gonna keep things on the up-and-up, Cap?" River jokes, talking to him like they're old buddies.

"As long as you aren't throwing me any high cheese, slugger. I'm ready to get a knock here." Cap swings the bat again for good measure.

"This could be a game-ender, ladies," River says to Holly and Emily. "Have we had our fun with this coconut?"

"Yeah, we've had fun!" Emily confirms, jamming her fist into the palm of her baseball mitt. "I want to see Cap hit it."

Holly steps back and sinks to the sand next to Jimmy and Fiona; Emily joins them. The other fishermen act as de facto outfielders, though it's clear that they've had too many beers and not enough sleep in the last twenty-four hours to do much ball chasing.

"All right, Cap. I'm gonna throw you a knuckleball with this hairy piece of fruit just in case you get plunked. You ready?"

"I was born ready, youngster." Cap crouches low, bat on his shoulder. He tightens his grip and shifts his feet. On his face is focused determination mixed with total amusement.

"Here she comes," River says, winging the coconut in Cap's direction. Everyone watches it sail cleanly through the air at low speed and with no spin. Cap pulls back and then slices through the air with the bat, teeth gritted as he makes sharp contact with the coconut.

They all watch, open-mouthed, as the coconut explodes on contact, shards of shell and husk raining down over the water. Coconut meat and water spray in all directions and Cap puts an arm over his head, covering himself from the fallout.

"Wow, that was cool," Emily says with awe, leaning her head on her father's shoulder.

"Gives new meaning to the term 'spray hitter,' don't it, slugger?" Cap says, tossing the bat at River gently.

River reaches out and grabs it by the barrel with one hand casually, plucking it from the air. "Indeed it does."

"I'll drop your new friend off at the B&B if you like," Cap says to Holly. "I'm headed back that way."

"Thanks, Cap," she says, giving him a one-armed hug. "And thanks for the game," she says to River. "That was fun...and unexpected."

"You're welcome. And you'd better get used to it, Mayor," he shoots back at her with a wink. "At least while I'm around. 'Fun and unexpected' are my stock-in-trade."

11

JAKE IS HELPING IRIS CAFFERKEY CHANGE A TIRE ON HER GOLF CART IN front of North Star Cigars when Holly pulls up to the B&B the next morning after stopping to get breakfast at Mistletoe Morning Brew. He's crouched with one knee on the hot pavement, sweat already drenching the back of his dark shirt as he cranks the cart up with a jack and assesses the flat. Iris is talking to him animatedly, hands waving in the air as she clucks around Jake, watching him work.

Holly pulls into the B&B's lot, her tires kicking up sand as she rounds the corner without braking. She has a chocolate donut clamped between her lips and she's steering the cart with one hand, a paper cup full of hot coffee balanced in the other. Holly doesn't have time to stop and visit with them this morning, and besides, the memory of Jake quietly leaving the bar the night before while she downed two beers and lavished her attention on River is still fresh in her mind.

"...a severe weather warning for Turks and Caicos, and with it, information about how to prepare..."

Bonnie is pacing around the office when Holly walks in. Her eyes are glued to the screen of her laptop, a weather report blaring from the speakers. "Thank God—you're here!" she says, reaching for Holly's coffee and purse.

Holly hands them over and takes the donut out of her mouth, pushing her sunglasses up on top of her head slowly. "What's wrong? What are you listening to?"

"Oh, honey, *everything* is wrong. And I'm listening to the weather report. There's a storm brewing near Turks and Caicos." Bonnie's eyes are wide and magnified behind her reading glasses. Her perfectly liquid-lined lids flutter in consternation.

"Okaaaay. Well, Turks and Caicos is about seven hundred miles out into the Atlantic, so let's not panic just yet."

"That's not all."

Holly sits down, rubbing her eyes. When she'd finally gotten home and into bed after the evening of coconut baseball, it was already well past midnight. "Okay, lay it on me. I'm ready."

"We're going to need a professional carpet cleaner to pay us a visit. The Seashell Suite smells like the scene of a gastrointestinal crime. Major vomit-fest."

"No—is it that guy who threw up on the boat on the way here?" The glimmer of an impending headache thrums steadily.

"No. That guy is in the Palm Tree Pagoda. Old Slugger is in Seashell, and he had a *rough* night," Bonnie says, shaking her head. (She'd been more than tickled the night before to find out that River once played minor league ball for Holly's rival team.)

"River?" Holly asked. "He's sick?"

"I've never seen anything quite like it in all my born days, sugar." Bonnie grimaces like she's remembering something heinous. "Bill came down this morning and asked for extra sheets and towels to take up to him, and I'll be honest: he wasn't looking too chipper himself."

Holly inhales deeply through her nose, considering. "You'd think that a bunch of guys who spend most of their time on boats could handle a cross country trip, a forty mile boat ride, and a few beers."

"You'd think." Bonnie sits down, busying herself with shuffling papers on the desk. "Oh. And there's one more teeny-tiny thing."

"Jesus. What now?"

"Your mother called. She'll be here at seven-thirty tonight." Bonnie peers at her boss over the top of her reading glasses. "She said plans changed for Alan with work, and that if they were going to come, it had to be now. She also said they'll be fine in any room you put them in."

"But we have a full house!" Holly wails, pushing back from the desk. "We've only got twenty rooms, and nineteen of them are booked. If I have to move River out of The Seashell Suite to get it cleaned, then I'll have nowhere to put my mom and Alan."

"Yeah, you are in a pickle there, sweetheart," Bonnie agrees, chewing on the tip of a ballpoint pen. "I'd say your mom could stay with me, but that woman is so cold, I'm afraid she'd use my powder room and freeze the septic tank. I'm pretty sure Coco pisses icicles." As awareness about what she's saying dawns over her, Bonnie lets the pen drop to the desk with a clatter. "Oh my God!" Her hand flies to her mouth. "I'm sorry, honey—that's your mother I'm talking about. I'm not myself this morning, Holly Jean, I swear. Forgive me."

"Oh, please. No offense taken." Holly waves her off. It's no secret that Bonnie and Coco aren't huge fans of one another, and there's really nothing that Bonnie can say about Coco that Holly hasn't already thought herself.

"Okay, here's what we'll do: I'm going to call Fiona and see if she can take a look at River, maybe give him some anti-nausea medicine or something. Then we'll check out his room to see if it's salvageable for the rest of his stay. I'll deal with where to put my mother once we get him taken care of," Holly says. She's got to take this one step at a time, and conquer one crisis before moving on to the next.

"Good plan. I'll go check on breakfast to make sure that things are set for the rest of the guys. I haven't seen a single one besides Bill, but I'm guessing they'll be up and hungry before too long."

"Fabulous. Is there anything else?"

Bonnie stops in the doorway. She turns back, one hand on the knob, and gives Holly an amused smile. "All of that wasn't enough for you, sugar?"

Holly takes a long sip of coffee, considering. "Yeah, unless the sky is falling, then I guess that'll probably do for now."

12

Dr. Potts runs from room to room, checking on symptoms and making sure everyone has a Gatorade handy to stave off dehydration. She's determined that what they're dealing with is a raging case of food poisoning, most likely brought on by dinner the night before.

"This is a total nightmare," Holly says, her head planted on the front counter of the B&B, arms wrapped around her skull like a child trying to block out bad dreams. She's popped four Advil already and they've barely put a dent in her headache.

Fiona stops on her way through the lobby and sets a hand on her friend's messy ponytail; she musses her hair gently. "I won't lie, kid— this is pretty bad. But it seems relatively mild so far. Let's just keep an eye on these guys and see what happens, okay?"

Holly lifts her head and looks at Fiona from across the bamboo desk. "I haven't even told you the worst part yet."

Fiona's face falls. "You ate the shrimp, too?"

"No. My *mother* is coming tonight."

"Wait—you mean I finally get to meet the infamous Coco?" Fiona holds on to both ends of the stethoscope around her neck as she eyes Holly.

"Yeah, you will. Her broom lands around seven-thirty. You'll know she's here by the dark clouds that roll in with her."

"Come on, Hol—she can't be that bad," Fiona scoffs. "Nobody's mother is perfect."

"I know, I know. She could have left me in a basket on the doorstep of strangers...so that's something, I guess." She tips her head from side to side, granting that her mother might possess at least a small kernel of human kindness. "I'm pretty sure she only comes down here to criticize me. She just sucks the air out of the room and leaves behind a gaping void. Wait and see."

"Well, if it makes you feel any better, I'll keep my hospital-grade oxygen tank handy in case the air gets too thin." Fiona reaches across the desk and pats Holly's hand before heading down the hall to check on her patients again.

"And don't believe anything she says about me, Fee," Holly calls out to Fiona's retreating back. "We've lived together for less than five years of my entire life!"

Which is true: Coco popped in and out of her life intermittently during childhood, spending a few months on the island here and there, but always fleeing again when excitement beckoned. Oddly enough, the resentment between the women runs both ways; whenever they're together, Holly and Coco react to one another like the south poles of two magnets.

How can things have swung so wildly in the other direction in just twelve hours? Holly inhales deeply at the front counter, steeling herself for certain disaster.

By six o'clock, most of the men have stopped puking up their stomach lining. Holly, Fiona, the triplets, and Maria Agnelli are emptying buckets and pans, handing out more Gatorade, and making sure everyone is comfortable for the evening. They drag the throw rug out of the Seashell Suite and leave it behind the B&B, and with about a gallon of bleach, the bathroom cleans up well enough for River to stay in his room.

Holly is exhausted after a day of sick men and weather reports. She sits on the edge of the bed in the Lemon Tree Loft—the sole empty room, and the only one with a second-floor view of the small lemon grove next door to the hotel—and mentally berates herself for serving the fishermen tainted shrimp. Logically she knows it isn't her fault, but there's really no one else to blame. The lemons outside of the window are waxy and bright yellow against the darkening sky, and Holly stares at them for a minute, imagining their crisp, clean, citrusy scent. With a sigh, she gets up and starts arranging the room for her mom and Alan. She snaps the top sheet in the air over the bed, letting it drift to the mattress like a falling feather. There are bathroom towels to re-stock, and a vacuum to run, and she's just plumping the pillows on the bed when her phone buzzes in the back pocket of her cut-off shorts.

"We're at the dock waiting for yooooou!" Coco calls out in a sing-song voice. "Come on down!"

The sound of her mother's voice grates on her instantly. "Hey, Coco. I'll be down there in five minutes."

Holly slips her feet into her flip-flops in the lobby and exits through the side door that leads to the pool deck. The underwater lights glimmer like blue topaz in the near-darkness. Waves of refracted light hit her face as she passes the deep end of the pool, glancing in to make sure that there are no fallen leaves to skim. The deck chairs sit still and empty like ghosts, and the tall palm trees around the pool give it the feel of a secluded oasis, though Main Street is just on the other side of the fence. Holly straightens a few chairs, then lets the metal gate to the deck fall shut with a soft *clink* behind her. The sound of the pool filter's steady hum fades into the distance, giving way to night sounds as she leaves the B&B. Old-fashioned lantern streetlights cast a dim glow on Main Street, and in the quiet of evening, the soothing sound of the ocean crashing onto the beaches reaches the B&B.

At the dock, Coco waits next to three expensive looking suitcases. A large purse dangles from her shoulder. "Hi, baby!" she calls out, making her way over to Holly with careful steps on her thick wedge heels. She claps the palms of her hands together excitedly; it reminds Holly of a seal.

Coco's skirt is only an inch or two longer than Holly's shorts, and her hair is cut into a sharp, flattering, chin-length bob. As always, she looks like Holly's sultrier, more worldly, slightly older sister, and her youthful body only adds to the illusion.

"Can you believe I'm a mother to a thirty-year-old?" she asks Alan in a stage whisper, pulling Holly in for an airy hug. "Look at her— she's a grown-up!" Coco eyeballs her the way a farmer might assess his livestock before taking it to auction. She runs a hand over Holly's sweat-dampened, flyaway hair, her lips pressed together tightly as she concentrates on the details of her adult daughter. She turns back to Alan. "She's a grown-up who needs a shower and a little concealer, but just *look* at her!"

Holly rolls her eyes.

"Yes, she is a lovely woman, Coco," Alan says, a hint of exhaustion in his voice. He lifts the first of his wife's suitcases and carries it over to Holly's cart. "How are you, kiddo?" he says to Holly quietly.

"I'm okay. How was the trip?"

"Long," Alan admits, heaving their bags onto the golf cart.

Coco slides into the front seat of the cart and gets settled with her purse in her lap. She waits for Alan to load the luggage. "Why are you just *okay?*" Coco's forehead creases ever-so-slightly. Her frowns have diminished to mere furrows of the brow with repeated deliveries of Botox to her nerve endings, and her changes of expression are now no more than light twitches. "Aren't you happy that I'm here?"

"No, it's got nothing to do with you, Mom. I'm happy that you're here," she says. She knows that this is what Coco wants to hear.

"Alan! Did you hear that? She called me *Mom!*" Coco crows, turning around in her seat to look at her husband.

"I heard." Alan slides onto the back seat of the golf cart—the one that faces out—and holds two bags on his lap, the other two wedged onto the seat next to him. The back of his balding head nearly meets the back of his wife's perfectly dyed and styled hair.

"Anyway, I've got you set up in the Lemon Tree Loft." Holly releases the parking brake.

"Now, why didn't Grandma and Grandpa name all of those rooms after Christmas things, too?" Coco asks, her face disapproving. This line of questioning comes up during every one of her visits. She always finds things to pick apart and suggestions to make, and she seems deeply troubled whenever she encounters something on the island that doesn't fit with the holiday theme. It's like she's reading a novel and keeps stumbling on plot holes that she just can't overlook.

"The B&B is mine, Coco. Remember? I opened it when I came home from college."

"Right. With your *degree*, of course." Coco looks out into the darkness, holding her purse tighter on her lap. Holly's college education has always been a point of contention between them because Coco never liked that her parents were paying for it out of what she saw as her own future inheritance. "But the B&B belongs to *the family*, Holly," she says firmly. "Your grandfather bankrolled your every whim, including college and a whole hotel," she says in a lower voice, almost as if she's thinking it in her head and doesn't meant to utter the words aloud.

Holly drives in silence, refusing to take the bait. She hangs a hard right into the parking lot, purposely hitting the pothole in the driveway and jostling her mother, who gives a yelp.

"Sorry," she says with a shrug, not sorry at all.

They park and unload the bags at the back door of the B&B.

"Is this a *rug* out here?" Coco stands in the parking lot, her long, bare legs holding an aggressive stance as she stares at the rolled-up carpet from the Seashell Suite. She points at it like she's pointing at a dead bird in a cage, or at a rancid, maggot-infested piece of meat.

"That's a long story," Holly says, hoisting one of her mother's bags. "But basically the B&B is at full capacity and we had an incident in one of the rooms." In the darkness, the rug looks like it's been rolled up to hide a body, and Holly briefly imagines Coco's dark hair spilling out one end, her wedge heels poking out from the other. She blinks fast a few times, erasing the vision from her mind.

"Are you kidding?" Coco's manicured hands fly to her face. "Full capacity? How did you manage that? We must be making a pretty penny with all of these guests. Or at least enough to cover the overhead—for once," she says with a snort, flinging out a hand and whacking her husband on the chest conspiratorially.

Holly ignores all of it. "I booked a weeklong stay for a group of fishermen from Oregon. We're providing the food, lodging, and entertainment for the week." She ticks the items off on her fingers. "We're branching out into eco-tourism and a few other things," she adds, some small part of her secretly hoping to impress her mother with her business acumen.

"That's great, Hol," Alan says, one bag in each hand. He smiles kindly from behind his rimless glasses, the light breeze lifting his thin, sandy blonde hair and ruffling it.

"Yeah, it's exciting for us." Holly opens the back door to the B&B, holding it open for her mom and her stepdad. "Except that they arrived yesterday, and in their first eight hours on the island, I managed to give all but one a really excellent case of food poisoning."

Coco pauses in the doorway, giving a hard laugh. "No you didn't."

"I mean, I didn't do it personally, but they all ate the shrimp last night, and...well, it does add up."

"Okay, as long as it isn't something contagious, then we can stay here, right Alan? But the first whiff I get of the flu, we're packing up and moving over to your place, Holly." Coco brushes past her, making her way through the darkened hallway with Alan on her heels. "Got it?"

"Yeah, Mom. I've got it." She rolls her eyes behind her mother's back for what feels like the fortieth time in the last fifteen minutes. "If anyone is sick, you're taking over my place."

Alan reaches out and touches her shoulder reassuringly as she leads them up the stairs to their room, and the look he gives her as she helps them get their bags into the Lemon Tree Loft tells her that they're on the same page: she and Coco will share a house when hell freezes over.

13

HOLLY TOSSES AND TURNS ALL NIGHT, WORRYING ABOUT HER B&B FULL of sick guests. The fact that Coco is on the island for an undetermined length of time doesn't help her fall into an easy slumber, either. She gets up early, makes a cup of strong coffee with a splash of cream and two sugars, puts on her Yankees hat, and takes Pucci down to Pinecone Path for a stroll.

She's alone on the beach, as she knew she would be, and the sun is just barely rising over the horizon to the east. Pucci gallops towards the water like a horse racing through a forest while his mistress sips her coffee from a travel mug. Holly dips her toes into the cool surf, watching as her dog stops romping in the waves every so often to make sure she's still following close behind. He shakes his wet body from head to tail, sending a shower of water droplets shimmering into the morning light. They round the bend in the sand that leads to the Ho Ho Hideaway, and Pucci runs ahead, bounding up the steps to the bar. He disappears from Holly's sight, leaving his paw prints in the sand.

"Pooch! Here boy!" She whistles for him.

"He's up here, Mayor. Just saying good morning." Joe Sacamano's deep voice comes from the bar's beachside porch.

"Oh, hey, Joe." Holly stops at the bottom step and leans against a wooden post. "I figured I'd be alone out here."

"No such luck, kid." Joe sits in a tall chair with his bare feet up on the railing, watching the waves. "You're up and at 'em early."

"So are you. In fact," Holly says, consulting her watch, "did you even go to bed, or did you pull an all-nighter for old times' sake? You'll pay for that later, you know."

Joe chuckles. "Her dog attacks me with affection at six-thirty in the morning, and then she attacks me with jabs about my age!" Pucci sits on his hind end next to Joe's chair, looking up at him expectantly. "All right, I'll scratch you under the chin, you old mutt," Joe says, eyes crinkling at the corners.

"What *are* you doing here this early?" Holly asks, giving Pucci a low whistle so that he'll leave Joe alone; the dog completely ignores her.

Joe lifts his own mug of coffee and sips it, smacking his lips together a few times. "Oh, I've been awake for hours. Just wait till you're old, girl—the days get longer and the nights get shorter, but the real pisser is that you have less and less to do with your waking hours."

"That's a cheerful thought." Holly sits on the bottom step and watches as Joe pets her pup.

"It's life. It beats the alternative."

"Which is?" Holly takes a swig of her coffee.

"Which is not being alive."

"Oh. Good point." The dog ambles down the stairs, finally settling at her feet in the sand.

"So Coco's on the island," Joe says. It sounds more like a statement than a question.

"As always, I'm amazed how quickly information spreads. Do you all have some secret Facebook page or something where you update each other in real time?" Holly takes off her hat and lets the early morning breeze blow through her uncombed hair.

Joe smiles, his eyes searching hers. "No, there's no top-secret Facebook page for old timers. I'm sorry to disappoint." He runs a hand through his white curls. "I could just see it on your face."

"Great. She's been here less than twelve hours, and it's already destroying my face."

"It'll take more than twelve hours and a flighty mother to destroy such a pretty mug," Joe says, standing up. "Want me to top off your coffee?" He reaches for her cup. "I just brewed another pot." Holly hands her half-empty travel cup over to Joe and waits while he goes inside and pours her more coffee, his bare feet scuffing across the smooth wooden planks of the open bar.

"Thanks." Holly takes the fresh coffee from him. "Hey, Joe? Can I ask you something?"

"Of course you can," he says, sitting back in his chair and propping his feet on the railing again. Steam rises from the hot liquid in his mug and he blows on it.

"When I was a kid, did you guys think it was weird that my mom wasn't around much?"

Joe considers her question, watching the waves in the distance. "I don't know if we thought it was weird so much as we thought it was just life. But keep in mind that you're asking for advice from a man who spent his twenties and thirties traveling the world with musicians who did hard drugs for breakfast. Most of them had their accountants send money home to support wives and kids they barely spoke to, so my view on family life might be a bit more skewed than most."

"Yeah, but those were *men*. I'm talking about a *woman* who hated being a mother so much that—"

"Now hold on there," Joe says, putting up a hand to stop her. "Are you holding her to a different standard just because she's a woman? A parent is a parent. And you can be a good one or a terrible one whether you're a man or a woman. I should know." He wraps both hands around his coffee mug, leveling his gaze at her.

Holly raises her eyebrows, waiting for more.

"My kids will tell you that I'm barely a dad to them. In fact, one of my daughters told me that I'm her *father*, but not her *dad*. That particular honor goes to the electrician my ex-wife married while I was on the road."

There are a million questions that Holly is dying to ask, but she doesn't. She digs her big toe into the sand at the foot of the stairs and waits for Joe to go on.

"But let me set you straight right off the bat: it wasn't because I didn't love them. There is no more powerful love than the kind you feel for your kids." Joe puts one hand over his heart. "In my mind, I was doing what was best for *them*. And—let's be honest here—I was doing what was best for me. I was a better musician than I was a family man, and I knew that their mom would find someone who could give her what she wanted. And she did," he says, pulling the hand away from his heart. "Sometimes we make hard choices, but it's because we want what's best for everyone involved. Do you see what I'm saying?"

Holly sets her Yankees cap back on her head, pulling the brim down low. "I think so. You're saying that Coco did what was best for *both* of us."

Joe smiles sympathetically. "Probably. It might feel like she made a selfish choice, but look around you, Holly." Joe grips his mug with one hand, pointing out at the wide beach with the other. "Look at what you have here. There's no way you'd have this life if you hadn't been raised by Frank and Jeanie. You think a teenage mom could have given you paradise?"

Holly follows the sweep of his hand, taking it all in. She nods, slowly at first, then more definitively. "You're right. I know you're right, Joe."

He lets his hand fall to his knee. "If it weren't for the choices your mother made, you wouldn't be where you are. You wouldn't be dragging this community into the future with your big ideas, and you wouldn't be living with a bunch of old geezers who all act like we're your grandparents."

"Thanks, Joe," Holly says quietly.

Joe smiles at her fondly over the rim of his mug.

Holly stands and takes the three steps up to the porch, leaning in to kiss him on the cheek. "All right, well, I guess Pucci and I will mosey on."

"See you around, Mayor."

When Holly glances back at the Ho Ho Hideaway from the water's edge, Pucci trotting along at her side, Joe is still watching her, bare feet on the railing, coffee in hand.

Coco is at the front desk of the B&B when Holly arrives, decked out in tight yoga pants and a racerback tank top that shows off her firm breasts and her equally firm deltoids and triceps. She's wearing a full face of make-up, and her hair is flat-ironed into a shiny sheet of chocolate. Holly catches a glimpse of her own reflection in the mirror over the front desk: puffy eyes from not sleeping well, unwashed hair spilling from a baseball cap, chapped lips, wrinkled t-shirt. She braces herself for the inevitable critical commentary on her appearance.

"Honey! I wasn't sure when you and the redhead rolled in, so I've been handling things up here," Coco says, ignoring the fact that her daughter looks like she's just spent the past month being held hostage in a place with no running water. Coco picks up a small stack of papers and thumbs through them. "You got a call from your accountant in Miami." She puts a hand up next to her mouth and whispers loudly, "I think *someone* might have forgotten to pay her quarterly taxes."

Holly unclips Pucci's leash and shoos him toward the back office. He knows well enough to head right back there, and he also knows well enough to stay clear of Coco, who dabs at her eyes with a Kleenex whenever Pucci is around. (She claims that he triggers her "latent dog allergies.")

"And the lady from the kitchen came in to find out whether she should make a real breakfast for your guests, or just tea and dry toast." Coco tosses the messages onto the counter when she's done reading them. "Oh, and then Cap Duncan stopped by to talk to you about the weather and a boat trip of some sort." Coco clasps her hands together on top of the desk. "That's all." She beams brightly at Holly like a child waiting to get a reward for good behavior. "Now, how can I help out around here today?"

Holly aches all over from tossing and turning all night. "I think we've got things covered here, so why don't you and Alan go out and explore the beach, or go have lunch at the Jingle Bell Bistro. You can use the B&B's golf cart to get around. The key is in that drawer by your hip, and the cart is parked in the lot right next to mine." She points at the desk and makes a break for the hallway that leads back to her office.

"But I want to help you! And to get a feel for what goes on around the island. You know, I really don't visit enough or ask enough questions," Coco says, her hand on the corner of the waist-high bamboo desk as she follows Holly to the hallway. "We both know that I never spent much time here when you were younger, so I feel like you have this whole world filled with people and things that I know nothing about."

Holly stops walking, her back still to her mother. Her talk with Joe on the beach had really helped to shed a different light on Coco's choices over the years, but more questions? More visits? No—definitely not. These are both unacceptable options.

Holly turns around slowly, a smile plastered on her face. "Well then, I guess we need to immerse you in island life and in the business side of things while you're here, don't we?"

Coco follows her to the office, obviously pleased to be given access to the island's inner workings. She pulls out Bonnie's chair and sits down, back straight, ready for action. "So, what should we do first?"

Holly sets the coffee mug she's been carrying around all morning on the corner of her desk and opens her laptop. "First we should check our email, and next we should prepare for the redhead to blow in and immediately kick you out of her seat."

Coco's eyelids flutter. "Let's do the email. I think I need to get the password to that. And maybe some of our bank account information, and probably copies of our taxes for the past few years."

Holly doesn't like any of these suggestions, and what she likes least of all is the self-assured way that Coco refers to everything as "ours": *our* bank accounts. *Our* taxes. Just hearing those words makes Holly grind her teeth in anger.

"Actually, I'll get us logged in to email, if you can run to the kitchen and get me a cup of coffee with half & half and two packets of sugar, please." She picks up her mug and holds it out without looking at her mother. More coffee is the last thing she really needs or wants, but the ability to send Coco on an errand pleases her.

Coco pauses, pencil in hand, a fresh yellow notepad at her elbow. A tart reply is written all over her face, and Holly waits patiently as her mother wrestles with the desire to speak her mind.

After a brief internal battle, Coco pushes back from the desk, eyes narrowed. "One coffee light and sweet, coming right up," she says. Coco straightens the hem of her tank top before she stalks off down the hall, head held high.

Holly quickly logs out of everything, clears her browser's history, and then reopens just her email. She double-checks that the filing cabinet in the corner is locked, and shoves a few of the files that she and Bonnie are working on into her desk drawer.

Once everything in the office is on lockdown, Holly sits and stares at her email inbox, chin resting on her laced fingers as she waits for her mother to come back with the coffee. Christmas Key will become a ski resort and its visitors will sleep in igloos on snow-covered beaches before she'll give Coco the keys to the kingdom.

14

THE MEN TRICKLE INTO THE LOBBY AROUND ELEVEN O'CLOCK, SHADOWS under their eyes, cheeks gaunt and scruffy. In comparison to their rowdy excitement on the night they arrived, they look like a placid, unexcitable bunch.

"We've got toast, oatmeal, coffee, a fruit salad, and lots of water and juice in the dining room," Bonnie says as they file past the front desk.

"They look a little worse for wear," Holly whispers, "but I feel like maybe we've come out the other side." She mentally tallies the men as they entered the ballroom, hoping she'll count all nineteen.

"Some of 'em are still green around the gills, hon," Bonnie says. "Hey, did you get back to Cap yet about the fishing trip? He called again while you were walking your mother around the B&B. And incidentally, thank you for keeping her out of our office while I drank my first cup of coffee."

"No problem. She was getting way too comfy at your desk, so I thought I'd move her out of there before things got ugly."

"She was sitting at my desk? Are you planning on firing me and taking on Coco as your assistant?"

"Please. I would rather chew off my own foot and let a baby alligator cut its teeth on the bloody stump," Holly says without even pausing to consider such a horrifying scenario.

Bonnie is distracted as Bill Hammond makes his way through the front lobby. He's the last of the fishermen to emerge for breakfast, and he ambles past with a smile for Bonnie.

"Hi, doll," she says to him, wiggling her red-tipped fingers. "Sleep well?"

Bill nods back at her, giving her a wink on his way to the dining room. "Like a kitten next to a fireplace," he says, patting his round belly. "Now I'm ready for some breakfast."

"Mmm, mmm, mmm." Bonnie shakes her head, still looking appreciatively in Bill's direction as he walks away.

"You're totally unbelievable," Holly says. "It's like your man-radar is set to go off in the presence of any human fueled by testosterone and T-bone steak."

"I was born this way, sugar." Bonnie bites her lower lip as she does a little hula-salsa hybrid for Holly's benefit. "Hey, do I look like Shakira?" she asks, face serious.

"Like *Shakira*?" Holly chokes on the words.

They look at each other and collapse into a fit of laughter.

"What's going on?" Coco demands as she walks in. "What did I miss?"

"Looks like we all missed something," River says, poking his head through the open doorway.

"Oh no," Bonnie dabs at the corner of her eyes, "this was all my fault. Well, actually it was all Shakira's fault." The mention of Shakira sends Holly into round two of the giggles.

"I see tears of laughter, so it couldn't have been that bad," River says, patting the doorframe with his hand.

"You can come all the way into the lobby, you know." Coco says, looking him up and down with interest as he hovers in the doorway. "We're a bunch of real nice ladies who won't bite." She runs her fingers through her hair in slow motion, popping a hip alluringly.

Holly looks on, sobered by the reality of her mother brazenly flirting with River before breakfast.

"I just wanted to see what was on the docket for today." River turns his attention to Holly. There is amusement in his eyes as he studiously avoids glancing back at Coco.

Holly clears her throat. "Um, right. I need to call Cap Duncan to make sure you're still on for the boat trip, but I wanted to see if you all were feeling well enough to be on the water. And we have our daily summer storm to deal with, so I'll see what time he thinks you should go." Holly hides as much of her body behind the front desk as she can. Having River see her in her wrinkled t-shirt and shorts is bad enough, but standing next to her overly-groomed mother makes her feel like a wet mutt standing next to a show dog.

"On the water is the only place most of us really want to be," River says. "Even if we're not feeling quite like ourselves yet, we're still more than ready to get out there."

"Well, there is fun to be had on dry land," Coco says, a hint of suggestion in her voice as she inserts herself back into the conversation.

River runs a hand over the scratchy whiskers on his cheeks. He looks like he wants to respond—there is definite mischief in his eyes—but he thinks better of it and nods thoughtfully instead. "Okay... well, just let me know what we can do to get out there on that boat."

"Of course. I'll get ahold of Cap right now. Should I call you in your room?" Holly hopes that her professional tone somehow cancels out her mother's embarrassing overtures.

"That'll work. I'm in the Seashell Suite—the one that smells like the inside of a stomach. And by the way," he says, his handsome features scrunched into a slight grimace, "I'm really sorry about that."

"No! That's not your fault," Holly says. "I don't know what happened, but I take full responsibility, and I—"

"Let's just forget about it, okay? Honest. We're tough guys; we'll come around." River pulls back from the doorway, patting the wood frame one more time like he's bookending their conversation. "Just holler at me when you've got something, okay?"

"Sure thing."

"Holly," Coco says when he's safely out of earshot. "I know I wasn't around much during your formative years, and I might have missed out on some important opportunities to show you how things are done." She leans backwards to watch River walk down the hall, then places her palms flat on the front counter and turns her attention to her daughter. "But honey, what are you *waiting* for?"

"Ladies and gentleman, my mother," Holly says, spreading her hands like she's presenting Coco to an audience.

"I'm serious, Holly!" Coco leans across the counter and grabs Holly's wrists. "If you weren't already dating Officer Hotpants, then I'd stop joking around and start fixing you up with that gorgeous specimen."

"Oh, speak of the devil..." Bonnie says under her breath. She straightens a stack of papers on the desk as the front door opens and Jake walks in.

"Jake." Holly's eyes widen with guilt like a teenager caught in the glare of a flashlight as she sneaks back into the house after curfew.

"Hey. I heard things were crazy around here," he says to Holly and Bonnie, taking off his hat politely and holding it in both hands. "Hi, Coco. How are you?"

"It's a little steamy around here for my taste," Coco says, picking up a brochure from the counter and fanning herself like she's having a heatstroke. "But other than that, not too bad. How are you, handsome?" She shifts seamlessly from flirting with River to flirting with Jake. As always, Holly is impressed (and somewhat annoyed) at how smooth Coco is; if she'd stuck around Christmas Key long enough, *she* could have been the sole politician on the island, because who wouldn't vote in a charmer like Coco as mayor?

Jake trains his gaze on Holly as he answers. "I've been better. But I wanted to make sure our visitors were up and on their feet again, and to offer my help if you all need me for anything."

"Thanks for stopping by, Jake. Everyone is up and feeling better. I think we're good right now."

"Well, just holler if you need anything." He nods at Bonnie and Coco and heads back out to his police cart. The women watch him through the front window, their three heads tilting in unison as Jake leans over to pick up a coin from the sidewalk. He turns and holds it aloft for them to see, grinning like he's just found the golden ticket. It's a quarter.

Holly gives him a half-hearted thumbs-up.

"What was *that* all about?" Bonnie asks, one fist on her hip.

"Maybe his last paycheck didn't clear," Holly says, watching him drive away.

"No, not the quarter. I mean him coming in here like that."

"I have no idea." Holly raises her eyebrows and shakes her head.

"Your man was just dropping in to see how things were going," Coco says. "I think it's sweet."

"I was about to tell you that I broke up with Jake a few months ago," Holly says to her mother. "So he's definitely not my man anymore. And these guys from Oregon are important to us. Their visit here means business for all of us, so my flirting with one of them would be unprofessional." She can hear the defensiveness in her own one-sided argument even as she's making it. Bonnie and Coco exchange a look; for once, they appear to be on the same page. "*Seriously,*" Holly says. "I can't. I really can't."

"Look, if you two broke up recently, then you might think there aren't enough miles between you and Jake, but let me give you some advice that's as old as time, dearest daughter of mine," Coco says, tapping her acrylic nail against the desktop with authority. "The best way to get *over* a man is to get *under* another one."

Bonnie hoots in agreement. "Ain't that the truth!"

"Now, I need to go and track down my darling husband so that he can take me to lunch." Coco tosses her head and holds out her palm. "Where are those keys to the golf cart again?"

Holly fishes through the drawer for the keys and hands them to her mother.

"Sugar," Bonnie says after Coco disappears up to the Lemon Tree Loft to find Alan. "You know I'd almost never agree with a word that comes out of your mother's mouth, but on that issue, truer words have never been spoken. And it's not very often way out here in the middle of nowhere that a viable option comes to *you*.

Young men around this place are as scarce as a hen's teeth. I'm just saying."

"You're not wrong," Holly sighs. "I just don't want to mess up this visit. It's so important to our overall plan. I need to keep my head focused on the business part—"

"Shh, shh, shh," Bonnie shushes her, holding out a hand to stop Holly. "You can be damn sure that if the gender roles were reversed, any man who was the mayor of this island would have no qualms about throwing some bait at a group of female visitors to see if he got any bites."

Holly nods reluctantly. Bonnie isn't totally off the mark, and she knows it.

"Now if you'll excuse me," Bonnie says, pulling a tube of lipstick out of the top drawer of the front desk, "I reckon I'll go and check on that handsome Bill and make sure he's got everything he needs." Bonnie turns to the framed mirror hanging behind the front desk and touches up her bright pink lips, the reflection of her own face and Main Street over her shoulder looking back at her. "And I know you're headed out to talk with Cap about that fishing trip, but you might want to swing by your place and take a shower, doll."

Holly looks down at her disheveled clothes, wishing she'd taken the time to shower first thing in the morning before heading out for her walk with Pucci.

"I say this with all the love in my heart, but you're looking a little worse for wear." Bonnie wrinkles her nose and blows Holly a kiss. "Oh, and you might want to slap on some deodorant while you're at it, sugar."

15

—————

"I DON'T KNOW THAT IT WILL DO THEIR STOMACHS MUCH GOOD, BUT I could get them out there later in the afternoon," Cap explains to Holly over the counter. They're standing in his cigar shop, debating the timing of a boat excursion.

"That could work," Holly says. "I mean, I promised them world-class fishing, and I really need to come through at some point."

Marco flies from his perch in the corner of the store and lands on Cap's shoulder. He turns one shiny, black eye to Holly and stares her down.

Cap looks dubious. "I think you need to learn more about fishing, girl."

"Is afternoon too late to catch anything?"

"Naw," Cap says, chewing on a toothpick. "We could catch some tarpon after dark, but we've got a major storm headed our way that's going to change everything."

"C'mon, Cap. You're not talking about that Turks and Caicos storm, are you?"

"Sure am, half-pint. You been watching the weather channel, or you too busy playing Barbies to notice something as insignificant as a tropical storm?"

Holly takes a step back from the front counter, stunned. She looks at Cap from under the brim of her hat.

"Really, Cap? *Barbies*?" Her face feels hot. That mentality right there is exactly the uphill battle she's been fighting ever since she stepped into her position as mayor. Just because practically everyone on the island has known Holly since she was a toddler with a tattered doll in one hand, her round baby belly poking out above her bikini bottoms, it doesn't mean that she'll always be a little girl. She blinks her eyes rapidly and takes a few more steps away from Cap.

"I'm busting my butt to do good work on this island, and I have everyone's best interests at heart," Holly says emphatically, jabbing a finger at him as she speaks. "You know what? Never mind. Just call Bonnie and make the arrangements for the fishing trip, will you?" She heads for the door.

"Aw, kid, no." Cap holds out a rough, square hand. "Don't go. I'm sorry. Sometimes I say dumb things—you know that."

"Jamming" by Bob Marley comes on over the speakers in the shop, filling the air with mellow background noise. She pauses, one hand on the doorknob.

"That's a sign, you know," Cap says, taking advantage of her hesitation.

Holly takes a deep breath. She's tired and stressed, and she doesn't want to blow a gasket when it's really her who's out of sorts and not everyone else. Besides, she knows in her heart that Cap didn't mean to get under her skin. "What's a sign?"

He points at the speaker on a shelf high up on the wall. "Bob's on. Nobody can be mad when Bob Marley's on, even if the person who made them mad is a total jackass."

Holly laughs in spite of herself. "Is that an official rule? That Bob erases all bad feelings?"

"I think so." He shrugs. "Oh, and also that you have to dance with whoever is closest when Bob comes on."

"Dance?" She looks at him with suspicion. He might be apologizing in his rough, Cap-like way, but she hasn't totally forgiven him yet. "I'm not sure I feel like dancing."

"I bet you do." Cap sets Marco on the back of his chair and comes around from behind the counter. He pulls her into a loose-armed embrace, the white hairs on his upper chest exposed by a rakishly unbuttoned Hawaiian shirt. Cap is so much bigger than Holly that it's easier just to give in to his goofy, relaxed swaying than to try and resist.

"See? You're smiling on the outside. And I think on the inside you're forgiving me, right?" He spins her around in a lazy circle, the ceiling fan turning slowly overhead like a tired dancer on her pole at the end of a long night.

"Of course I forgive you, Cap, come on. It's just that Coco is here, and the fishermen got sick, and now there's this damn storm..."

"Yeah, tough breaks all around. And having Coco here can't be easy. Sorry, kid." Cap turns Holly under his arm one time, setting her free as the song ends.

"Yep. She's on a mission to learn everything she can about the island and how we run things. It seems weird that she's suddenly interested, but I'm trying not to read too much into it." Holly leans across the counter, adjusting the bill of her Yankees cap.

"Never read too much into other people's actions—most of the time it's got nothing to do with you anyway." Cap reaches across the counter and taps the brim of her cap, knocking it down an inch so that it covers her eyes.

"Solid advice," Holly says, straightening her hat so that she can see him again.

"Okay," Cap says after a pause. "So what we have here is a tropical storm with winds at sixty-four knots, which is about seventy-four miles per hour." He points at a big map of the Gulf, Caribbean, and Atlantic that's hanging on the wall. "Last time it made landfall was near Nassau, so we're looking at it heading our way in the very near future. We really need to think about battening down the hatches, as they say," Cap says, running his hand over the wispy ponytail that runs down his neck.

Holly presses her hands to her cheeks, staring at the tiny dots of land on the mostly blue map. "So...you think we're going to get hit?"

Cap sniffs, nodding his head firmly. "Definitely. I think we're looking at a question of when, not if, and really—as is always the case with storms—how hard."

"This is unbelievable, Cap. I've got all this stuff planned, and it seems like every day some unseen force is turning it all upside down."

"Some people call that Murphy's Law, my dear."

"Well, I call it shitty luck."

"That, too..." Cap clucks his tongue at Marco.

"So do you think we have time to at least get them out on the water this afternoon before it gets too choppy? I can start rounding up the troops around here and thinking of things we can do while we wait for the storm to pass. And I need to meet the boat this afternoon and pick up our food delivery so that we have supplies."

"I can get 'em out on the water for a while, but I have some bad news about that boat."

"What?" Holly's stomach plunges like an elevator loosed from its cables.

"That's what I was trying to call you about all morning: they radioed to let us know that delivery is suspended until the storm passes. They don't want their boats to get stuck out here."

"Because that would be terrible, right? To be stuck on Christmas Key?" She pulls an exasperated face. "Dammit, we need food! I was counting on that delivery, Cap," she says.

Cap's thick white eyebrows jump into his hairline. "Yeah, I would imagine you were." Marco flaps his wings twice before lifting his feathered body from the back of the chair. With a few lazy wing dips, he crosses the room and lands Cap's shoulder. "But luckily for you, you have the best neighbors in the world," he reminds her. "And, if I were mayor of this fair isle, I'd snap out of the 'woe is me' frame of mind as soon as possible and start calling on those neighbors for help."

Holly chews on the inside of her cheek, thinking. "You know what, Cap? You're right." She holds a hooked finger up to gently chuck Marco under the chin.

"Yeah, sometimes I get it right," Cap says. "Sometimes, but not always."

"Oh, you do all right, you old pirate," she says. "Thanks for the dance."

Holly jogs back to the B&B, dodging slow-moving golf carts on Main Street. Now that she knows it's coming for sure, she can already feel and smell the impending storm.

16

The first order of business is getting the men out on a boat before the storm sweeps in and keeps them locked up for at least another twenty-four hours. Holly heads straight back to the B&B and knocks on the door to the Seashell Suite. River throws it open; he's grinning down at her, leaning lazily against the doorframe.

"So the mayor delivers messages in person, huh? I was only expecting a phone call from your people, but this works too." He's shirtless. Lean, muscular, lightly tanned...and shirtless.

Holly wills her eyes not to fall below his chin. "Yep. I deliver messages. I also bus tables, wash all of the linens around here, and answer my own phones."

He cocks an eyebrow at her.

"Okay, sometimes my assistant answers the phones."

River chuckles. "Well, every good politician needs an assistant, and I hear you're a damn fine mayor."

Holly can't help it: she looks down. And back up again. On the taut skin that covers his strong, rounded shoulder is a tattoo of a baseball. It's filled in with the vertical green, white, and orange stripes of the Irish flag. A few inches below the clavicle on that same side, in the fold of skin between his ribcage and armpit, is a thick, raised, pink scar. Her eyes linger.

"So you've been hanging around the mean streets of Christmas Key, getting the four-one-one on our local governing body?"

"Not really, but I might be interested in getting the four-one-one on the local governing body." There's just enough humor in his eyes to water down the suggestiveness of his words.

"All right, all right," Holly says, holding up her hands in mercy. She can hardly keep her knees from buckling beneath the weight of all this innuendo. "I think you're getting stir crazy after being cooped up for too long."

"Maybe so," he says, his eyes challenging her to back down. "Wanna come in? Or I could come out and take you for a drink at that bar down the street—what's it called? Frosty's?"

"Yeah. Jack Frosty Mugs—or just Jack Frosty's." Holly picks at the paint on the doorframe with her thumbnail, avoiding River's gaze. "But I'm not sure that's a good idea."

"Right—business hours. I get it: politicians drinking midday is frowned upon."

Holly gives a quiet laugh. "Something like that."

"Nah, I understand." He pushes away from the doorframe and puts another foot of distance between them. "It's the cop, right?"

Holly's eyes fly to his face. "Is it that obvious?"

River turns both palms up and the corners of his mouth turn down. "Kind of. I guess."

"God, that's terrible." Holly frowns. Her baggage with Jake shouldn't be on display for everyone to see.

"Relax—honestly." River's voice is reassuring. "It's not that obvious. I saw him eyeballing me in the bar that first night after dinner, and I've been around the block enough times to know when a guy is trying to stake his claim."

Holly isn't sure why she feels the need to explain, but she does. "It's over between us. We're just trying to figure out how to share this island."

"That's cool. It just felt a little...complicated."

"It is." Holly exhales and stops chipping away at the paint with her thumbnail. "Anyway, I wanted to let you know that Cap Duncan will be taking you guys out on the boat this afternoon."

"Really? That's excellent." River folds his arms across his bare chest, allowing her to change the subject without further comment.

"If we get rain and storms—which we almost always do—they'll probably end around three. Why don't we meet in the lobby then, and I'll have Cap join us."

"Got it, Mayor." River smiles down at her again. "And thank you for arranging everything."

"Please. It's no problem at all." Holly turns away and tucks her hair behind her ears. She waves awkwardly over one shoulder, trying not to look at his naked torso again, but failing.

About halfway down the hall, she stops and turns back; he's still watching her. For some reason, all the talk she's been spewing about not mixing business and pleasure is suddenly a distant memory, and the idea of Jake staking his claim makes her want to be extra clear about the fact that there's no claim to stake.

"Hey," she says, suddenly feeling that same sense of elation and spontaneity that she had the other night while they'd tossed a coconut around on the beach.

River raises his elbow over his head and leans against the door-frame, waiting.

"I'll see you in a couple of hours, slugger."

17

THE FISHERMEN TRUDGE BACK INTO THE DINING ROOM AT SEVEN-THIRTY, wind-swept and boisterous once again, debating waves and marlin, ocean depths and mangrove snapper. Because they ate a late breakfast, Holly sent them out on the boat with brown bags full of snacks: granola bars, shiny apples, and bottles of water. Now their intended lunch is spread out in the B&B as an informal dinner, and the men grab plates at the head of the buffet-style offering, constructing sandwiches from the cold cuts and condiments as they go.

Through the north-facing windows of the dining room, the sky is blue behind a backdrop of mangroves and palms. But after spending the afternoon monitoring the maritime weather service and manning the phones in the office, Holly knows that they're in for at least a minor storm.

With all of the men seated at the round tables, cans of soda or bottles of beer cracked open, and thick sandwiches piled high on their plates, Holly calls for their attention. She feels as anxious as she did calling the last village council meeting to order (though certainly less exposed, as her yellow and white striped bikini is well-hidden under black shorts and a hot pink Christmas Key B&B t-shirt.) Several strands of hair have fallen loose from her French braid, and her t-shirt sleeves are rolled up onto her shoulders so that it looks like a muscle shirt.

"Thank you again for being here with us." Holly looks out at the crowd, steepling her hands in front of her chest as she speaks. "We're so happy that you're here on Christmas Key with us, and we love your adventurous spirit and your patience as we do our best to get you out on the water for as much fishing as possible."

A few of the men raise sweaty bottles of beer at her in a toast before tipping them back to wash down their sandwiches.

"I'm hoping that the short boat trip you took today is just the beginning of a great week, and that the rocky start we've had isn't an indication of how the whole trip will go. That said, I do have some interesting news to share." This gets everyone's full attention. "As you may have heard from Cap while you were out on the boat, we've got a tropical storm headed in our direction."

The men lean back in their chairs, ready for more info.

"While you were fishing, I got us completely prepared for the next twenty-four to forty-eight hours. Our normal shipment of food and supplies was supposed to come in today, but with the threat of an imminent storm, that got pushed back."

River sits at the table right in front of Holly. He catches her eye and then looks down at his sandwich with exaggerated sadness, his face contorted into a pitiful frown like it might be the last food he'll see. Holly looks away from him so that she won't laugh.

"Now, lucky for you all," she goes on, "not only have you landed on the most festive island in the Keys, but you also ended up with a bunch of people who aren't afraid to chip in and act like neighbors. Several of our local ladies have offered up meals from their own kitchens, and they're hard at work right now baking us lasagnas, frittatas, and banana bread, and everyone I know is checking their shelves for board games, flashlights, batteries, and extra pillows and blankets. We'll make the dining room here our main gathering place, and for as long as we have wild weather to deal with, we'll have home-cooked food, entertainment, and," Holly folds her hands together, looking around at the faces of her guests, "we'll have each other."

The men are quiet, digesting the sandwiches and the news simultaneously.

"Well," Bill Hammond says, standing up and pushing his chair back. He pulls out the napkin that he's tucked into the collar of his t-shirt. "It's true, we did come here to fish. But we're a bunch of old geezers—and a couple of young bucks," Bill nods at River and at his own son, Josh, "who love adventure. And as long as we've got food—"

"And beer!" calls a man from one of the other tables.

"—and beer," Bill agrees, "then we're going to survive. And when it's all said and done, I still plan to have caught me a bunch of big old fish!"

The other men cheer loudly.

"Now, how'd you all know I was coming?" Bonnie asks in a sassy drawl, sweeping into the room with Buckhunter on her heels. She bows and curtsies, pretending that the whooping and hollering is for her. "Actually," she bats her eyelashes, "I know all of this hullaballoo is really for Buckhunter. Who am I kidding?"

Holly turns back to the men, her hands poised like Vanna White showcasing a prize. "Here's Bonnie with our good friend Leo Buckhunter, and Mr. Buckhunter with our good friend Bud Light." More cheers and laughter from the crowd.

Holly finally lets the breath she's been holding escape from her chest. Everything is going to be fine. Her CD player is on a table at the back of the room next to a tower of discs to choose from, and she's got a stockpile of batteries for flashlights and radios. The men carry on talking over sandwiches and beers, and the noise level in the room rises back up to where it was before Holly's big announcement. She's amazed at how flexible and easygoing this group of guys is: no one even batted an eyelash at the threat of being stuck inside the B&B while a storm rages outside.

While Holly and Bonnie clear dinner away, islanders begin to drop in with supplies to give or to loan, and with covered dishes to stash in the kitchen. Some even decide to stick around and ride out the storm at the B&B for fun, and others have brought their own slippers and toothbrushes along so that they can stay amongst neighbors for safety and companionship. The triplets bring a bunch of pillows to sit on, and a rousing game of gin rummy starts up on the carpet near where Holly's podium usually stands at village council meetings.

The mood is downright festive—kind of like the final night of a convention where everyone stays late in the hotel ballroom to drink and carry on—when Coco walks in on Jake's arm. She's dressed for dinner in tight white jeans, pink strappy heels, and a loose, colorful blouse. Holly immediately unrolls the sleeves of her t-shirt and tries to flatten out the wrinkled cotton with her palms.

"What's going on here?" Coco asks, slipping her arm out of the crook of Jake's elbow.

"Tropical storm headed our way," Maria Agnelli says, walking right up to Coco. She stands a full foot shorter than Coco, but shoots her a steely look that's all business. "It's gonna be a real rat bastard, Coco—kind of like that boy who knocked you up and left you all those years ago." She puts a wrinkled hand out to take Coco's smooth one.

"Oh, Maria, for heaven's sakes," Coco says, letting the older woman hold her hand. The reminder of her unplanned teenage pregnancy sits there awkwardly for a minute. "So how are you holding up, you old dear?" Coco asks loudly, leaning in to Maria's ear.

Maria recoils, obviously offended that someone would feel the need to yell at her. "My ears are holding up just fine. My feet aren't so great, and I don't have much left in the butt department, but I can sure as hell hear you." Maria lets go of Coco's hand, then pulls on Holly's arm, motioning for her to bend down to hear. "I'm going to go and see if I can't scare up a game of Truth or Dare with these guys. And good luck with that old bag of bones," she says in a stage whisper, giving the tiniest jerk of her thumb in Coco's direction. "You can put lipstick on a pig, but it's still a pig, you know."

"Always lovely to see you, Maria!" Coco calls after her as Mrs. Agnelli joins the Cafferkeys at their table.

"So we've got games and food here, huh?" Jake is still standing behind Coco. "It looks like some of the other islanders are ready to pull an all-nighter here. Maybe I should stick around just in case things get rowdy."

"I'm sure things won't get out of hand here, officer. But you're welcome to stay if you want to."

"Well, it looked like you had everything under control the other night at Jack Frosty's," Jake says simply. "So I'm sure you can manage anything that comes up around here."

Holly nods, folding her arms. She knew that night in the bar with River was going to come back and bite her eventually.

"Hey, look at that," Jake says, nodding at a table surrounded by fishermen. "Poker. I'm gonna see if they have room for another player."

Jake squares his shoulders and approaches the table of men; they stop what they're doing and look up as he introduces himself. A few stand and offer handshakes, but Jake directs his words at River, who stops shuffling the deck of cards and nods at whatever Jake is saying. Before Holly has a chance to walk over and see what's going on, Jake pulls out a chair and antes up, tossing some bills from his wallet onto the tablecloth.

Holly decides to stay away for a while and just watch the game from afar. She makes the rounds, talking to Alan and her mother, then sitting with Heddie and Iris for a while to kick around ideas for brides who might decide to do destination weddings on Christmas Key. By midnight, several of the men have folded at the card table and gone back to their rooms to catch a few winks, and Coco and Alan have finally turned in after huddling at a table with the triplets and their husbands for a few hours of wine and conversation.

The first licks of the storm have officially reached the island, and Holly is in the kitchen with Bonnie and Fiona, eating the brownies that Iris brought and sipping leftover champagne from the fourth of July straight out of the bottle.

"Now that he's not sick and I'm not worried about him choking on his own vomit anymore, I can definitely say that your baseball player is hot," Fiona says, breaking off another piece of brownie.

"He's not *my* baseball player, Fee." Holly seals some leftovers in a container and wipes her forehead with the palm of her hand. Even though she showered and changed, Holly never had a chance to catch a nap, and after her restless night she's starting to feel dull around the edges.

"I don't know about that, sugar. I think he'd like to slide into your home plate."

Holly drops her chin, looking at Bonnie tiredly. "Really? More innuendo, Bon? I thought the frisking and the 'concealed weapon of love' stuff with Jake was your best work."

Fiona laughs, brownie crumbs flying from her mouth. "Sorry," she says. "But did he actually frisk you?"

Holly blows the hair out of her eyes and carries a stack of saran-wrapped plates over to the counter next to the fridge. "I seriously can't handle either of you right now. I'm way too exhausted to think about Jake frisking me on Main Street. And really, Fee, we should be discussing *your* love life right now."

"Mine?" Fiona feigns innocence, holding a hand to her heart like she's shocked. "But it's so boring."

"Honey, Buckhunter is many things," Bonnie says, "but boring is not one of them."

"Did you..." Fiona turns to Holly, her hand pointing at Bonnie.

"Tell Bonnie you've got the hots for Buckhunter? No."

"No need, Dr. Potts. You might be able to diagnose diseases, but I can diagnose a serious case of lovesickness at fifty yards. It's a gift." Bonnie winks at them.

"Lovesickness?" Fiona blanches. "Ew. Not even."

"I don't know. It's definitely some sort of sickness," Holly teases, reaching for a chunk of brownie.

Fiona ignores Holly's jab. "We're just having fun." She gives a casual shrug. "It's nothing serious."

"So you're admitting that you two are playing doctor?" Holly raises an eyebrow at Fiona.

"Or maybe he's been doing body shots off of you after the lights go out at Jack Frosty's?" Bonnie offers.

"Jesus. What is it with you two and the work-related double-entendres?"

Bonnie and Holly make eye contact and, without words, agree to drop the subject—for the time being, anyway.

"So, did you see those two boys out there, sugar? They're locked in battle over *you*," Bonnie says to Holly. She's turned her attention to moving food around on the shelves of the refrigerator to make room for the Tupperware containers full of lasagna and pasta salad.

"I saw." Holly takes two cookies out of a Ziploc bag before handing the bag over to Bonnie. "But they're not fighting over me, they're just being men. Neither one of them wants to lose at poker." She bites into an oatmeal raisin cookie, her face twisting and contorting like she's just bitten into a tart lemon. "What kind of cookies *are* these?" Holly turns to the sink and spews crumbs. She spits twice, trying to get the horrible taste out of her mouth.

"If those are the oatmeal raisin, then Maria made them. I think she used capers instead of raisins this time. Here, drink this and throw that bag of cookies in the trash." Bonnie pulls a bottle of water from the fridge and sets it on the counter. "Now, if this were the animal kingdom, I'd say those boys are either fighting to the death, or trying to establish who the alpha male of the village is." Bonnie mutters a few words under her breath as she reshuffles the containers of food to make them all fit in the fridge.

"But since it's not the animal kingdom?" Holly ignores her friend's frustration and hops up onto the edge of the stainless steel counter to sit and drink her water.

"Well," Bonnie says, holding onto the door handle with one hand. "Then I think they're hashing out who gets to take you back to your side of the island to play Tarzan and Jane once this storm passes."

"Wait—so you think they actually believe," Holly slides down from the counter, straightening her shorts with one hand and holding her water bottle in the other, "that whoever wins a *poker* game has some chance of getting into my pants as the grand prize?"

Bonnie thinks about it for a second. She picks up a damp rag from the counter and starts wiping down the island in the middle of the kitchen. A knowing smile plays at the corners of her lips.

"Bonnie!" Fiona laughs. "Are you serious? Have you ever let a card game decide which man you're going to date?"

"Honey, no one ever said anything about a *date*, did they?"

"Bonnie Lou..." Holly shakes her head in amazement. "You are too much."

"That's what they all say." Bonnie cocks her head saucily and tosses the wet rag across the kitchen; Holly catches it with one hand.

"River is kind of adorable," Fiona says, licking the chocolate frosting off her fingers.

Holly drains the water bottle in one big gulp and then recaps it. "Yeah, he is. And today when I went to his room to tell him about the fishing trip, we had a moment."

"A moment? Tell everything sugar—leave no detail unshared!" Bonnie leans against the counter, face eager.

"Well, he invited me in—"

"Oh, sweet Moses!" Bonnie picks up a cold jar of mayonnaise from the counter and holds it to her neck like she's trying to keep from overheating. "I can't believe that man invited you in!"

"The real question," Fiona says, reaching for another brownie, "is did you go?"

Holly scoffs and tosses the empty water bottle like a missile towards the recycling bin. She makes the shot. "Of course not, Fee. I'm the mayor. I don't spend my afternoons in the hotel rooms of male tourists."

"That's right, love. Never visit a strange man in his hotel room during daylight hours," Bonnie says, wagging a finger smartly.

Fiona throws back her head and laughs. "Excellent advice, Bonnie. Okay, so it was probably wise not to go into his room, but if you have the chance to get to know him better, I think you should go for it."

"Doctor's orders?"

"Doctor's orders." Fiona takes a big bite of brownie.

From the sound of the wind and rain outside, the storm is rapidly picking up momentum. The women stand there together in companionable silence for a few minutes, passing the bottle of champagne around and listening to the rain pelting the roof and windows.

"So this is where you three are hiding out," Jake says from the doorway.

"Hey, Jake," Fiona says with a smile. "I haven't seen you in ages."

"It's been, like, two days," he says, giving her a puzzled frown. "And I'm pretty sure I almost ticketed you a few days ago on December Drive for tailgating me."

"You were driving slow and I had an appointment with some waves and sand after work."

"Yeah, yeah, yeah. Just watch the lead foot and the reckless driving, huh?"

"Yes, sir." Fiona gives him a sloppy salute.

"Anyway," Jake looks at Holly, "we're taking a five minute break. You wanna come out and watch me empty these fishermen's pockets at the card table?"

"Jake," she says with a warning note in her voice. She doesn't like the idea that he's playing too aggressively against their guests.

"Don't worry. Any man who bellies up to a poker table knows the stakes."

"And what exactly are those stakes?" Bonnie asks.

Holly and Jake lock eyes for a second. "The whole pile of chips, as far as I can tell." He backs into the swinging door, bumping it out with his backside. "See you ladies out there."

Bonnie gives a low whistle, her face awash with admiration. "Honey, I am IM-PRESSED. Getting two men to fight over you like this is some kind of ninja-level man-eating."

"Oh, come *on*," Holly says, grabbing Bonnie's elbow. She drags her into the hall, heading for the dining room as Fiona follows close behind, still holding the champagne bottle.

"Hoo-hoo-hoo!" Bonnie whoops like a chimpanzee as she trails behind Holly. "You Jane, me Tarzan!"

Holly stops in the doorway of the dining room; Bonnie and Fiona nearly bump into her from behind. There, at a round table in the center of the room, are Jake and River. They're facing each other, eyebrows furrowed in concentration as they examine their respective hands of cards. Standing behind them are a mix of locals and fishermen, their arms folded across their chests as they make small talk and watch the two men square off.

A pool of light from overhead falls directly on Jake and River like they're performing a play on stage. Their profiles are both strong and handsome, their gazes intense. With Jake's short dark hair, five o'clock shadow, and deep tan, he looks like a chiseled actor on the set of a movie. In contrast, River's straight, sandy-colored hair is mussed, he's grown in the start of a blonde goatee, and his sharp blue eyes dart around keenly, humor dancing on his face as he spies Holly. His look tells her all she needs to know about what will happen next.

River takes the toothpick that he's been chewing on from between his teeth and holds it with one hand. "You ready?" he asks Jake.

Jake nods and lowers his cards, spreading them flat across the tablecloth. Three kings and two sevens: a full house. The men watching the card game whistle and a few clap.

Outside, the wind is howling and palm fronds are tapping against the windowpanes like the fingers of unseen ghosts. The lights inside the B&B flicker.

Casually, as if it happens to him every time, River lays out his cards in a fan: a ten. An ace. A jack. A queen. A king.

"Royal flush!" Joe Sacamano shouts, holding up a glass in toast. "Nice work, young man." Everyone starts talking again as if they've been holding their collective breath, waiting to see the outcome.

"Good game, officer," River says politely, scooping the separate piles of cash into one big one. "I think I'm gonna quit while I'm ahead." He stands and folds the wad of bills in half, tucking it into his shirt pocket and patting it exaggeratedly. "Might need to throw the deadbolt on my door tonight, right Mayor?"

Holly is watching Jake's face as he turns up both palms and makes a show of being a good sport. "I wouldn't worry too much," she says, turning to River. "Crime on Christmas Key is nonexistent."

He leans in to Holly, putting his mouth next to her ear just briefly. "Yeah, but if I do get robbed, I'm pretty sure the cops won't come running to help me."

Holly's stomach does a flip; she knows Jake is watching this whole exchange.

"Hey, it's only midnight," Bonnie says cheerfully. "What should we do now?"

All that Holly wants to do is head home and go to bed, but that won't happen until after the storm has passed.

"Hide and go seek?" River suggests.

Bonnie snorts. "If you let a bunch of old people loose to hide at this time of night, someone is bound to fall asleep in a closet or under a bed while they're waiting to be found."

"Aww, I don't think you're giving them enough credit," River counters. "How about 'Two Truths and a Lie'?"

"That could be fun," Holly says. She looks around the room.

"Let's see if we can get a game going." River walks up to the table where the triplets are still sitting with their husbands. Gen has her head on her husband's shoulder, but lifts it and looks at River with a sparkle in her eyes. Holly knows that if he gets the triplets, then they'll help him sell the idea and he'll have nearly everyone on board.

Sure enough, in less than five minutes River has a group of about sixteen people seated in dining room chairs in a big circle. Holly shakes her head in amazement and pulls up a chair of her own.

"So, the idea is to tell us three things," River explains. "Two that are absolutely true, and one that is a bald-faced lie. But the lie has to be believable enough that we might fall for it. And then after you tell us three things, we have to vote on which one is the lie." River looks around at the faces of fishermen and islanders, checking to see that everyone is on board. "Got it?"

"Cap, you look like a man with enough of a past to kick butt at this game. Wanna go first?" River nods at him.

"All right," Cap says, rubbing his hands together eagerly. "Here are three things about old Cap: one, I learned how to live completely off the land anywhere in the world just in case I ever got shipwrecked someplace. Two, I took a break from sailing the seas in my early twenties to serve as a gunnery sergeant in the United States Marine Corps during Vietnam. And three, my parents were first cousins who fell in love and moved across country so that they could marry and raise a family together."

The room is silent. People flick glances at one another to try and gauge which of Cap's statements might be the lie.

"The lie has to be the one about your parents being first cousins," Heddie says, her thin hands folded in her lap.

"Although it would explain a thing or two," Joe Sacamano says. The crowd erupts in laughter.

"I vote for the Marines as the lie," Holly says. She can't even picture Cap with short hair and in uniform.

"You're both wrong," Cap says. "I have no idea how I would live off the land in Siberia or Antarctica."

"So, hang on here just a second with your scandalous self, Cap Duncan," Bonnie says. "Your parents were first cousins? Are you sure you all weren't from the South?"

Everyone laughs again.

"I'll go next," Jake says, raising a hand boldly. Heads turn in his direction. "So, number one," he clears his throat and sits forward on his chair, elbows on both knees. "I speak four languages: English, Spanish, Cantonese, and Italian. Number two, I'm a huge fan of every sports team in Miami." He pauses here, letting his eyes fall on Holly. "And number three, when I got to this island, I fell in love with everything about it. Absolutely everything."

There is a tentative shifting of bodies as people look back and forth between Jake and Holly. No one speaks up to guess which of his statements is a lie.

Holly feels the heat of being put on the spot. It's like she's been turned inside out and everyone can see what she's thinking and feeling. Her ears ring in the quiet room while she waits for someone to guess which of Jake's statements is a lie. Technically there are two: he definitely doesn't speak Cantonese, and she knows he doesn't love *everything* about Christmas Key.

It only takes about thirty seconds for someone to guess that Jake only speaks three languages, which leaves his veiled declaration of love sitting there like an undetonated bomb. The awkward moment passes, and the game continues, but Holly doesn't feel like playing anymore.

After a few rounds of truths and lies and a lot of laughter, the crowd disperses. Several of the fishermen head to their rooms to sleep, calling out their thanks to the locals for the food and games as they exit the dining room. River catches Holly's elbow as she's straightening tables and chairs.

"I know you can't go home until the storm is over, so why don't you take my bed and catch a few winks? Here," he says, handing her his room key. "I'll stay down here, promise." River holds up a hand like he's taking an oath.

"Oh, no, thank you," she says, setting down the chair she's just picked up. "Really—I can't. You go ahead and sleep a bit. I need to do a couple of things in my office anyway."

"You're sure?" He looks at her quizzically.

"Positive. But seriously, thank you." It takes everything in her not to snatch the room key from his hand and take him up on the offer. "And thanks for getting a game going. I'm going to have to hire you on full-time as our island event organizer if you keep entertaining us."

"I prefer 'Games Manager' or 'Steward of Fun'—something catchy like that." He's joking with her, his eyes twinkling, but Holly is too tired to pick up his easy banter and run with it.

Bonnie materializes at her side. "You turnin' in for the evening, slugger?"

"I couldn't convince the mayor to borrow my bed for a few hours and get some sleep herself, so I guess I'll call it a night." He looks at Holly one last time.

"Goodnight," she says, busying herself with the chairs again.

"Night, ladies."

"Sleep tight, Tarzan," Bonnie whispers to him as he brushes past her.

Holly gives her a light shove.

18

THE TAIL END OF THE STORM WHIPS ACROSS CHRISTMAS KEY AROUND
seven the next morning. The lights flicker repeatedly in the kitchen,
and everyone stops what they're doing and stands perfectly still (as if
this will somehow keep the electricity from going out completely). It
blinks and buzzes a few times, then comes back strong. The small
group of kitchen workers cheers.

Their hoots and hollers wake Holly up in her office. She rolls
over, stretching out the kinks in her neck and shoulders as she tries to
remember where she is. She managed to catch about four solid hours
of sleep by curling up on Pucci's dog bed (he kindly took the spot
under her desk, watching with interest as his mistress curled up into
the fetal position on his bed like a lean, furless canine). Pucci is up
immediately and sniffing Holly the second her eyes open.

"Thanks for letting me hog your bed, buddy," she says, accepting
a wet nose to the cheek.

She puts the maritime news report on in her office while she
checks her email, and the sounds of a subdued breakfast filter
through the B&B.

From the news reports, it seems like everything is finally about to
wind down enough for the islanders to disperse, and there's a distinct

possibility that the fishermen could get out on the boat again as soon as the storm passes. Holly emerges from the office bleary-eyed and with messy hair. She left her flip-flops in another room at some point, so she pads through the hallway barefoot now, peeking into the laundry room and behind the front desk, wondering where her shoes could be.

In the dining room, everyone is up and piecing together their hodgepodge breakfasts from the random assortment of leftovers and baked goods that the kitchen staff has pulled out of the fridge. Two giant tureens of hot coffee and a stack of white china coffee cups make it all look more presentable, but there's no hiding the fact that they're dining on cold pasta and deviled eggs from the kitchens of the locals. Holly twists her hair up into a loose bun and wraps an elastic around it.

"You look like you need coffee!" Coco says brightly, swooping in on her without warning. She's already showered and dressed in white shorts and a bright tank top. Her hair and make up have been freshly applied, and she smells like gardenias. Holly looks down at her own bare feet, wondering how someone who loses her shoes and sleeps on a dog bed is even related to a woman who probably irons her silk pajamas and sleeps in coordinating lipstick and nail polish.

"I *do* need coffee," Holly says, stepping around Coco so that she can fix herself a hot cup of java with cream and two sugars.

"Did you sleep at all last night, honey?" Coco coos, trailing after her. "I would offer to let you shower in my room, but Alan is still up there sleeping...and I'm sure you'll be able to head back to your place soon and freshen up, right?"

Holly doesn't respond as she pours her coffee. It's only after she's gotten it just the way she likes it, stirred it with a silver spoon, and taken her first sip that she turns around. "I slept in my office—a little. And it's fine. I'll go home as soon as I get things settled around here this morning."

"Oh. Okay."

Coco follows her to a table, perching on the edge of the chair next to Holly's as she sips her coffee and takes in the breakfast scene. Most of the fishermen are there, as are the islanders who stayed in the B&B's dining room all night. Holly holds the rim of her coffee cup to her dry lips; she can't even imagine what she must look like.

"So, do you think we can get back to business here after you go home and shower?" Coco sweeps a hand through her shiny hair, eyes cutting around the room. "There's still a lot of ground for us to cover while I'm here."

Holly is about to give a withering, sleep-deprived answer when Bonnie and Bill walk into the room at the same time.

"Whoa," Holly says from behind her coffee cup. "This just got interesting."

"Sugar, hi," Bonnie says, blinking several times as she pulls out a chair at the round table.

"Hi yourself, you little minx," Coco says, nudging Bonnie with an elbow. "How was last night?"

"Pardon me?" Bonnie gives a sniff of disapproval as she sits down.

"Come on, you're not fooling me for a second with that innocent act. Everyone in the room can tell that you just spent the night with that man, and we all know that you've been lusting after him for days," Coco says, nodding in Bill's direction.

"Honey, if you're calling me a harlot, then may I remind you," Bonnie shoots Coco a look, "that it takes one to know one?"

"Huh," Coco huffs. She stands up, smoothing her shorts against her thighs. "Excuse me."

"That woman," Bonnie says, shaking her head as Coco walks away. "I try, Holly, I really do."

"I know you do, Bon." Holly picks up her coffee cup. "She isn't easy to deal with after four hours of sleep on a dog bed, so she can't be much fun after a sleepless night filled with steamy, unbridled passion."

"Oh, don't I *wish* my night had been filled with unbridled passion, sugar," Bonnie says, shaking her head. "But unfortunately Mr. Bill Hammond and I are not coming from the same place; we just happened to walk in at the same time."

"Then where were you last night?" Holly frowns and takes another sip of her coffee, holding the cup with both hands.

"Prepare yourself." Bonnie makes a grim face.

"I'm prepared."

"I couldn't find anywhere to rest my head, so Cap took me across the street to his place."

"No!" Holly shouts, scandalized. She sets her coffee cup down so hard that hot liquid sloshes over the side and immediately stains the tablecloth.

"Oh, lordy—it's not what you think! He made up his pull-out couch for me, and the whole thing was as boring as all hell." Bonnie brushes it off with the flick of a wrist. "Really, I promise."

"So you're not going to take up with Cap the way that Fiona's taken up with Buckhunter?"

"Honey, no." Bonnie reaches over and takes Holly's hand in hers. "I solemnly swear that I will never spend another night with Cap Duncan...and not just because that man saws more wood than Paul Bunyon!"

They snort like schoolgirls, collapsing onto each other's shoulders in conspiratorial laughter.

19

THE STORM LEAVES THE ISLAND WRAPPED IN A COCOON OF CLEAN, COOL air. After making sure that the islanders and the fishermen are situated for the day and that everyone who crashed at the B&B has a ride home, Holly climbs behind the wheel of her wet, muddy, formerly pink golf cart, and heads for home.

Everything outside is heavy with moisture. The eaves of the buildings are dripping, and the sound of raindrops falling from palm fronds makes a series of loud splats on the ground. The road is pitted on dry days, and now it's like driving through a maze of mud puddles, the golf cart bumping along slowly as Holly navigates her way through the sludge. She swerves to avoid fallen branches and leaves, and pauses as a turtle lazily crosses the road. The sky is clear blue; everything feels green and washed, like a new start.

At home, Holly draws the curtains, cranks up the air conditioning, and turns off her phone. The hours of sleep she got in the office were fitful and uncomfortable, and she needs about three or four more—and a long, hot shower—before she can even think about what comes next. Sleep comes in like the tide, pulling her under instantly.

Seven hours later, she claws at the blanket that covers her face, and blinks as the room comes into focus. Her house is dark and cool, and she feels supremely hungover, though Fiona drank the lion's share of the champagne in the B&B's kitchen the night before. She yawns and stretches.

Moving the curtain aside next to her bed, Holly looks out at the dense foliage around her house. The trees are a deep emerald green in the late afternoon sunlight, and the bright colors of her tropical plants pop against the greenery like sprinkled confetti. The sky is awash in color, pinks bleeding into oranges over the ocean in the distance. Holly drops the curtain and pulls off the tank top and underwear she wore to bed, tossing them into her laundry basket.

In the shower, she cups her hands and lets the water stream down her forearms. A smile spreads across her face as she remembers River standing in the doorway to his room, shirtless and smirking down at her. Holly turns under the water and wets her hair, thinking of River and Jake squared off at the poker table. Then the memory of Jake's awkward profession of love during the game of 'Two Truths and a Lie' comes back to her and her smile fades. For as good as she feels about being honest with Jake and setting him free, there's an equal part of her that questions the wisdom of letting go of someone who feels so comfortable—so familiar. Especially on a remote island filled with men who are old enough to be her grandfather.

Holly turns off the water, and it trickles to a stop as she stands there thinking. She used to believe that Jake was like an oasis in the middle of a parched desert. He was a bright dandelion in a field of weeds. Even after she broke things off with him, he reminded her of a giant bacon cheeseburger with extra cheese and onions at a vegetarian buffet...until River showed up. Even with his familiar smell and easy way of making her laugh, Jake pales in comparison to River.

River is a motorcycle ride under the stars with the hot night wind whipping through her hair. He's a dive from a high cliff into uncharted waters. River is like putting all of her money on one number at the roulette table in a flashy casino at three in the morning on the French Riviera.

And River will be leaving in less than a week.

She pulls a fluffy yellow towel from the cabinet in the bathroom and wraps it around her body, clipping her wet hair off her back with a plastic barrette while she dresses.

"Hol?" a voice calls from the living room. As usual, her front door is unlocked, though unannounced visitors are few and far between. "Holly? You back there?" It's Fiona.

"Just got out of the shower," she shouts back. "Be there in a sec."

Holly digs through her dresser drawer for a bikini top and bottoms, settling on a mismatched set. She covers the bathing suit with a lime green wrap dress, then lets her wet hair fall on her back. After running a comb through her tangled waves, she gives up and twists the whole pile into a bun on the top of her head, securing it with a handful of bobby pins. With a swipe of pink lipgloss and a pair of hoop earrings, she feels like a new woman.

"You look about a hundred times better," Fiona says from her spot on the slipcovered couch when Holly comes out of the bedroom. Fiona is flipping through a copy of *Oprah* magazine from the coffee table, her feet tucked under her skirt on the couch cushions. "Good quizzes in this issue. Mind if I borrow it so I can take them and find out what my true calling in life is?"

Holly smiles dazedly like someone who's still coming out of the fog of a good nap. "Sure. Go for it." She pulls a piece of gum from a pack on the kitchen counter and then ties a white cardigan around her waist. "But I can save you the ink and the time: just do what Joseph Campbell said and follow your bliss."

Fiona leans back, tossing the magazine onto the coffee table and running a hand through the air in front of her face like she's reading a marquee sign. "*Follow my bliss*," she says dreamily. "I think I already did, right? I ditched my overbearing boyfriend, and then I ditched snowy Chicago for paradise. That's pretty blissful, isn't it?"

"Hmm," Holly says, sticking the gum in her mouth and balling up the wrapper. "I thought your 'bliss' was a little more to the west." She nods her head in the direction of Buckhunter's cottage.

Fiona throws a pillow at her friend from the couch. "Good lord!"

she cackles. "I guess I need to work on my stealth moves if I'm going to be making house calls to your next door neighbor."

"Or maybe just park your cart in the bushes and walk over to his place when it's totally dark," Holly suggests. "And don't forget to take your shoes in with you."

"All right, Sherlock, you got me."

"Damn," Holly says, looking at her watch. "I need to get my head back in the game and start thinking about tonight. It's getting late."

"Yeah, you disappeared on us and you weren't answering your phone. That's why I made the trip out here to the back forty. I needed to make sure you were still alive."

"I turned my phone off." Holly digs it out of her purse and switches the ringer on. "Let's head back to the B&B and see what needs to be done."

"Your mom helped Bonnie all afternoon," Fiona says, a smirk spreading across her face as she tosses the magazine on the coffee table and stands up. "It was...entertaining."

"Oh, I'm sure. Wait—you got to meet my mom? I'm sorry, in all of the chaos last night I totally forgot to introduce you."

"Bonnie introduced us after things calmed down at the B&B. She even suggested that your mother come back to the office with me so that I could show her what I do."

"She didn't."

"She most definitely did. And I totally shot that down by telling your mother that I just got a new mammogram machine at the office, and that I needed a woman in her forties to test it out on since all of my patients are generally much older. Surprise, surprise: she magically found something else to do with her afternoon."

"Stop—I can't even!" Holly inhales as she laughs, picturing Coco's face when a woman she's just met offers to squish her breasts between the metal plates of a mammogram machine. "I have so many things to say about all of this, but I just can't," Holly says, resting her fingertips on her forehead and rubbing her temples. "And you know what? I'm not even sure anymore that Coco being here is my biggest problem, which is really saying something."

"I hear you, Hol. I really do. And not that you're asking, but I think your biggest problem is actually which gorgeous man you're going to let clear the cobwebs out of your—"

"Don't say it!"

"—bedroom. I was going to say *bedroom*. Jeez." Fiona pinches her friend on the arm. "However, as your primary care physician, I *do* need to point out that sex has definite health benefits that would lessen your current stress level, and you really need—"

"AND we're all done here," Holly says loudly, talking over her friend. "What I really need is a freaking miracle to come my way and turn this ridiculous streak of bad luck around so that the fishermen actually have a good time while they're here." She picks up her bucket purse and throws a chapstick into it.

"I can think of one way to show the fishermen a good time..."

"Yeah, Bonnie's got that angle covered—at least she's working on it."

"Shut it!" Fiona says, following Holly out the front door. "Is it that one that she keeps winking at?"

"Naturally."

"She's a feisty old broad, that one. Wait—he is single, right?"

Holly flips on the porch light before closing her door. "Yeah, he's here with his son, but he's divorced."

"Well, more power to her," Fiona says with approval. "Life is short."

"And she spent the night at Cap's last night," Holly says with a hint of salaciousness.

Fiona stops in her tracks. "I'm dying right now. Absolutely dying. Are you messing with me? Bonnie and Cap?"

"Yeah, I'm messing with you. She slept on his pull-out couch because there was nowhere to crash at the B&B."

Fiona heaves a sigh of relief. "I'm not sure I have enough penicillin on hand to keep up with the romance on this island," she jokes.

"You know," Holly confides as they continue walking down her sandy driveway. "I actually turned Jake down a couple of weeks ago at the Ho Ho."

"What? Why? Isn't there some clause that allows for an occasional hot, drunken night with an ex, no strings attached?"

"That's exactly what he said. I just wasn't drunk enough, I guess. And that stunt he pulled last night during the game..."

"Oh, I thought that was sweet—awkward, but sweet. He's obviously feeling threatened by River, and he's trying to remind you that he still exists. Which is a big job, because your baseball buddy is giving him a real run for his money."

Holly rolls her eyes. "How can I forget he exists when he's underfoot all the time?" She throws her purse onto the seat of her golf cart. "Follow you to the B&B?"

"Sure." Fiona slides onto the bench of her own cart and nods at Holly's ride. "Looks like you've got company there again. He was waiting on the roof of your cart when I pulled up."

Holly sits down behind the steering wheel and stares at Marco. He's perched on the dashboard, watching her. "You again?" she says to the bird. "Okay, let's roll, buddy. I'll drop you back at Cap's." Marco climbs onto the cupholder and grips it with his talons while she backs up onto the road.

Cinnamon Lane is bathed in the hazy light of a summer evening. Fiona takes the unpaved road at top speed, bumping along over dips and gullies, her long hair glinting in the golden sunlight where it penetrates the shadows. Holly follows close behind.

20

"You organized this?" Holly watches Coco bustle around the B&B's kitchen like she owns the place. Which, technically, she partially does, but seeing her *act* like she owns it is unsettling for Holly.

"It was nothing, really. Cap had a freezer full of fish for the men to grill on the beach, and between all of the women on this island, I know we'll have a buffet loaded with side dishes," Coco explains, pointing to a spot on the counter where Maria Agnelli is setting down a casserole dish as if on cue.

"It's a tray of spicy meatballs with clam sauce," Mrs. Agnelli says, bracing her weight against the counter with a spindly arm. "And you know what they say about clams," she whispers behind one arthritic hand. "They're a bit of an aphrodisiac!"

"I think that's *oyster* that works as an aphrodisiac, Maria," Coco says. "But I'm sure it's delicious."

"Ah, well." Maria waves a hand in front of her like she's swatting away a fly. "It's probably all hooey anyway. Food of any kind will win your way into a man's heart, but a nice set of buns will get you into his pants." She totters off, leaving Coco shaking her head.

Holly watches her go. "Do *not* eat that," she says, pointing at Mrs. Agnelli's meatball platter once she's out of earshot.

"Why?" Coco leans over, lifting the corner of the tin foil from the dish and sniffing. "It smells amazing."

"Because the last time she brought a dish to a pot luck, she rolled her chicken cutlets in Cap'n Crunch instead of bread crumbs, and the other night she put capers in her oatmeal cookies."

"What about the time she put hot dogs in her Jell-o mold?" Bonnie asks as she breezes in, setting a Tupperware container on the counter. "I brought corn puddin'," she says, patting the lid of her dish.

"Thanks, Bon."

"Does Maria eat like that at home?" Coco wrinkles her nose.

"Probably. But she eats at the Jingle Bell Bistro several times a week, and I know the triplets take turns having her over for dinner, so she's not starving." Holly isn't too concerned about a tough old bird like Maria Agnelli, but she is a little worried about sharing Mrs. Agnelli's creative cuisine with their unsuspecting guests. "So, again, you organized this, Mom?"

"She called me Mom again," Coco says to Bonnie as an aside. "And yes, I did." She runs her hands back and forth under the faucet in the sink. "I thought since you were sleeping and maybe wouldn't be back over here tonight, you know..." She shifts her weight from one wedge-footed leg to the other, shaking off her hands. "I know you don't think I'm very helpful, Holly, but I really want to be."

Holly hands her a clean dishtowel to dry her hands. There is no part of her that wants to shower her mother with gratitude, but even she has to admit that Coco putting something together in her absence is a thoughtful gesture.

"Thanks, Mom. I mean it." Holly busies herself with searching cupboards for plastic cutlery and paper napkins. "I know it will be great."

The fishermen look thrilled to be outside on the beach. Iris and Jimmy have moved their outdoor grill down to the sand from the patio behind the Jingle Bell Bistro, and the smell of grilling fish wafts through the air. Everyone appears to be enjoying the clear evening on

Snowflake Banks, and Coco has managed to spread the word far and wide, which means that there are nearly as many islanders at the barbecue as Holly had seen when she looked out from her podium at the last village council meeting. Fiona is standing with Buckhunter under a palm tree, handing out bottles and cans of beer from a cooler, and the locals are moving through the crowed, chatting with each other and the fishermen. It's quite a turnout.

It looks like a cocktail party on the beach, and with everyone in their colorful t-shirts, and the sun setting over the water, it feels like a staged magazine shoot. Holly sets her purse on the sand and digs out her phone. So far she hasn't been tempted to capture much of the fishermen's visit (somehow middle-aged men stricken with food poisoning or a group of people stranded in the B&B's ballroom during a storm don't sound like particularly captivating Instagram photos), but this scene—this one right here—looks like one that would make someone want to visit their island.

Holly frames her shots and starts taking pictures. Fiona and Buckhunter smiling at River and Josh as they exchange a few words and hand over sweaty bottles of beer. Jimmy Cafferkey's jolly red face as he stands behind the grill, his white apron smeared with blackened char from the barbecue. Maria Agnelli laughing up at something Jake is saying to her, her wrinkled hand clutching his strong arm. Holly snaps one more of Bonnie with her fiery red hair, wearing a red-and-white checked blouse and jeans, her face the picture of contentment as she looks out at the sunset.

Holly closes her camera app and looks around. It's like she disappeared into her house late that morning and fell into a slumber like Sleeping Beauty, and when she emerged in the evening, the island was draped in pastels and smiling faces. Gone is the storm. Disappeared from memory are the sick guests. Everywhere she looks are people talking and making jokes like old friends. Holly saves her pictures into a file that she keeps on her phone for social media; she'll go through them in the morning and post the best ones.

The triplets are making their way across the sand, toting insulated bags full of food from the B&B's kitchen. Holly drops her phone into her bag and hurries over to offer them a hand. They set everything up on a long folding table that the men have dragged out onto the beach, loading it up with twice-baked potatoes wrapped in foil, grilled corn salad with tomatoes and croutons, homemade dinner rolls, tortellini salad, red cabbage slaw, and baked macaroni. A light breeze lifts the edge of the tablecloth, and Holly inhales the scent of salt water, barbecue, and good food. She really does owe Coco for putting this dinner together.

In full darkness, with the bonfire raging and the crowd sated with dinner and drinks, Holly kicks off her shoes, sits down, and digs her feet into the cool sand.

"I'd like to make an official complaint to the Chamber of Commerce," says a voice from behind her.

"Oh?" Holly says mildly, not turning around. "What complaint would that be?"

"Christmas Key is tempting me to throw in the towel on my real life and move down here," says River.

"She is a force to be reckoned with. A tantalizing temptress. A real man-eater."

"We are talking about the island, right?" River frowns, still standing over her.

"Maybe," Holly replies.

"Wanna take a stroll?"

"Are you suggesting that I disappear into the night with a stranger?" Holly asks, finally looking up at River's face.

"You've seen me without my shirt, watched me whip your ex-boyfriend's tail at poker, and held a bottle of Gatorade to my lips so that I wouldn't get dehydrated while I was throwing up all over the floor of your B&B. I don't think we're strangers anymore."

"True," Holly says, holding out a hand. River takes it and pulls her up. "Which way should we go? We're on the south side of the island; if we go west, we'll wrap around the beach and run into Pinecone Path, which has a wooden boardwalk. If we go east, we'll eventually run into the dock and pier at the end of Main Street."

"Surprise me."

"This trip hasn't surprised you enough already?" She leads him west towards Pinecone Path.

"It's been interesting. Not many fish caught yet, but, oddly, I'm having a good time."

"That is odd, given the circumstances." She wobbles intentionally as they walk, her bare arm brushing against his. The advice from Bonnie and Fiona—and even her mother—fills her head: *go for it. Have some fun. If the mayor of this place was a man, he'd have some fun with gorgeous female visitors...*

"So tell me about Christmas Key. All of it. I want to hear the history," River says, walking next to her with his hands in the pockets of his cargo shorts.

"Really? All of it?" The waves break and wash over her bare feet as they walk farther away from the bonfire. She looks up at his face.

"Yeah, start at the beginning. I know you grew up on the island, but how did you end up here?"

"My grandparents bought the island when I was a baby, and we moved out here while I was still in diapers."

"So you're a real island girl, huh? Running around this rock in the middle of the ocean in a bikini, swimming with the dolphins, keeping geckos for pets?" Every person Holly has ever met off the island has the same kind of questions about a childhood that, to them, sounds like *The Swiss Family Robinson.*

"Yep, all of it," she says. "In fact, my first pet gecko was named Kermit."

"Kermit?"

"Big Muppets fan here."

"I was a rather committed Muppets fan myself," River admits.

"All the cool kids were."

"So, your grandparents bought the island, and Coco is their daughter?"

"That's pretty much the sum total of it, but it's kind of a long story."

"Well, I've got time." River copies her earlier move, weaving a little so that he bumps into her with his arm.

The contact of their bare skin sends a shiver up Holly's spine, and she turns around and starts walking backwards, still facing him.

"You want to see where I live?" she asks impulsively, pushing all nagging doubt from her mind. There's something about his honesty and curiosity that makes Holly want to pull back the curtain and show him the real island, not just the version she hopes to sell to visitors. "My grandparents built everything on this island from the ground up, and our family property is really special to me."

River stops walking. "You'd take me there?"

She stops walking and looks up at him in the moonlight, searching his handsome face for something—anything—that might stop her from taking the plunge. Is this all too good to be true? This great guy showing up here when she's single, wanting to hear all about her life and her island? She brushes a stray hair out of her eyes.

"Yeah, I want to take you." Her lips curl up in a smile so big that she feels like her face might crack. The whole thing is completely out of left field: Holly Baxter bringing a strange man of an appropriate age back to her house...she almost pinches herself to make sure it's not a hallucination. "But you have to help me collect some shells on the way."

"Shells?"

"Preferably whole ones. We can rinse them off at my house."

River shrugs. "Okay. Shells it is."

Their footprints leave a trail behind them in the wet sand as they wander up the beach, picking up shells in the moonlight. River calls out to her from ahead when he finds a good-sized white mollusk. He holds it up, it's curved body like a pearl glowing under the light of the moon.

"It's so pretty!" Holly says breathlessly when she catches up to him. She takes it from his hand. "I have about fifteen good ones here." She's holding them in the front of her dress the same way she'd held the lemons and limes with her shirt in the kitchen. The fronts of her tanned thighs are exposed as she pulls the fabric of her dress out and lets River drop in the shells he's collected. "Let's go up through those trees." She nods into the darkness beyond the beach. "We're not far from my house."

They traipse through the seagrass that lines the edge of the beach, then high-step over tangles of mangrove roots and rocks. Holly leads the way up her darkened driveway, past Buckhunter's quiet bungalow, and to the front door of her own house. She lets them in, still holding the edge of her dress with one hand.

In the bright kitchen, Holly carefully places the shells inside a colander and sets it in the sink.

"Nice little shack you have here," River says, checking out the house.

Her heart pounds as he looks around, and she wonders if she's making a huge mistake by bringing him here. But Holly's proud of the clean white walls, the simple furniture, and the pops of turquoise and lime green that she's scattered around. He stands in front of her white wood bookshelf, admiring the framed photos and the haphazard stack of CDs.

"If you want something to drink, help yourself," Holly says, raising her chin at the refrigerator. She turns on the water and runs it over the basket of shells, rinsing off the sand.

River walks to the refrigerator and looks at the old picture of her standing on the undeveloped island that's stuck to the front of the fridge. "Is this you?"

"I haven't changed at all, have I?"

"Not really. You're still cute as a bug's rear." He opens the refrigerator and takes out two bottles of root beer. "This okay?" he asks, holding one bottle in each hand.

"Perfect. Glasses are in that cupboard behind you." She nods over his shoulder, her own hands wet under the faucet. "And I think it's actually *cute as a bug's ear.*"

"Oh, potato, po-tah-to," River says, popping the tops off of the root beer bottles and pouring the foamy liquid into two glasses. He sets them on the counter and stands next to her at the sink, holding the dishtowel in both hands so that she can place the wet shells there. As she does, he gently rubs each one dry and then sets it on the counter. "Now, tell me more about your island life, Mayor."

"Okay, well, my mom got pregnant in high school," Holly says, starting way back at the beginning. "And my grandpa decided that Miami was too fast and dangerous for his family. He wanted his granddaughter to grow up in a safe place with lots of good people around, and he wanted it to be paradise. So one day he and my grandma took a boat trip way out here to see what was past Key West…"

She talks comfortably, rinsing shells and handing them to River one by one. As she does, she tells him all about Christmas Key and its origins, about her grandma's long battle with cancer, and about everyone who lived on the island—even the people who'd come and gone, or who had lived there and passed on. She tells him about Coco's wild ways as young mother, and (without meaning to) she launches into her concerns about her mother's sudden interest in Christmas Key.

River just listens. Occasionally he asks a well-timed question, but mostly he listens.

"I'm pretty sure the only thing I'm leaving out of this verbal tirade is my blood type," she jokes, turning off the water. "You haven't even had a chance to tell me anything about you."

"Are you kicking me out now?" He folds the dishtowel in half and sets it on the counter.

"I wasn't planning on it," Holly says, setting her clean shells in a bowl and leading River out to her lanai.

"Then maybe I'll tell you a few things besides the tale of my illustrious baseball career, which you already know. Whoa—" River stops, looking at her wall of shells. "This looks like quite a project."

"It is." Holly stands before the half-finished wall, the bowl of shells resting on one hip. She admires her work so far. "I feel like it's going to take me at least another year to finish it."

"How long have you been working on it?" River runs his fingertips over the shells that are already dried and embedded into the plaster.

"Off and on for a couple of years. I only put my most favorite shells up there, and I only work on it late at night when I can't sleep."

"And you figure tonight you won't sleep?" He nods at the bowl full of shells in her hands, his eyes serious and heavy with suggestion.

Holly isn't sure what to say. She looks down at her feet. When she looks up again, River has taken a step closer to her. He pulls the bowl out of her hands gently and sets it on the table. Just like that, the life stories and fizzy root beer are forgotten, and the buzzing current of electricity that's been running between them since the moment they met takes center stage.

River takes her hands in his; Holly hasn't been this close to a man who isn't Jake since college, and this nearness feels dangerously unfamiliar. The humidity pulses around them. Even with the overhead lanai fan turned up high, her lime green dress clings to her breasts and thighs.

River runs a hand up her bare arm. When she doesn't back away, he does the same thing with his other hand. He stands before her, his thumbs tracing lines gently up and down the skin of her outer arms. It's her turn to take a step closer.

"I do have just one other question," River says, his voice low.

"What's that?"

"I've already had some major firsts in the past few days. It was my first time throwing up pink seafood, first time beating a cop during a game of cards, and my first time riding out a tropical storm," he says.

Holly chuckles. "You crossed some big things off your bucket list this week, my friend."

"I did. And I thought maybe I'd round it out by kissing a true island girl under a tropical moon for the first time. What do you say?"

Holly dips her chin so that he can't see her face. This good-looking stranger washed up on her shores, and in just a few short days he's complicated everything. It isn't even her lingering loyalty to Jake (although his presence is another kink in the hose), but more that she knows what a ridiculously short shelf-life this fling has.

She turns her head up to him, lips parted, heart skipping lightly in her chest. After a lifetime of safety and stability, of choosing people and things that are solid and present, Holly desperately wants to choose excitement. Breaking things off with Jake was her first step towards trading certainty for adventure, and now River's presence is making her feel like a champagne bottle that's about to lose its cork. She's determined to let loose, to bubble over. The unknown is—for the first time—a very real destination for her.

"I guess after all of that, then I say if you wanna kiss an island girl, you'd better kiss an island girl," she whispers.

River pauses for one second, two seconds, searching Holly's eyes as they silently acknowledge that split second before something happens for the first time—something that can't be undone. Then River pulls her close, the heat of their bodies like a forcefield around them.

Holly lips melt into his, her pulse quickening at the feel of his fingers tangling lightly in the loose hairs at the base of her neck. He pulls her even closer, the front of his hard body running the length of hers. She lets her hands explore his chest, then wraps her arms around his torso as his lips part questioningly. It *is* different than kissing Jake, and she lets the newness of River's touch sink in.

Holly can taste the root beer they sipped in the kitchen, and her knees feel like they might give way before River gently picks her up by the waist, holding her off the ground. He parts her legs and wraps them around his waist, holding her thighs in his strong arms. Before kissing her again, River looks into her eyes, searching deeply to make sure she wants him to keep going. She does.

His lips still on hers, River backs her up against the part of the wall that she hasn't yet plastered shells onto; she gasps as the rough stucco touches her skin, her hand reaching out and clutching at the textured mortar and shells like a rock climber searching for something to cling to. Her breathing is more insistent as River presses his body firmly into the crook of hers, pinning her to the wall. He is taut and hard against the bare flesh of her inner thighs, the lime green dress pushed up around her waist. River runs his hands over the knots of her bikini bottom where it ties on her hips.

With one hand, Holly reaches for the collar of his shirt, pulling at him hungrily. The snap and crackle she's felt between them since he first climbed into her golf cart at the pier is real, and she knows now that a kiss was inevitable—at the very least a kiss. She's wrestled with doing what's right as mayor, and now she's giving in to what feels right to her as a woman.

"Do you want me to stop?" River whispers into her ear, nibbling on her neck.

"I don't think I want you to stop," she laughs throatily, the tingling chill of his kisses leaving a trail of goosebumps on her skin. "But I might need you to pause."

River pulls back, his eyes hazy as he looks into hers. "Pause? Okay, we can do that." He sets her on the ground reluctantly, lowering her slowly so that her dress falls over her lower body again, covering her bikini bottoms.

"That against-the-wall move was very forward of you, my friend," Holly says, a huge grin on her face as she tries to pull together a few scraps of composure.

"Hey, no time to waste here, Mayor. My ship sails in a few days." River leans down to her, meeting her lips with his own again.

Holly wraps her arms around him, setting her cheek against his chest. "I know," she says, looking out into the darkness beyond her lanai. "That's the problem."

River is quiet for a minute. "That I'm leaving?"

She nods into him, her cheekbone rubbing against the warm fabric of his shirt. "It complicates things. Even more than they already are."

He wraps his arms around her more tightly in response. "I know it does." After holding her quietly for a second, River's body shakes with a silent laugh.

"What's so funny?" Holly asks, pulling back to look at his face.

"I just realized that I've never made out with a politician before," he says, still laughing.

"So you hit on me just to see if the power and prestige would rub off on you, huh? Are you trying to get us caught by the paparazzi—do you want me to get impeached for misconduct?"

"Paparazzi?" River ducks in mock worry, his eyes darting around the pitch blackness of the tall trees. "Do you think they're out there?" he whispers loudly.

"Maybe," Holly giggles, still holding his arms.

"Then we'd better go inside." River gives her a serious look, then bends over at the waist, butting his shoulder gently into her stomach like a linebacker and folding her in half. Holly cries out in surprise as he stands up, holding the backs of her thighs as she dangles over his shoulder.

With a show of unnecessary bravado, River throws open the door from the lanai and carries her into the house. Holly's laughing too hard to protest when he carries her back to her bedroom, and she realizes that she doesn't really want to stop him as he lays her softly on the bed.

"Oregon is about as far away as you can get from Christmas Key and still be in the lower forty-eight. You do know that, right?" She's looking up at his face.

River pulls his shirt over his head in one swift move, standing over her as he considers this fact. "I can come back anytime."

Holly nods, biting her lower lip. She knows there's a good chance that he might never make the trip all the way to her remote island again, but that doesn't stop her from wanting to make the most of the time he's there.

"Or you could come to Oregon." He puts his knees on the bed, one hand on either side of her head. "They don't make too much of the Mets-Yanks rivalry out there, so we probably won't get tomatoes thrown at us if we walk down the street together."

Holly reaches her hands up and runs her fingers through his hair as she pulls him lower. A night with River might make things more tense with Jake, but Holly's already decided that she's ready to deal with the outcome—whatever it might be.

"Shhh, just come here," she says, eyes shining in the darkened bedroom.

He does.

21

HOLLY COASTS THROUGH THE NEXT DAY, FIELDING CALLS FROM VARIOUS magazines and newspapers that she plans to advertise with. She and Bonnie are both lost in their own worlds, and they work across from one another all morning without their normal banter. It's a contented kind of silence, with each woman stopping every now and then to gaze out the window or into the distance.

The memory of River's face that morning is burned into Holly's mind. He'd been watching her with a lazy smile when she rolled over in bed, covered only by a sheet. Now she smothers a grin with one hand, hoping to keep the details of their night together under wraps.

"So what time will the guys be back from the Dry Tortugas? Eight?" Bonnie asks, double-checking the details of the fishermen's day trip.

"Yeah, they'll be here and hungry, I'm guessing. I was planning on having dinner set and ready for them at eight sharp. Do you think we should push it back any later so they can shower first?"

"No, I think they'll want to dive right in," Bonnie says.

"Mmmm, right. Good call," Holly says distractedly. She's squinting at the fine print on an advertising contract that's just come through as an email attachment.

"So what's up, sugarplum?" Bonnie asks from across the desk. "You're acting like a woman who's just stumbled into a state of nirvana. That smile on your face looks permanent."

Holly tucks her pencil into the bun on top of her head and leans back, putting her bare feet up on the desk. "It feels like it might be."

Bonnie takes off her reading glasses and sets them on top of her laptop's keyboard. "Details, please."

Holly can't help it: her face cracks into a satisfied smirk. "He came to my house last night."

"OH MY GOD!" Bonnie shouts, clapping her hands together. "I knew it was going to happen!"

"But he's leaving in a few days, Bon." Holly chews on the side of her thumb nail. "So, I don't know...it's kind of like a combination of nirvana...and purgatory."

"Yuck," Bonnie says. "Is there any way to ignore the fact that he's leaving and have some fun right now?"

Holly stands up and paces across the small office. "No. Of course not," she says. "I can't ignore it. And that makes me wonder if it's part of the fun, you know? That he's leaving and so everything is more..." She flails around, searching for the right word.

"Thrilling. Intense. Passionate," Bonnie offers knowingly. "Yeah, it does make things a little steamier when you know you'll never be picking their laundry up off the bedroom floor while they nap in front of a football game, doesn't it?"

"Probably. But it was the first time I've been anywhere near a naked man other than Jake since college, so it was pretty exciting anyway." She opens the drawer of the filing cabinet closest to her and pretends to search for a file.

"Good for you, honey!" Bonnie says. "I'm not even going to do the math on that one, but it's about damn time."

"And he makes me laugh, Bon." Holly slams the drawer and spins around, leaning her back against the filing cabinet. "He keeps me on my toes, and we have a sort of..."

"Chemistry?"

"Exactly. It's like when we're together I'm always the best version of myself, you know? And last night was amazing."

"I get it. Believe me, you don't have to sell me on this." Bonnie holds out one hand and shakes her head back and forth like she's hearing the gospel from the mouth of a preacher. "I am one hundred percent in favor of any man who makes you laugh and have a good time."

Holly walks to the window, staring out at Main Street. "I'm just weighing the pros and cons, that's all. You know how I am."

"I do." Bonnie picks up her reading glasses and slides them back on. "But don't overthink it, sugar. Just let the man make you happy."

Holly pulls the pencil out of her bun and puts on her Yankees cap, sliding her feet back into her espadrilles. "You're right, Bonnie. Listen, I'll be right back."

"I'll be here," Bonnie says, beaming at her boss as she hurries down the hall.

Jake is standing next to his cart at the curb in front of the B&B when Holly pushes through the front door. He's sipping a cup of coffee and making small talk with Cap.

"Mornin', kid," Cap says to her. "Hey, I'll see you later, Jake." Cap salutes casually before looking both ways and crossing Main on his way back to the cigar shop.

"Hi," Jake says.

Holly kicks the tire of his cart with the toe of her shoe.

"That's police property, you know," he says sternly, nodding at where her foot connected with the tire.

"Oh. Sorry."

"I'm kidding." Jake nudges her with one arm, cup of coffee still in hand. "What's eating you this morning?"

"Nothing, I just wanted to come and say hi."

Jake takes off his sunglasses. "I was going to see you home after the barbecue last night, but you disappeared."

"Yeah, I ran some stuff back here to the B&B, and since everything was under control on the beach, I just went home. I was tired." She tugs on the brim of her cap, pulling it down to shade her eyes so that he won't look into them and see her lie.

Jake nods slowly and swirls his coffee around in the cup.

"Anyway, I have a few things to do, so I'll see you around." Holly takes a few steps away from him, wishing she'd had the good sense to stay inside the B&B.

"Hey, Holly?"

"What?"

When she turns back to him, Jake is staring at her, a serious look on his face.

"Don't make a fool out of me. If you want to see this guy, then see him—I can't stop you. But don't expect me to be waiting around when he picks up anchor and sails off into the sunset. Understood?"

Holly nods once, her eyes focused on Cap's front door across the street. When she looks back at Jake, he's already climbed into the cart and punched the gas. His cart jerks away from the curb.

The dock at the end of Main is quiet. There's no ferry anchored there and no one coming or going. Holly ambles to the end, stopping at the weathered navigational sign to admire the handiwork of friends and neighbors both past and present. She touches her grand-father's painted sign, feeling the way the sun and rain have warped and battered the wood over the years. There is a hardy strength—a tenacity—to the sign that brings her comfort; these are the qualities she most admires, they are the things she wants to carry in her own heart.

Holly walks down the dock and sits at the end. In the distance, a boat of undetermined size moves slowly on the water. She wraps her arms around her shins and pulls her legs into her chest, resting her chin on her knees. Life on the island is usually so calm, so without drama, that the past month feels like a bumpy plane ride through stomach-churning turbulence. From the last village council meeting, to all of the work she's done for this group of fishermen, to suddenly finding herself with not one but *two* men to choose from, Holly feels like her world has tilted on its axis.

And the strangest thing about all of this upheaval is that she actually kind of likes it. She's always labored under the illusion that security brings a sense of calm, when what she really needs in her life is some commotion. A pinch of uncertainty. A few projects where the outcome isn't guaranteed.

The sound of the waves lapping against the pier lulls her as she watches the light dancing on the gentle waves. Eventually, the boat on the water disappears from view completely. Holly squints at it until it looks like a piece of dust on a camera lens. The boat takes so long and turns into such a tiny speck before it vanishes that it looks like it's reached the edge of a flat Earth and simply fallen off.

22

HOLLY IS STANDING AT HER KITCHEN SINK AFTER HAVING DRINKS ON THE lanai with Fiona, who bid her adieu and then walked directly over to Buckhunter's place. It's kind of a trip watching her best friend carry on with her next door neighbor, but Holly is happy for them, and she loves seeing Fiona glow with the promise of a new relationship.

She's rinsing dishes absentmindedly, setting each one gently on the rack in the dishwasher, when she catches a glimpse of her own image reflected in the kitchen window. Her face goes up in flames at the memory of River pinning her against the wall on the lanai, his strong hands holding her up while he kissed her. He'd been gentle but commanding, insistent and tentative at the same time. It had been so long since she'd had a "first time" with someone other than Jake that she'd nearly forgotten how passionate it could be.

Holly rests a cobalt blue shot glass on the counter and bends to pick up a dishtowel that's slipped from her shoulder to the floor. When she stands up abruptly, her elbow knocks the shot glass off the counter and sends it flying. As she reaches for it helplessly, it skitters across the counter, rolls off the edge, and hits the tile floor, shattering on impact. Holly stands where she is, looking at the shards of blue glass near her bare feet. In order to get around them, she shakes out the dish towel the way she might unfurl a blanket on the grass for a picnic, then sets it gingerly on the tile. She steps onto it, scooting across the room with both feet on the towel so as not to step directly on the glass.

The collection of blue glass dishes and glassware had been her grandmother's, and breaking a piece bothers her. Holly always loved seeing the sunlight filter through her grandma's blue dishes as they rested in the cupboard, the glass doors on both sides letting the light shine through. She'd been thrilled to use them again when she moved back into her grandparents' house after Frank's passing, and seeing the glass all over the floor fills her with regret. She should have been more careful.

As Holly pulls a broom and a dustpan from the narrow closet in the hall, she bumps into the wall and a piece of paper flutters down from one of the two shelves overhead. She glances up: there, on a shelf just above eye level, is a three-ring notebook peeking out at her from between her photo albums and her framed college diploma. Printed on the spine in her grandfather's blocky handwriting are the words *Christmas Key: A Long-term Prospectus for Paradise*. It's the collected ideas of Frank Baxter, something he worked on for years as his vision for the island grew and changed. Holly has memories of him pecking away at his typewriter, and she runs her fingers over the indented letters that her grandpa lovingly pressed onto the pages with the hard punch of the typebars on his sky blue 1968 Royal Aristocrat. She picks up the piece of paper that fell from the shelf; it's a note, written in Frank Baxter's hand.

January 13, 1994—$5,000 First Union Bank, Miami. Call L.B.

She reads it over and over, wondering what it means. What was going on in 1994? She was nine that year, and probably racing through the mangroves and pines with Emily, chasing imaginary unicorns and pretending to be princesses. In 1994 her mom had been twenty-six and living in Georgia with two other girls, cocktail waitressing and bar-hopping. Her grandparents were still alive and well, inviting their friends to move to the island and vetting strangers who wanted to come and live with them on Christmas Key.

It's strange, but the one thing that strikes her most about the memories of that time isn't that her grandparents were still alive, but that her mother had been away from her, and she hadn't even really missed her at all. She'd been so happy with her grandma and grandpa and their idyllic island life that she never bothered to question their living arrangement.

Holly pulls the *Prospectus for Paradise* down from the shelf and tucks the twenty-year-old cryptic note into its pages for safe keeping. She feels the weight of the notebook in her hands and thinks of the chain of events that put it there: the broken glass; the dustpan and broom; the falling note. She's thought of her grandparents so much lately that it feels like they're somehow reaching out to her to offer guidance. She holds it to her chest tightly for a moment, then takes her broom back to the kitchen to clean up the broken glass.

23

For a change of scenery, Holly drives down Main Street and turns left onto Pine Cone Boulevard. She takes it straight past the cluster of houses known as Turtle Dove Estates, stopping her cart in the sand on December Drive where it runs into Candy Cane Beach. She generally favors the beaches on her side of the island, but first thing in the morning, the most beautiful view of the sun rising over the water is on the east side at Candy Cane Beach.

Holly sits in her beach chair with a coffee mug wedged into the white sand next to her right foot. The *Prospectus for Paradise* is open in her lap. She started re-reading it from the beginning the night before after watching the sun go down from the deck of the Ho Ho Hideaway, Joe Sacamano's Christmas Key rum warming everyone's bellies as they waited for the easy dinner of snapper and potatoes in tinfoil to cook over the small bonfire on the beach.

She could tell River wanted to come home with her again, but she'd left him playing darts at the Ho Ho with the other fishermen and had slipped away on her own. Holly climbed into bed alone with the prospectus and a glass of wine, only breaking from her reading to call Fiona so that they could kick around some ideas about why Coco might be so interested in the island all of a sudden. She'd lain there in bed, covers tucked under her armpits, talking into the speaker-phone as she sipped her wine.

"Do you think she wants to retire here with Alan and live rent free?" Fiona asked from the comfort of her own bed across the island.

The cicadas chirped in the dark outside of Holly's bedroom window. "No, I think there's something else brewing," Holly guessed. "Like an idea for some sketchy business that she wants to run some-where remote—away from prying eyes. That's more Coco's style."

"I bet she wants to launder money through the B&B," Fiona joked. "She's going to bring the glitz and crime of the big city to Christmas Key come hell or high water."

"Right? I'm sure she'll bury her assets in the sand." Holly took off her reading glasses and rubbed her eyes. Beneath the joking was a very real, very uneasy feeling that was growing in the pit of her stom-ach. She hung up with Fiona and re-opened the notebook to page one.

A tropical oasis floats in the middle of the sea like an ice cube in a glass of whiskey. It fairly teems with wildlife and tropical flora and fauna. The sun makes its daily ascent and descent over the island like a rainbow, rising each morning from the Atlantic and dropping into the Gulf at night. From far and wide come people who want to share in this paradise. With them, they bring their histories, their passions, their gifts. They also bring agendas and desires that may or may not align with your own. Find ways to harness what works with your vision for development, and to ignore what doesn't. You have no other choice.

Now, sitting on the beach at sunrise, Holly realizes that he'd been right, naturally. In the years she's been running the island without her grandpa, she's gotten a crash course in making decisions based on what's best for Christmas Key. She's had to ignore agendas and desires that don't run parallel to her own, and to push her way forward even in the face of resistance.

She closes the book softly on her lap. Coco's motives are suspect, and her presence alone brings with it an agenda that Holly can't even fully imagine. There are so many thoughts and worries swimming through her brain that she doesn't know what to do first. But she knows she has to refocus. Even with River's visit winding down and with Jake throwing ultimatums in her direction, it's time to put romance out of her mind momentarily and figure out the real purpose behind her mother's visit.

Coco has taken to carrying a notepad around with her everywhere she goes on the island. She's got a million questions, and she's always ready to jot down her ideas (or her "lightbulb moments" as she's taken to calling them).

Holly rolls her eyes when her mother taps on the door to the office, pen in one hand, the damned notepad in the other.

"Is this a bad time?" Coco whispers in a breathy voice. She sounds like she's doing a bad Marilyn Monroe impersonation.

Holly motions for her to come in; she knows she can't stop Coco from mowing her down even if it is a bad time.

"What do you need, Mom?" She keeps typing on her laptop, hoping to send the message that her time is valuable and in short supply.

"I just have a few more questions about the island, and I wanted to pick your brain."

Holly inhales deeply, counting slowly in her head as she does. She exhales, saves what she's working on, and shuts the laptop.

"Okay. What." It isn't even a question, but more of a command to just get it out and get it over with.

"Well, your grandparents owned all of the storefronts on the island—all of the property, basically—and now the tenants pay rent each month to run their individual business. I've got that."

Holly nods, silently confirming.

"And they sold the property that the houses rest on to some of the villagers, but retained the land in other cases, letting them build there, but live rent free. Why would they do that?"

Coco slips into Bonnie's empty chair across from Holly. She crosses her bare legs slowly, waiting for an answer.

Holly chews on the inside of her cheek, trying to decide how much detail to give. "Well, by selling to some people, they were able to bring in a stream of revenue that would allow for more building. Of course, anyone who buys land can ultimately sell it as they see fit, but Grandma and Grandpa weren't worried about that. On the other hand, those who couldn't afford to buy, or who simply didn't want to, were allowed to build at their own expense on land that was pre-selected for them. But upon their passing—or if they choose to leave the island at any point before then—the land and any dwelling built on it reverts back to Grandma and Grandpa's estate."

"That seems like a pretty sweet deal for the tenants."

"It works well for us, too, since the islanders who don't own land all contribute to our local economy anyway. A few of them run businesses or volunteer, and they're all a part of our community. And they're building homes that we could potentially turn around and sell when the time comes." Holly takes a rawhide dog bone out of the drawer of her desk and tosses it to Pucci. He's sitting quietly on his bed in the corner, nose resting on his paw, big eyes trained warily on Coco. Pucci picks up the bone and tucks it under his chest before returning his gaze to Coco's knees.

"Hmmm, I suppose." Coco scratches a few words onto her notepad and underlines them firmly. "Now, I've gotten in touch with your accountant in Miami to talk about—"

"Actually, Coco, I have a question for *you*." Holly stands up from her desk and positions herself over her mother. "What exactly do you want here? Why the sudden interest in Christmas Key?" Her tone is suspicious. "After years of doing your own thing and not caring about the island, why do you suddenly care now?"

Silence falls over the small office. Pucci lets out a shuddering sigh and rolls over onto his side.

Coco taps the lid of the pen against the notepad in her lap. "Well, I wanted to gather as much information as I could—"

"Why?"

"Like I said, I had questions, and I wanted to know—"

"Why?"

"Holly, you're being very rude." Coco puts the pen down and glares at her daughter. "Let me finish."

"Fine. Finish—quickly."

"Okay." Coco folds her hands on top of the notepad in her lap and gathers her thoughts, breathing in and out a few times while Holly waits. "I've been looking into it, and I think we should sell the island." She looks down at Pucci on his dog bed. "I think this place is worth more as money in the bank than it is as a giant piece of property to be managed."

Holly is speechless. She opens her mouth to say something, but can only blink in response. "You...I can't..." She puts a hand to her chest.

"And Alan agrees with me." Coco lowers her chin and looks at her daughter squarely, obviously ready for a challenge and bringing her husband's support along as ammo for her argument.

"What do you mean, *Alan* agrees with you? Who cares what *Alan* thinks?" Holly spits. "How dare you even take his opinion into consideration here? This island has nothing to do with Alan."

"Alan is my husband, therefore I take his advice and opinion seriously." Coco lifts her chin haughtily. "And he's got a helluva lot more business expertise than you do, young lady."

"I majored in business," Holly reminds her, still standing and glaring down at Coco.

"*I majored in business,*" Coco says in a spiteful, mocking tone, turning the corners of her mouth down like a bratty child. "And what exactly has that college education done for us so far? Are you suddenly on the cusp of turning this island into a profitable venture? Do you honestly believe that you and a bunch of old farts can get a few fishermen to drift way out here, rent them some bikes, sell them a few boat rides, and suddenly call this place a travel destination?"

Holly is incensed. For the first time in her life, her vision is actually blurred by white-hot anger. She points at the door. "You know what? *Get out.* Go pack your stuff, get your husband, and leave my island. *Now.*"

Coco stands up, slowly pulling herself to her full height so that

she can maximize the two inches she has on her daughter. Her helpful, curious façade has fallen away completely, and her eyes are
narrow and beady as she physically backs her daughter into the
corner of the room. "You can't tell me to go away, little girl," Coco
hisses, moving in closer. "This is *my* island, because it belonged to
my parents." She jabs a finger at her own chest for emphasis. "And—
in case you've forgotten—you're *my* daughter, so you'll do as I tell
you."

Holly has never been in a physical altercation before, and she's
never wanted so badly to reach out and slap someone, but Coco has
her pinned so that her shoulders are nearly touching the wall
behind her.

Just then, Alan appears in the doorway, his face a mask of
innocence.

"Ladies, I just wanted to stop in and see if you felt like joining me
for coffee," he says, assessing the situation. "Oh. You're busy—got it."
Holding up a hand, he backs away, attempting an escape.

"Not so fast," Holly snaps. Her eyes are still on her mother's face,
which is mere inches from her own. Alan stops in his tracks. "I don't
want you and my mother discussing my personal business when I'm
not present, understood?"

"Holly, she has your best interests at heart," Alan says, holding a
handkerchief in his hands. "And I can't help it if I agree with her."

"Are you *kidding* me? You agree with her that we should sell the
island? Just get rid of the only home I've ever had? I would really love
to hear your suggestions about what I should do with my life next,
Alan." Holly slips away from the wall, stepping around Coco. She
folds her arms across her chest and squares off with Alan instead.

Her stepfather shrugs, unconcerned. "The resort offered to keep
the younger people on the payroll, and they promised to relocate all
of the older folks. It's not like you'd have to leave."

Holly is flabbergasted at the words coming out of his mouth. She
has a surreal moment where she feels like aliens have invaded the
island; her life is quickly turning into a horror movie. "Did I hear you
say they would *relocate* the older people? And wait, let's back it up

here for just one hot minute," Holly says, her anger threatening to get the better of her. "Exactly what 'resort' are you referring to?"

Alan turns to Coco, holding out a hand to her.

"Well, honey, I have a resort that's interested in purchasing the island," Coco says, the acidity of her former words replaced by an overly-saccharine sweetness. "They want to build a five-star resort here with villas and the capacity for eight-hundred guests. They think your Christmas theme is really cute," she adds hurriedly, "but we haven't worked out all the details on whether that will work with their overall vision."

Holly nods, jaw clenched. "First of all, don't call me 'honey.' Secondly, Eight hundred people. *Eight hundred*." She keeps nodding, trying to take in this new information without her head exploding.

"It would be the culmination of all that your grandfather dreamed of, sweetheart." Coco waves a hand, her long, manicured nails flicking through the air. "This would finally be a real tourist destination, not just some rinky-dink island full of people with more wrinkles than class."

"Jesus, Mom," Holly whispers, her steaming rage melting into a quiet puddle of sadness. She can hardly bear the weight of hearing her mother talk that way about the people she's known and loved her whole life; it truly sickens her. "That's not what Grandpa wanted at all. You don't know anything about this place." Completely against her will, her eyes begin to sting. She stares at her mother for a moment longer, and then at Alan. They feel like strangers.

"I want you gone," she says to Coco unflinchingly. "And I don't want you to breathe a word of this to anyone," she orders. "There's no reason to get people in a tizzy about this when it's never going to happen. Now get the hell out of my office. Both of you."

24

IN SOUTH FLORIDA, DAILY RAINSTORMS DURING THE SUMMER ARE AS predictable as politicians talking out of both sides of their mouths. For the second time in a week, the island is taking a lashing from a driving onslaught of showers, this one stopping just shy of tropical storm status. There's no need to congregate in a safe place like they had during the previous storm, but the rains are heavy enough that Holly has to rush home from the B&B mid-afternoon to roll down the thick plastic covers that protect her lanai.

She's on the tiled patio, sweat running down her front and back as she tugs at the cords to release the rolled-up sheets of plastic from the ceiling. One of the cords is tangled, and Holly fights with it as a steady flow of water streams in through the screens. The front of her body is totally drenched.

When the cord finally lets loose, the plastic unfurls like a tube of wrapping paper rolling down a flight of stairs. She jumps out of the way as it comes crashing down, the plastic now shielding her and her patio furniture from the water. The world on the other side of her lanai is suddenly a vision of plastic-muted trees and greenery, and the sound of the falling rain is muffled by the window covers.

Holly stands there, contemplating the strange dichotomy of summer in the tropics: it's entirely possible to be soaked to the bone with both sweat and rain at the same time, and to still be hot enough to feel like stripping off your shirt. So strip it off she does. She tosses her wet shirt over the back of a chair and unbuttons her shorts, letting them fall on the tile at her feet. Holly twists her long hair to wring out the water; it splatters on the tile at her feet.

A loud tapping startles her; Jake is outside of the lanai, looking in at her with one hand shielding his eyes like he's looking at the sun. His face is blurred and distorted through the screen covers just like the palms and mangroves in the distance, but she would know Jake's figure anywhere. Holly throws back the plastic.

"Jake, what are you doing here?"

He looks her up and down, taking in her bikini and wet hair. "Your top doesn't match your bottoms," he points out, still staring at her body.

"As usual, right?" She glances at her own mismatched top and bottoms, then back at his face. "I got soaked putting my rain covers down."

"I just wanted to make sure you were okay. There's a storm raging," he says through the downpour, his shirt and shorts plastered to his body. "Actually, I was over here helping Buckhunter get his cart out of a muddy ditch, so I thought I'd drop by." He runs a big hand across his mouth, wiping away the water that's dripping down the sides of his tanned face.

It's then that Holly sees the drooping collection of flowers in his other hand. They're hanging at his side, water falling from the petals.

"Officer Zavaroni," she says, pointing at the handpicked bouquet of pink hibiscus, banana flowers, and baby carambolas. "Are those for me?"

He looks at her from under his black cap, shifting his weight in the mucky grass. "Yeah," he says, suddenly looking like someone who's shown up at Christmas with a gift that he regrets bringing. "I know it's not the seventeenth, but...here." He holds them out to her.

"I can't take them through the screen—come around. I'll meet you at the front door."

Holly stops in the bathroom on her way through the house to grab her silk robe. Her wet bikini immediately seeps through the pink satin, leaving two round circles on the chest of her robe.

"Hey," she says, opening the front door but not inviting him in. She leans against the edge of the doorframe and Jake steps up onto her porch where the overhang shields him from the driving rain. "Not only is it not the seventeenth, but we're not even dating anymore, so anniversary flowers aren't necessary. Plus, you just told me yesterday that you had no interest in waiting around for me," she points out, taking the bouquet from him and putting the wet flowers to her nose.

"I just saw them and thought of you. Anyway, I'll go." Jake steps down one of the three stairs in front of her house.

"But thank you. I mean, for thinking of me." Holly sniffs the flowers.

"Oh," he says, stepping back up so that he's out of the rain again. "I know I said it was fine if you want to date that other guy."

Holly's eyebrows shoot up.

Jake pushes a puddle of standing water from her doorstep with the side of his black tennis shoe. "But it's not fine."

"Jake—"

"I'm done just sitting by and pretending like everything is fine while you continue to make huge mistakes."

The flowers drop to Holly's side as her hand falls. "Exactly what 'huge mistakes' are you referring to?"

"How about breaking up with me, just to start with. Um, let's see, bringing some other guy back to your house." He's ticking items off on his fingers, his face accusing. "And then shooting down your mother's idea without even considering it."

"You're kidding me." Holly feels the blood drain from her face. "My mother's idea. How did you hear about that?"

"No, I'm not kidding you. She told me about the resort, and I think it sounds like an interesting offer." Jake takes off his hat and wrings the water from it.

"Well I'm *not* interested. And the fact that you don't know that completely reaffirms that I made the right choice when I broke up with you, Jake." She puts her hand on the door like she might slam it at any moment, but she's more stunned than angry. "If you don't know me enough to understand that this island is in my blood—that it's a *part* of me—and that I'm not selling it off to some company so they can build a hideous, oversized resort here, then you don't really know me at all."

"I guess I knew that," he admits. "I just thought that maybe you'd eventually grow up and realize that you running this place forever isn't realistic. And that maybe cashing in on this amazing gift your grandparents left behind might free you up to live your life."

Holly takes a step back like he's slapped her.

"But it was never an either/or situation," she says, raising her voice to be heard over the rain as it starts falling more heavily. "I don't have to sell the island to grow up, and cashing in on Christmas Key won't mean that I'm living my life, Jake, it'll just mean that I've given up on my dreams." She searches his face for understanding. "And I'm not doing that."

Jake shrugs, looking beyond her face rather than straight into her eyes.

"Here, take these," Holly says, stepping forward and pushing the wet bouquet against his chest. "I don't want them."

Jake doesn't reach for the flowers; they fall at his feet.

Holly stands on her porch in her bikini and her wet robe and watches Jake get into his cart. He drives too fast through the big puddles on her unpaved driveway, water splashing all around his cart in his haste to get out of there.

Water pours through the treetops and trickles down to the already saturated ground, and Holly listens as her gutters funnel and dump even more water in an endless rush. The flowers from Jake are scattered all over her porch steps, their colorful buds drowned and their greens slick with rain like wet lawn clippings.

She stands there on the front porch and looks at Buckhunter's house, all closed-up and cozy and lit from within. She stands there thinking of the travesty of selling her beautiful island, and of the fact that the people closest to her would even consider that as an option. She stands there until the rain finally stops.

25

"Hey, I've been trying to catch up with you," River says. The gate to the pool area clangs shut behind him.

Holly took a quick shower and threw on a dry sundress after Jake left, then drove straight over to the B&B to skim fallen leaves from the surface of the pool after the summer storm.

"Sorry, I've kind of got my hands full with my mother right now." She pulls the skimmer out of the water and bangs it against the edge of the garbage can to dump out the soggy leaves.

"Is it that stuff about her wanting to sell the island?" River reaches for the skimmer and takes it from Holly gently. He dips it under the surface of the pool and drags it across the water in one smooth stroke, gathering a clump of palm fronds in the net.

"What?" Holly is instantly frantic. "How did you hear about that?"

He stops skimming and looks at her. "I heard her telling Bonnie about it at the front desk."

Holly turns on her heel and stalks across the pool deck without another word. She flings open the side door to the building and storms into her office.

"Bon!" she shouts.

"Heavens to Betsy, child! What are you howlin' about?"

"Coco," she says flatly. "What did she say to you? I need to hear it all—every word of it." Holly taps her finger against the top of her desk for emphasis.

"Oh, I squashed her like a bug, honey. Cool your jets," Bonnie says, waving a hand at her. "She started talking about how great this place would be if she could get someone to swoop in and turn it into a resort, and I told her that she has no business talking like that about a place her parents made with their own bare hands."

"Wow." Holly's jaw drops.

"And I followed that up by telling her she could drag her bony, nosey butt back up north if she doesn't stop messing with your head by showing up here and trying to play mother after all these years."

Holly snorts in disbelief.

"Yeah," Bonnie says, getting out of her chair. She's just getting warmed up. "I said that—all of it. And I know I should bite my tongue when it comes to Coco, but the time when I'll sit by and watch her play tug of war with your emotions has come and gone, doll. She can pop in and pretend to be interested in how things work, and she can think that you might let her sell this place without putting up a fight, but she *cannot* come down here and toy with a girl who's like a daughter to me. Not anymore, Holly Jean Baxter—not on my watch." Bonnie's face is heated, eyebrows raised like a woman who means business.

Holly isn't sure what to say, so she flings herself into Bonnie's arms, wrapping her in a fierce hug.

"Okay, okay, sugar." Bonnie rubs Holly's back as she hugs her tightly. "I've got work to do here, and you have a boy who's leaving this island in two shakes of a tail feather, so go take him to the beach or something, you hear?"

Holly pulls back, nodding.

"And don't worry: I won't tell a soul what she's got cooking," Bonnie says, pressing her lips together and pretending to twist the lock on her mouth with one hand.

River is still outside at the pool. He jabs the skimmer back into the water, breaking the blue surface like he's puncturing a layer of skin.

"Hey," Holly says as she walks out of the building.

"Hey what?"

"Wanna go to the beach?"

He stops skimming. "Don't you have work to do? Or mayoral duties to attend to? You seemed like you had something urgent to handle there," he says.

Holly pretends to think about it. "I decided to take the afternoon off." She walks backwards toward the gate, grinning. "You coming?"

"Really?" He looks at her questioningly, trying to decide if she's serious. "Hell yeah, I'm coming." River tosses the skimmer onto a pool chair and jogs after Holly to her golf cart.

They jump in like two kids who just snuck out the side door of school for an afternoon of hooky, and Holly pulls away from the B&B with a sharp crank of the wheel. River braces himself against the dash with one flip-flop clad foot.

"You're driving like a bat of out of hell, lady!" he shouts over the sound of the wheels crunching across rocks and shells.

Five minutes later, Holly screeches to a halt on the sand at South Pole Shore, about halfway between her house and the Ho Ho Hideaway. River feigns whiplash.

"Woman. You clearly need the ocean, so I'm not going to stand in your way," he says, still hanging onto the golf cart's roof as she jumps out and pulls her sundress over her head in one fluid movement.

"Race ya," Holly shouts over her shoulder, already running towards the shoreline in a turquoise bikini top and white bottoms. Before River is even out of the cart, she's splashing through the surf, diving headfirst under a wave. He watches her admiringly, stripping off his own shirt and tossing it into the golf cart before following her into the waves.

"So," River says, cutting through the water with strong arms. He catches up to her, slightly breathless from the chase. "I sensed some tension back there at the pool when I brought up your mom." River reaches the spot where Holly's treading water and he stops swimming. "Is everything okay?"

"Yeah," she says, spitting out a mouthful of saltwater. "We've obviously got some issues, but we're working on them."

"I gathered."

"It would help me a lot if you didn't repeat anything about the conversation you overheard between Coco and Bonnie." Her brown hair is dark and wet after the short swim, the long strands sticking to her skin like silken seaweed.

River reaches over and picks a piece of hair off of her forehead, smoothing it back onto her scalp. "My lips are sealed."

"Thanks." She reaches for him and pulls him close for a quick, salty kiss. "Want to swim out farther?"

"No. Not really." River smiles, pressing his lips to hers again. His dark blonde hair shimmers in the sunlight, and beads of water run down over his sharp cheekbones. "I'd rather stay here with you and talk about us."

"Us. Right." Holly looks away from him as her stomach clenches. She doesn't want to think about River leaving the island yet, and she doesn't want to have the "this has been fun but..." conversation. There isn't one ounce of regret in her for taking a wild leap and ending up in River's arms, and she definitely doesn't want him to leave wishing that he hadn't gotten mixed up with the crazy mayor of Christmas Key. "You know we don't have to do this, right? You came here for a vacation, and you're going back to your real life in a few days—I get that. I've got my hands full here anyway."

River's laugh is soft, his eyes amused.

"This is funny to you?" She blinks.

He shakes his head and pulls her close to him again, both hands on her waist. In surprise, she wraps her legs around his torso and her arms around his neck.

"You're a nut," River says quietly, standing upright and holding her under the water. With laughter in his eyes, he kisses her slowly. The cool water pools in her cleavage, her breasts pressed against his bare chest as the kiss goes on and on.

"Can I just say something?" Holly pulls back, her eyes grazing his slightly chapped lips. The desire to kiss him again is almost overpowering. "Okay, I *do* have my hands full, but I'm just..." She tries to find the right words as they bob together in the water. "I'm just getting all...you know, *this* over *you*." Her hand flutters in the air. "And I'm not ready to think about you leaving yet."

"You're pretty amazing," River says.

Her face flushes. They're far enough out in the water that the only sound is the slight lap of the waves and a seagull crying out in the distance.

"Even if you are a Yanks fan," he teases, pulling her closer until their bodies fit together again. "And for the record, *I'm* getting all, you know, *this* over *you*," River says, crossing his eyes and making a face. It breaks the mood. "Anyway, I'm just going to leave you with this."

"With what?"

"With this." River leans in and kisses her tenderly with his eyes open. She puts her hands on the sides of his face and holds him as they kiss, unexpected tears filling her eyes.

River pulls away slowly, one thumb brushing at her cheek. "Don't cry."

"I'm not crying." She wipes at her nose with the back of her hand. "I think I got sunscreen in my eyes."

Holly lets her body go slack as she spreads out on her back in the water, floating. Her hair drifts around her shoulders like the tentacles of an octopus, and her arms move in slow strokes as if she's making snow angels. She stays this way for a while, just watching the clear, limitless blue sky and listening to the underwater sounds.

"Hey," River says, grabbing her by the shoulder so that she'll pull her ears out of the water. "Is that what I think it is?"

Holly is upright instantly. "What? Where?"

"Out there." River points into the distance. "Right there."

The corners of Holly's mouth turn up slowly. "Yeah, it is." As they watch, a dolphin pokes its slick nose out of the water. Its body shoots up into an arc, diving through the air and cutting back into the water in a deep dive.

"Wow," River whispers, watching for it to reappear. "That was freaking amazing."

Holly grabs onto him and rests her chin on his shoulder. She looks out at the vast expanse of blue-green water where it meets the sky on the horizon. It feels like they're the only two people in the world, like two pieces of driftwood floating in an endless sea. She holds River tighter.

"Hey," he whispers in her ear, kissing her neck. "Didn't you say you had the afternoon off?"

"Mmmhmm."

"Wanna go back to your place?"

"That's too boring," she says, pulling back so she can see his surprised face. "I know a better spot."

A slow, sexy smile spreads across River's face, and he cups her body against his under the water.

They head to a secret cove east of the Ho Ho, a stretch of beach tucked into a nook right before December Drive begins. The tide is out just enough that they can burrow into the sand dunes on the beach towels Holly keeps in the back of her golf cart. There, they strip off their bathing suits to play in the surf, chase one another between the white trunks of the palm trees, gather shells, and lay together in the sand until the sun sets to the west, its golden light bathing their wet skin in flecks of glitter.

26

THE NEXT TWO DAYS GO BY WAY TOO QUICKLY. THE MEN FISH ALL DAY, Holly spends hours at the B&B scouring the fine print and filling out an application for an opportunity that she thinks might be good for the island, and everyone spends the nights dancing and drinking in the humid air on the deck of the Ho Ho. By the time the men sit down to their last big meal on the island, River and the other guys are sun-browned and peeling, with little white lines etched in the skin around their eyes from where they squinted in the sun on the water.

A pink hibiscus flower is tucked behind Holly's right ear. River spins her out as Joe Sacamano wails on his guitar, and then he reels her back in feverishly, holding her close. They move around the floor like they've been dancing together for years.

"Want to talk about tomorrow?" he asks as they sway to the music.

"Nope," she says, spinning out from him again and putting some distance between them. She backs up to him, her spine pressed into his chest as she holds both sides of her dress in her hands, shimmying against River's body seductively. She's long since stopped caring whether or not Jake sees them together, but he's kept his distance since dropping by her house during the rainstorm, so his presence isn't even an issue on their last night together.

The song ends and Holly picks up her clutch purse from on top of the bar. At the bottom of the stairs, River sweeps her into his arms like he's carrying her over a threshold, and she whoops happily, waving at Bonnie over his shoulder. Bonnie and the other islanders are still dancing and drinking as Joe starts a new song.

Without needing directions, River sets her down and leads her to the beach wordlessly. They hold hands in the darkness, following the water up the beach to where Holly's porch light shines through the thick trees. River cuts through the mangroves to her bungalow like he knows the island intimately.

Inside, Holly throws her purse on the couch and lets River lead the way. They kiss in every room, turning off the lights behind them as they move to the back of the house.

"You really don't want to talk about this?" he asks in the kitchen. The tile floor is cool beneath their bare feet.

"I really don't," she whispers, holding the lapels of his short sleeved Hawaiian shirt in her hands, her eyes trained on his collarbone.

"Not talking about it won't make it go away," River says, resting his chin on the top of Holly's warm head. "And I'd rather know that you want me to try and come back, or that you might come and see me sometime, than to be left wondering if you and the policeman are just going to pick up where you left off when I leave."

Holly pulls her head out from under his chin and looks up at him, fire in her eyes. "That's not happening," she says firmly. She shakes her head twice. "It's not."

"Whoa, okay." River puts his hands up, palms facing Holly.

"As far as you and I are concerned, I think we should just see where it goes. I kind of have issues with people leaving, and if I pretend like you're just going out for another day of fishing, then maybe I can get through this. And then, you know," she looks away from him, "if you call, you call. If not, then..."

"I get it." River puts his hands on her shoulders and gives her a gentle shake. "But I hope you believe me when I tell you that this isn't some vacation fling to me. I really like you, Holly. I like your island, I like your sense of humor, I admire your plans for this place, and I have no intention of leaving tomorrow and pretending like this never happened. Okay?"

Holly nods. "Okay." She takes a deep breath. "Okay."

"Do you want me to stay tonight? Or go? I'll do anything you want —just say the word." In his tone Holly can hear his desperation to please her.

"Stay," she says with certainty. "I want you to stay."

River takes her hand and leads her through the darkened house without another word.

THE NEXT MORNING, BONNIE STICKS CLOSE TO HOLLY'S SIDE AT THE dock, always ready to help out. Holly's overly efficient list-making and task-completing from behind her dark sunglasses are simply ways to keep herself occupied as the fishermen load their luggage onto the ferry, and Bonnie knows it.

"Did we print them receipts from the B&B for everything?" Holly asks, waving at Cap and Buckhunter as they pull up in their golf carts. Each man has two fishermen and several duffel bags piled onto their carts. Holly is still amazed at how her neighbors have pitched in and pulled together to make this visit a success. A knot of happiness twisted with melancholy fills her chest as she watches her neighbors shake hands with their new friends, saying their good-byes and laughing jovially about the mishaps that the fishermen survived on Christmas Key.

"Yep, got their receipts, and gave them the thank you notes and the travel brochures that you had printed up," Bonnie says efficiently.

Holly pretends to consult a list on her clipboard when she sees Coco and Alan approaching. The wheels of their suitcases make loud clacks with each roll over the boards of the dock. Coco has wisely avoided her daughter since their confrontation in the B&B's back office, and with both Bonnie's and River's promises to keep all talk of selling the island under wraps, there's been absolutely no mention of resorts or relocation.

Watching her mother stride down the dock, chin raised defiantly, Holly feels a headache pressing against the backs of her eyes like two thumbs pushing into soft clay.

"Holly," Alan says, approaching her alone. Coco hangs back, her long legs encased in a stretchy ankle-length black skirt. She shuffles the paperwork for their flight like she doesn't even see her daughter standing there.

Alan stops in front of Holly, his tall frame stooped over slightly. He has a rolling suitcase in each hand. "Listen, Hol, your mom…"

Holly braces herself. Her stepfather doesn't generally interfere with the prickly relationship between his wife and her only child, but Holly feels a lecture coming on, and she knows she won't like it.

"She wants to do the right thing here, and, to be perfectly honest, she's always wanted to do right by you," Alan starts, setting the suitcases upright and sticking his hands into the pockets of his shorts. He jingles the coins and keys in his pockets nervously.

"Alan—" This is not a conversation that Holly feels like having on the middle of the dock with nearly every islander crowded around and an extra nineteen visitors looking on for good measure.

"No, hear me out, Holly." Alan pulls a hand out of his pocket and holds up a palm to stop her. "I get that you two are like oil and water, and I also get that this island is a source of contention for you two right now."

"It's not a source of contention, Alan. My grandparents gave me a home, and *she* wants to take it away." Her last few words sound more like a little girl complaining to her dad about the unfairness of it all than she wants them to, and in no way is she—a thirty-year-old mayor and businesswoman—trying to plead her case to her mother's husband. She clears her throat and stands up straighter. There is absolutely no chance that she's going to let Alan play mediator here and offer an opinion about this island like it's any of his business.

"She's trying to solidify your financial future, Holly. She sees that this place could easily become a money pit," Alan says in a quiet voice, leaning down to her. "And she wants to keep you from ending up with no island and no money."

"Alan. That's not going to happen. This island is growing, and before you know it, Christmas Key will be a major tourist destination."

They both glance around at the group of middle-aged fishermen, at their duffel bags and sun-bleached baseball caps. Holly realizes that this particular group of tourists isn't quite the moneyed, cosmopolitan crowd that would indicate a major tourist destination, but it is a start and she's proud of what she's doing.

"Yeah, well...I'd ask you to at least look over any proposals that your mother puts together, okay? Don't be narrow-minded when it comes to your future, Holly. I say this strictly from a financial stand-point, and one from which I have nothing to gain, you understand?" Alan's face is serious. The placket of his button-up shirt flaps in the breeze; under it is a white t-shirt. Holly fixes her gaze on the thin gold chain that snakes out from under his collar and wraps around his neck.

She's considering just nodding in agreement to end this conversation when she catches Coco in her peripheral vision. Her mother is now standing under a palm tree with Buckhunter, of all people. From behind, she can see Coco's strong, sculpted shoulders flex and ripple under her loose tank top as she gestures heatedly. Buckhunter is frowning, and every time he opens his mouth to speak, Coco interrupts by throwing a hand up in his face.

Holly instinctively moves in that direction. Keeping everything calm and even-keeled in front of the fishermen is important to her, and her mother creating a scene just before leaving is totally unacceptable.

"Just hold up," Alan says, grabbing her forearm. "Your mom's got this one."

Holly yanks her arm away from Alan's grip, startled. He's never touched her before, except maybe to give her a casual hug on greeting or departure. His presumption about his place in her life at this moment has finally pushed her to a dangerous place.

"Get. Your. Hands. Off of me." Holly hisses in a low voice. "I'm a grown woman and I will not be manhandled by my stepfather."

She's more than ready to walk over and break up whatever is going on between Coco and Buckhunter, but when she turns back to them, Coco is already walking toward her with a smug look on her face.

"Let's get on the boat, Alan," Coco orders, large black sunglasses shielding her eyes from view. "And you and I are not done with this discussion," she says to Holly. "Not by a long shot. I'll be in touch. And I expect you to consider any serious offers that I can drum up."

"Don't waste your time, because I won't," Holly says stubbornly.

"Well, then this is going to be more painful for you than it needs to be."

Coco keeps walking, assuming that Alan will follow. With a deep sigh of resignation, he lifts a suitcase handle in each hand.

"Holly." Alan nods at her curtly. "Thank you for having us."

A nauseating, acidic burn roils in Holly's stomach she watches her mother and stepfather climb onto the boat. Her eyes search the crowd frantically for River. Nothing feels right. River leaving; Jake showing up at her house and insinuating that selling the island might be a good idea; Alan trying to appeal to her on Coco's behalf; watching her mother rail at Buckhunter for some unfathomable reason—it all makes her feel queasy and unmoored. She places a palm against her flat stomach, deeply regretting the iced coffee she inhaled that morning on an empty stomach.

"Hi, Holly," Emily says with a sunny smile, waving as she approaches.

Thank God—talking to Emily will calm her nerves. She reaches for her like she's reaching out for a hand to pull her from deep water.

"Hey, Em." She opens her arms to hug her friend. "I'm so glad you're here."

Holly smiles when she sees the shirt that Emily is wearing. Frank Baxter had ordered matching baseball shirts for both girls when they were teenagers, with three-quarter sleeves made of turquoise cotton. There's a giant palm tree on the front, along with the words

"Christmas Key" emblazoned in glittery script. On the back—just like a baseball team would—Holly's grandpa had put their names, and each girl had the two-digit number of the year she was born printed in sparkly turquoise. They'd both loved the shirts. Holly still wears hers to bed occasionally.

"I wanted to say good-bye," Emily says. "It was fun having visitors."

"It was, wasn't it? I'm trying to get more people to come to Christmas Key for vacation, and I'm working on some other stuff."

"They'll come." Emily nods confidently. "These guys promised to tell everyone about us. And especially about our clam chowder. They liked the food."

"How could they not? The Jingle Bell Bistro has the best food on the island!"

"In the world!" Emily corrects her.

"That's probably true," Holly agrees. "Listen, I need to say good-bye to a few people. I'll see you later, okay?"

"I know, you need to say good-bye to River," Emily whispers behind her hand. "He's cute, Holly."

"Oh, not just him. I have to go play mayor and say good-bye to the rest of the guys, too," she says, trying to shift the topic away from River. "But he *is* kind of cute," Holly whispers back from behind her own hand. She hugs Emily again and makes her way through the group of men as they lift their luggage and fishing rods onto the boat.

River is standing with Buckhunter and Fiona under a palm tree, surveying the scene. As she approaches, Holly eyeballs Buckhunter with curiosity; she's dying to know what Coco was ranting about, but if the conversation left Buckhunter flustered, he's not showing it. His face is a calm sea, his wiry arm draped over Fiona's bare, freckled shoulders like they're hanging out at a backyard barbecue. Seeing them together acting like such a *couple* is still a new thing for Holly, and she does a double-take every time sees them consult one another about something, or she catches a glimpse of Fiona drinking her morning coffee on Buckhunter's porch.

"Hey, chief," Buckhunter says, lifting his chin at her. "Quite the going away party you're throwing here."

"Not intentionally," she says, looking around. "I think we all kind of liked having new faces on the island. It's going to be weird when it's just us again."

"Mmmm," Buckhunter says in his gravelly tone, neither agreeing nor disagreeing with her.

"Let's amble down the dock." Fiona tugs at Buckhunter's limp hand hanging over her shoulder. She winks at Holly.

"All right, doc. I'll amble down the dock with you," Buckhunter teases, moving the unlit cigar in his mouth from one side to the other. "Let's roll." They wander off, Buckhunter's beat-up Birkenstock sandals slapping lazily against the wooden slats.

"So." River's hands are on his hips. He straightens his shoulders and looks around like he's assessing the area.

Holly twists the end of her long braid with one hand. She hopes the brim of her baseball cap is enough to shield the sadness in her eyes from his view.

"This went way too fast," River says. "I wish we could rewind and start it all over."

"Even the food poisoning?" Holly squints up at him, laughter in her eyes.

"Well, it wasn't my favorite part of the trip, but I'd do it again if I had to."

"What was your favorite part?" she asks in a quiet voice, cocking an eyebrow at him suggestively.

"Hmmm..." River gives her a long meaningful look that makes her stomach feel like she's riding a sailboat through a storm.

She tosses the braid over her shoulder and moves as close as she can without actually touching him. They're both aware of the fact that about forty sets of eyes are taking in their good-byes, and Holly is determined to keep things light and tear-free.

"For the record," River says with authority. "That police officer really blew it when he let you get away." His eyes crinkle at the corners. "If you were my girl, I promise I'd never make that mistake."

Holly turns her eyes to the glare on the water intentionally so that she won't have to look at River. "It kind of seems like I'm the one letting *you* get away," she says.

"True. But if you tried to keep me, it would probably count as a hostage situation of some sort."

Holly kicks at a pebble on the dock, sending it skittering into the water. "Right. I wouldn't want to get all *Silence of the Lambs* on you."

River laughs loudly. "That could get creepy fast."

"It might," she says. "But we'll talk. You know, you can Facebook me. Follow me on Instagram. Tweet at me: @xmaskeymayor."

"Are you serious?" He laughs. "@xmaskeymayor? How did I not know this?"

"Yeah, it's true. I try to keep up a steady stream of pictures and updates about the island, but I've had my hands pretty full for the past week or two."

River pulls his phone out of his pocket. "I'm following you right now—I swear."

They spend the next ten minutes hunched over the screen, the warm skin of River's arm brushing against hers as they follow each other on all of their social media accounts. They take a picture of themselves under the palm trees at the dock, laughing as River posts it to his Facebook page. But beneath the laughter is the somber feeling of an impending good-bye.

"All aboard!"

The fishermen make their way through the crowd, shaking hands, slapping backs, and waving to the islanders. Holly turns her phone off and drops it into her purse.

"Maybe I should hire you to be our sports and recreation organizer," she jokes, walking alongside him as he follows the other guys to the boat.

"Can I telecommute?"

"You can, but I think you'd have to visit every so often to make sure you were up-to-date with what's happening on the island."

River stops behind two of his friends, waiting for them to board. "It's a deal."

There's an awkward moment when Holly pauses and wonders whether she should throw herself on him in front of everyone, but River solves the dilemma by dropping his bags and lifting her off the ground.

"Thank you kindly for all of your hospitality, Mayor," he says in her ear. The juxtaposition of his formal words and their intimate embrace makes them both laugh.

"I'm going to miss you," Holly says into his neck as she holds him tight, her feet dangling a foot off the ground.

"Kiss her!" comes a shout from the boat. Holly and River turn their heads to see Bill's son Josh hanging off the stern of the boat, a goofy grin on his sunburned face.

River sets Holly on her feet, his hands still on her waist.

"Lay one on her, slugger!" Bonnie hoots.

With his eyes, River asks for permission; Holly winks back, granting it. And so he takes her into his arms gently—leaning her back just enough that the move looks dramatic—and puts his lips to hers. The small crowd around them cheers.

"Alright, I think it's time," River says, pulling her upright again. "I'll talk to you soon?"

"You know where to find me." Her eyes search his for a moment; he bends to pick up his bags. Holly watches as he lifts his luggage up onto the boat, her heart clenched with disappointment.

Once the men are on board and most of the islanders have scattered, Bonnie and Holly stand together on the dock, waiting for the deckhand to unmoor the boat. The vessel bobs on the water and the morning sun glints off of the windows so that it's impossible to see inside. It's better that way because Holly isn't sure if she wants to watch River leave, and she knows she doesn't want to make eye contact with her mother again. Instead, she and Bonnie link arms and stroll back towards Main Street together.

"Back to real life," Holly says wistfully, watching her sandaled feet as she matches her steps to Bonnie's.

"Well, real life ain't half bad, sugar. And we've got work to do, so that'll distract us. Nothing like some good old-fashioned work to keep us busy as bees in a hive."

Holly isn't so sure. She lifts her Yankees cap off of her head and puts it back on again, readjusting it. "I don't know if it'll keep my mind off of men entirely, but you are right about one thing, Bon: we have some serious work to do."

27

HOLLY DIVES BACK INTO WORK WITHOUT HESITATION. First thing Monday morning she opens her email to find a message from her mother: Coco and Alan are spending a couple of days in Miami, and they plan on taking a few meetings before heading back to New Jersey. Coco has an appointment with Holly's accountant, they're looking into the vendors they use for anything that isn't grown on the island, and they'll be having dinner with two potential buyers who've shown interest in Christmas Key.

The email fills Holly's stomach with lead. She works hard to distract herself and keep from sending a nasty reply. They book a few rooms in September and October for people who want to visit the island, sort through a pile of mail, and Holly posts a few pictures from the fishermen's visit to her social media accounts. At noon, she leaves Bonnie in charge so that she can drive home to have lunch and take a walk on the beach.

Holly takes her tuna sandwich and a root beer out to the lanai with her grandpa's prospectus. She lays the book open on the table in front of her. His words and intentions are right before her eyes:

There may come a point where the elbow grease required to maintain a whole community seems daunting. The idea of selling paradise to anyone willing to buy it might cross your mind. You may even entertain an offer or two, but you have to resist them. Take a walk through the black, red, and white mangroves. Count the cabbage palms that surround our bright buildings, partake of the alligator pear tree's fruits. Search the seagrass beds for queen conch, and admire the different breeds of sea turtles that swim in our waters. And then keep moving ahead— towards progress, towards change, towards new challenges. Always keep moving.

Knowing that she's working to build on her grandparents' dream will have to keep her strong as she goes head to head with her mother in the coming months. With her grandfather's legacy in her hands, and the place she loves as passionately as she loves any human on the planet at stake, Holly needs to find the strength to both forge ahead and to hold her mother at bay.

She's been using the strange note she found in the prospectus as a bookmark—the one dated January thirteenth, nineteen ninety-four —and she's glanced at it so many times that the words written in her grandpa's ballpoint scrawl have become like background noise to her each time she tucks it between the pages of the bound prospectus. What could he have possibly meant by *Call L.B.?* And why would he have done a five thousand dollar transaction at First Union Bank in Miami? Who knew? More than twenty years later, it probably isn't even possible to find out. There's no way to track his decades-old banking online, and she doesn't have much information to go on anyway.

Holly leaves her dishes in the sink and wakes Pucci from his afternoon nap so that he'll follow her out the front door. Sunlight filters through the treetops overhead, and the rush of the ocean is near. She walks through the dense foliage near her house, and Pucci bounds ahead of her as he always does. Marco is back on her side of the island, flapping and squawking as he moves from tree to tree. He picks up Holly's trail on her way to the beach and follows overhead like an avian drone.

"You see what I'm up against?" she says to Pucci and Marco, pretending that her words are of interest to them. "My mother doesn't care; selling the island right out from under us won't mean anything to her."

Pucci dodges under a bush, his hind end sticking straight up in the air.

"Pooch!" Holly calls, whistling. "Come on out, boy!" With some reluctance, Pucci backs out of the bushes, giving his body a firm shake. He makes a run for the water.

The broad expanse of white sand unfurls before them, tall green palm trees bending to reach the water like graceful ballerinas. Pucci runs from sand dune to surf, dodging happily as he ducks in and out of the cool water, but Marco sees the immense beach before them and picks a high branch to observe it all from. He squawks at Holly.

"What's up, Marco?" She stops under his palm tree. "You can fly yourself around this island like you own it, but you get to the sand and chicken out?" She watches him affectionately, hands on her hips, head tipped back so she can see him from beneath the brim of her cap. "Okay, off you go, then," she says, pointing at the thick trees behind them. Marco gives a flap of his wings and takes off for the safety of the shady mangroves.

Holly follows Pucci. She kicks off her sandals and digs her toes into the sun-warmed sand. She pulls the bill of her hat down to protect her already freckled nose, breathing in the smell of the ocean. Her grandpa was right, of course: all she needs to do is take in the natural beauty of the island. The ability to wander freely over this giant lump of sand, miles of blue sky overhead, is all that she needs in life.

Each step on the beach reconfirms her history with this place, and each breath of the tangy salt air reminds her of the oneness she feels with her island. It's a sense of peace and companionship like nothing else; no living, breathing man or person gives her the feeling of being rooted to something the way that Christmas Key does, and the gratification she gets from working with her neighbors to improve their home is like the whipped cream and cherry on top of it all. As her grandpa said, maintaining it all is daunting sometimes, but there's nothing on earth she'd rather do.

Holly takes off her t-shirt and shorts, drops her hat on top of the pile in the sand, and chases Pucci into the ocean. He pants joyfully when he realizes that his mistress is in the water with him, and he keeps pace with her, paddling alongside Holly with his front paws as she dives under the surf, letting the water swallow her whole. As the waves push her to and fro, she rolls over onto her back, and stares up at the cloudless sky.

When she's done swimming, she carries her clothes in her hands and lets the hot sun overhead dry her hair and bikini. Holly takes the long way around December Drive by foot, following Pucci over sandy paths and through undeveloped plots of land as she makes her way back to the B&B. Just before she reaches the road where she knows she'll run into her neighbors, she stops on the sand to put her shorts and t-shirt on over her dried bathing suit.

This freedom to swim and roam on her lunch break—to commune with nature and the island's animals at whim—has infused her with a visceral love for her surroundings, and it leaves her feeling even more territorial about Christmas Key than ever.

Holly crosses through the lemon grove behind the B&B, waving at two of the triplets as she ducks into the lobby. She's ready to answer some emails.

28

Coco,

I received your message and I understand your intent. Please feel free to do as much research and financial investigating as your heart desires. I've walked through the mangroves and counted the cabbage palms, and I'm ready to keep moving—towards progress. I'm ready to battle you endlessly to hang onto the only home I've ever known, which also happens to be the most magical place on the planet.

Holly

She hits 'send' and then answers her ringing desk phone.

"Christmas Key B&B, this is Holly."

"Holly Baxter? This is Wayne Coats from NBC's *Wild Tropics*. Am I catching you at a good time?" The voice is smooth and tinged with the crisp edge of good breeding and an expensive boarding school education.

A surge of adrenaline flows through Holly. In her hand is a heavy ballpoint pen, poised over a pad of paper. "No, this is a perfect time," she says, steadying her voice.

"Good, good. Listen, we got your application and we're interested in having you go through the interview process for *Wild Tropics*. I wanted to talk to you a bit more about what we're looking for, and what we'll need from you."

"Okay, excellent." Holly scribbles on her pad of paper to make sure the pen is working. "I'd love to hear more about the project."

"*Wild Tropics* is our newest reality show, as I'm sure you know, and we're hoping to make it a combination of *Survivor* and *The Real World*, but set on a tropical island. The contestants will have challenges to complete, but we want to plop them down in a place where they have no ties and no resources and just watch them assimilate. We want to explore some of the bigger themes like individual versus community, and sort of watch them rise above adversity. And I think Christmas Key would be a fascinating setting for the show. What do you think?"

"I think I'm interested." Holly grins, dropping her pen as she switches the phone from one ear to the other.

"Well, it would certainly be beneficial to you as an island looking to boost tourism. *Wild Tropics* could put you on the map in a big way. As an added bonus, every reality show spawns its own set of devoted followers who want to see where their favorite shows are made."

For the next ten minutes, Holly listens as Wayne walks her through the details of the network's vetting process. She chews on her lip, taking notes and smiling.

Fiona is walking by the window of her office as she wraps up the call, and Holly waves frantically, trying to get her attention. Fiona keeps walking like she doesn't see her.

"Right, that sounds good," Holly says to Wayne Coates. She grabs a pink eraser from the drawer of her desk and pegs it at the glass pane that separates her from her friend. Dr. Potts jumps in surprise when the eraser hits the window. She leans in, cupping her hand over her forehead and squinting until she spots Holly.

Holly waves her in as she wraps up the call. "Great. I'll wait for your email. No—thank *you*," she says into the phone, watching Fiona as she steps into the office.

"Hey, what's up?" Fiona is breathless. "I'm on my way to work."

Holly sets the phone on the desk. "That was a guy from NBC."

Fiona waits, her face blank.

"You know, from *Wild Tropics?*"

"Right! Oh my God!" Fiona sits down in Bonnie's empty desk chair, resting her oversized straw purse on the floor by her feet. "I forgot about that. What did he say?"

"I filled out the application as soon as you sent me that article about the show looking for a location, and I included all of our social media links and some background info on the island. He said he thought it was 'charming' and 'potentially perfect' for the show."

"Hol, this could be just what you're looking for!" Fiona says, sitting on the edge of her chair, hands over her heart. "I'm totally freaking out! Can you imagine the publicity we'll get if they make that show on Christmas Key?"

Holly shakes her head. She's in shock just thinking of the possibilities.

"You need to tell Coco to cease and desist with her plans to pave paradise and put up a parking lot, because this could be a serious game-changer."

"I know," Holly says, her hands falling to her lap. "I'm kind of in a daze here. And some of the people from the network want to fly out and visit the island."

"Do you have to run this by everyone at the next village council meeting?" Fiona scratches at a mosquito bite on her freckled upper arm.

"Yeah, I still need to figure out how to present it." She waves the thought away. Ultimately, the choice is hers to let the cast and crew use the B&B, and each islander can decide for him or herself whether or not they wish to be on camera. That will be an individual decision, but if she invites the show to film there, then it'll happen whether she gets a majority consensus or not. There is the potential for a major backlash that could make the whole process really uncomfortable for the production team, but Holly knows her neighbors well enough to know that some of them will be tickled at the thought of being a part of a reality show. And it hasn't even happened yet, so she's not going to start worrying about it when they're still in the interviewing stage.

Fiona picks up her purse and slides her phone out to check the time. "I'm stoked to hear what happens next, but I need to get to the office and open up. I've got an appointment with Mrs. Agnelli in ten minutes, and she'll cuss me out if I keep her waiting too long."

"Okay, go and check some blood pressure," Holly says, blowing her a kiss. "And thank you again for sending me that link—you totally hooked us up with this opportunity."

"Sure. No problem. Glass of wine tonight?"

"I'll call you, okay?"

Fiona stands up, the keys to her office in one hand. "Sounds good, chica."

Holly watches Fiona through the window as she crosses Main Street, and replays her conversation with Wayne Coates in her head while she waits for Bonnie to come back from lunch. What chance do they have, really? She isn't even sure if they're the only island currently under consideration, but how many places could they possibly find that are both wild and tropical, yet still semi-populated and developed? Wayne said they want an island that's inhabited, and he thinks the Christmas-theme would be a perfect backdrop for the show, but...she's not sure. She chews on a pencil, inhaling its woody scent absentmindedly.

Her computer chimes softly, and she clicks on her email. Nothing new there. In the background she has another screen open, with the island's Facebook account on one tab and the local weather report in another. There's a message notification on Facebook; she opens it and sees River's name.

I've started this message about eight times, just so you know. I tried "Bonjour, Mayor!" and "Dear Holly,"...and then "Hey, how are you?" But it all felt cheesy. So I'm just launching into it. Anyhow, what's new? We got home safe and sound, and no one threw up over the side of the boat this time. I really missed the rainy weather here (haha) and there's no way I miss the sun, white sand, fishing, or, you know...you. Hope you're doing well. Before I erase this whole thing again, I'm just going to hit "send."

Holly reads and re-reads the message, tugging on her lower lip as she does. It's weird to think that three months ago, her days were happy but nondescript, each one running into the next with only stunning sunrises and tropical sunsets to bookend them. But now —*now* things are getting interesting. She has a producer from NBC casually calling her desk phone and the potential exposure that a reality show might lead to, and an incredibly handsome former baseball player messaging her from across country just to say that he misses her. The stuff with Coco is less thrilling but by no means less exciting, because the anticipation of her mother's next move is keeping her on her toes.

Hey yourself, stranger. I'm great—actually, more than great. I just got a call about a reality show that's looking for a tropical island to shoot on... and whadda you know? I know a tropical island that would make for a pretty freaking amazing backdrop to a reality show! So there's that. And then some cute guy from Oregon just sent me a message on Facebook. Plus the sun is out, and I've already been to the beach today (no dolphin sightings to report). So yeah, things are really good. But it would be nice to have someone to walk the beach with other than Pucci and Marco...

She sends her return message pinging across the miles. Bonnie hasn't come back yet, but she's probably just running late or grabbing an afternoon coffee. Holly shuts her laptop cover and sets her sunglasses on top of her head; she's going to talk to Buckhunter.

29

BUCKHUNTER ISN'T AT THE BAR YET TO PREP FOR HAPPY HOUR, SO HOLLY gets in her cart and heads back to her side of the island to find him. Her neighbors are out and about on Main Street, running letters to the postal box in their plaid shorts and sandals, and waving at her from slow moving golf carts. She waves back, bumping onto the unpaved road of Cinnamon Lane in her own cart.

As she swerves under low-hanging palms, Holly thinks through what she wants to say to Buckhunter. Actually, it's less what she wants to say, and more what she wants to know. Her mother has never pretended to be a fan of Buckhunter's, but seeing them talking at the dock made Holly feel like there must be a piece of the puzzle that she's missing altogether. She pulls into her own driveway, skidding to a stop and kicking up a cloud of dust in the process.

"Buckhunter!" Holly calls, leaving her purse and baseball hat on the bench seat of her golf cart. "Leo! I see your cart—I know you're here!"

"Hey there, Mayor," Buckhunter says, stepping off his deck and into the grass. He moves like a mildly curious tortoise. "What can I do ya for? The good doctor isn't here, if that's who you're after."

"I'm not looking for Fiona. In fact, I just saw her on Main Street."

"It's still a little early for happy hour, but you two are already thick as thieves, huh?" Buckhunter chews on the end of his cigar and swirls his coffee around in his tin cup. She stands there, still staring at him but not speaking; he scratches his scalp roughly. "Come on up for a coffee?" he offers, nodding at his porch.

"I will, if you don't mind."

Buckhunter looks surprised; he clearly hadn't expected her to accept the offer. "Well, come on, then." He leads her up to the porch. "Get you anything in that java, ma'am? Cream? Sugar? Splash of whisky? I make a mean Irish coffee," he says, holding his mug aloft as proof.

"I'll have whatever you're having," she says boldly, sitting in one of his hand-carved wooden chairs, but leaving his prized rocker open for him.

"Be right back." Buckhunter disappears into the house. Holly can hear him whistling and banging around in the kitchen.

"So what's the nature of this unexpected visit, Miss Baxter?" Buckhunter asks without a trace of sarcasm. He hands her a mug.

Holly sips the coffee, nodding her approval as she swallows the sweet, rich drink. The whiskey gives her the extra boost of courage she needs. "Thanks for this," she says, setting it on the wide plank of the chair's arm. She takes in the thick trees that surround the property. "I guess I wanted to come by and talk to you about my mother."

Buckhunter's body language shifts. He leans back in his rocking chair, holding the coffee cup in both hands like a shield in front of his body. "Huh," he huffs.

"I saw you two arguing at the dock, and I want to know what's going on."

Buckhunter shakes his head firmly—just one shake. "You don't." He drinks his coffee, eyes fixed on a point in the yard.

"What do you mean, I don't? How do you know what I want?" She scowls.

Buckhunter exhales through his nose. "Your mother is a real gem, Holly. A real piece of work, that woman is."

"This is not front page news." She's impatient and ready to hear the truth—whatever it is.

Buckhunter rocks back and forth in his chair, watching her with a steady gaze. "I mean...I was given instructions to keep my mouth shut, which I've done for a long time. But you're a grown woman." He strokes his gray-blonde goatee. "How much do you honestly want to know?"

She pauses, the coffee cup halfway to her lips. How much *does* she want to know? Is she going to hear some disgusting tale about Buckhunter and her mother? Or worse?

"No." She's up and out of her seat in a flash, nearly knocking the coffee from the arm of the chair. "No, no, no."

"Holly," Buckhunter says, putting up a hand to calm her down. "Hold your horses, girl."

But she's already stumbling down the stairs, trying to block out the sound of his voice. "This was a bad idea, Buckhunter. It was so, so bad. I'll just go now if you promise to pretend this never happened."

"Holly!" He's right behind her. "Hold on."

"Please, no. Don't say it—I..." She doubles over at the waist, her body physically recoiling from what she thinks he's about to say. "I swear I won't tell anyone that I figured it out if you just promise not to say it."

Buckhunter's confusion comes out as a hard laugh. "Tell anyone what? What have you figured out?" He looks genuinely puzzled.

Holly tries to keep walking, but he reaches out and grabs her by the wrist.

"I don't want to talk about it, Buckhunter. I knew this day would eventually come. I feel like an idiot—we've been living next door to each other for three years." She can feel the anger and embarrassment pinching at her windpipe, taking her breath away.

"Come and sit, Mayor. You're on the verge of hysteria." Buckhunter leads her back to the porch, and though she wants desperately to flee, something inside of her collapses and she follows him. He gets her situated in her chair again, facing him. "Now pick up that cup of coffee and take a sip. There, yep, just like that. Get a good swig of it."

He watches as she brings the cup to her lips with a shaky hand. Her phone buzzes in her pocket; she ignores it.

"I can't hear this, Buckhunter. Please," she begs, her eyes watery.

"Jesus, woman. What in the hell are you getting at?"

"I don't judge you, I swear. I just thought...I guess I thought you'd have darker hair." She points at her own head. "I thought she liked South American boys."

"Wait—are you trying to say that you think I'm your *father*?" His eyes are narrow, forehead creased. "Because I hate to disappoint you, darlin', but I am definitely *not* the kind of guy who would have knocked Coco up, even as a dumb teenager."

Buckhunter is not her father? *Buckhunter is not her father!* Thank you, thank you, thank you! Relief brings her senses back and restores the circulation to her extremities while she gives a silent prayer of gratitude.

"Then what are you talking about? What's so top-secret that you've been given instructions not to tell me about it?" Her breathing is returning to normal, her heart rate slowing.

"I mean how much do you want to know about your whole family? There's a lot that I'm guessing no one ever bothered to tell you, island princess, and if you don't even know who your daddy is, then I'd imagine you're living in the dark about a lot of things."

Holly lifts her chin just slightly, miffed at being called 'island princess.' She snorts. "Okay, I'm game. What exactly do you know about my family that I don't, Buckhunter?" Her confidence—badly shaken for a minute when she thought she might actually be living next door to her father—is back. "You come here and rent this house from my grandparents, set yourself up as our *neighbor*, and we barely know you! I mean, I like you fine. You're an amazing bartender and a pretty damn good guy to have around the island, but it's always stuck in my craw that we live within shouting distance of one another on *my* property and we're not even family."

He nods, giving her a look that says, *fair enough.* "I see your point. I do. But that's not entirely true."

"Which part?"

"I'm not a stranger, Holly."

She braces herself for the impact of whatever comes next.

"I've known your family for years—Frank, Jeanie, even your mother."

"How?" she croaks, still expecting him to reveal a torrid romantic tale of lust and heartbreak that somehow involves Coco even if it didn't result in, well, *her.*

"Okay," he starts, looking out into the mangrove trees again as he rocks in his chair. "It's a long story."

"So start telling it," she demands.

Buckhunter laughs at her tone. "Slow down there, missy. You aren't really steering this ship right now, are you?" He lifts his coffee cup and takes another sip, swallowing and smacking his lips in what feels like slow motion. "Anyhow, as I was saying, I've known your family for years. And now with your mother making the choices she's making about the island, I think it's time for you to hear this, because it actually does involve you."

Holly makes an *okay, lay it on me* gesture with her hands.

"There are secrets in every family, Holly. And sometimes the people you love surprise and disappoint you." Buckhunter rolls an unlit cigar between two fingers while he talks. "I know your grandparents because they sent me money every month for as long as I can remember. Your granddad would pick me up for spring break every year and take me fishing, and they never forgot my birthday."

Holly waits for understanding to wash over her. Without more information, she can't imagine why her grandparents would give him money or take him on vacations. Was Buckhunter some sort of charity case? It's just not making sense.

"My mother and I lived in a tiny house outside Savannah, and she worked nights. She was a nurse." His eyes glaze and he looks faraway. "My whole life, it was just the two of us. And every month, she waited for that check to come so she could buy me an extra gallon of milk, or a new pair of shoes, or send me to football camp. We had a good life, but she never let me forget that we'd been blessed by her decision to bring your grandfather into our lives."

"Buckhunter..." Holly leans forward, elbows on her knees. She is thoroughly vexed. "What in the *hell* are you trying to tell me here?"

"When my mom was younger and still in nursing school, she was a real beauty—an absolute doll. She had this wavy light brown hair, and sparkly, clear blue eyes. She could have been a movie star—no problem." Buckhunter had obviously inherited his own icy blue gaze from his mother. "She and some girlfriends took a trip one summer from Savannah down to Miami Beach. They were looking for some nightlife and sun, but what she found instead was a charming older man at a card table. And what *he* found was a naïve girl who just wanted to be loved."

"Wait—are you talking about—"

"Frank. Yeah. I'm talking about your grandfather."

"But..."

"But what about your grandmother? Yes, your grandparents were married at the time. Your mom was born about six months after I was."

Holly's first instinct is to slap him in the face—to make him take those words back—but she can't bring herself to move. This whole thing has to be a bad joke. Her grandparents' love had never wavered —not even for a moment, and definitely not for a weekend on Miami Beach with a nursing student who looked like a movie star.

Holly's mind races wildly. Buckhunter waits, letting her process everything.

"So—my mom..."

"Is my sister."

"Jesus." Holly stands up, setting the mug of coffee on the wooden planks of the deck. "I don't know how to deal with this." She feels unsteady on her feet. How is it possible that her beloved grandfather *cheated* on her grandmother with some nursing student? And how is she supposed to believe that Coco has a brother, and that it's *Buck-hunter*? Holly holds her arms across her stomach protectively.

"Why don't you go take a breather. We can talk later," he suggests, standing up from his own chair. They face each other on the porch. Buckhunter is still holding his coffee cup.

She nods mutely.

With no recollection of running across the grass to her golf cart, no memory of the bumpy drive back down Cinnamon Lane, and no idea how she got there, Holly ends up in the chair at her desk, facing a chipper Bonnie. Her baseball cap is still in her shaky hands, her muscles quivering from the shock.

"Hey, sugar," Bonnie says, smiling at her from over her open laptop. "Busy around here, huh? Feels like you and I haven't spent even a hot minute here together all day."

Holly nods dumbly, her eyes glazed and unfocused.

"While we were at lunch we got an email from a bride who'd like more information about how we can help her throw her dream wedding on Christmas Key. Says she saw an ad in the *Miami Herald* and she followed us on Instabook."

"It's Instagram, Bon," Holly says in a raspy voice. Her head feels loose on her neck and she's struggling to hold it up.

"Honey? What's eatin' you?" Bonnie is watching her with the kind of concern you see on someone's face when they realize that all is not well and that they might need to call for back-up.

Holly takes a deep, ragged breath—in through the nose, out through the mouth. She runs her hands over the smooth aluminum cover of her closed laptop. "I just found out that Buckhunter is my uncle."

30

"No," Bonnie says, shaking her head like that will make her words true. "That's impossible. Leo Buckhunter is *not* your uncle."

"Apparently it's not impossible, Bon. Buckhunter's mom was a cute, young nurse vacationing on Miami Beach when she met my very married grandfather. I'm sure you can imagine the rest." Holly feels like her head weighs forty pounds; the desire to rest it on her desk is overpowering.

"So wait just a second here." Bonnie taps a manicured finger against her half of the desk. "Are you telling me that Frank Baxter had an illegitimate baby with some floozy, and that that baby is *Buckhunter*?" Her face is incredulous.

"That's what he says. He and Coco are," she pauses, swallowing hard, "*brother and sister,* and he knows all the details about her wanting to sell the island."

"Okay. Then this is—and I'm still trying to fit the pieces together in my pretty little head, mind you—but this is actually *good* news, sugar."

"I seriously have no clue how you see this as good news," she says, forehead still planted firmly on her desk.

"It's good news because it means he probably has some stake in this island. Do you think your grandparents put him in their will?"

Holly lifts her head slowly, her hair falling into her eyes. "I don't know. Maybe. I haven't thought that far ahead yet." She blows the hair out of her face and searches for her phone blindly on the desk. "I always figured it was just fifty-fifty with me and Coco. No one ever told me that for sure, but she never completely makes decisions without my input."

"And your grandparents never told you how they were splitting things up?" Bonnie probes gently.

"I guess...maybe. But not in so many words. It was just understood that I'd run things, and that Coco and I would come to an agreement on anything major. Bonnie, I need to call someone. Who do I call?" She flicks through the contacts in her phone, trying to decide who to get on the line. "Accountant? Attorney?"

"Uhhh, probably attorney, sweetheart."

Holly chooses a name in her contact list and waits for the line to ring. Her attorney's secretary picks up after three rings and redirects her call to the lawyer that her grandparents retained when they first bought Christmas Key. Bonnie gets up discreetly with her iced coffee in hand, pulls her pink t-shirt down over her round bottom, and leaves the office so that Holly can speak privately with the lawyer.

It's a quick conversation: the attorney knows about Mr. Buckhunter and was given explicit instructions not to discuss it with Holly until she called to ask. The will is iron-clad. A copy of the document will be scanned and emailed to her within the hour.

Bonnie comes back with a computer printout in hand from the front desk, sipping her iced latte through a neon yellow straw. "Got a rundown of our bookings for September so that we can look at dates with that bride who wants to start talking details," she says, sitting down across from Holly. She peers over the frames of her reading glasses, waiting patiently to hear what the lawyer had to say.

Holly taps the back of her cell phone against her bare thigh as she turns the information over in her head. "Okay. Interesting turn of events."

Bonnie pulls off her glasses and sits down in her chair.

"After my grandma died, Frank took a trip to see his attorney and to change the will. He was very firm about not sharing the information with anyone until there was a good reason for us to know."

"You mean like Coco wanting to sell the island?"

"Right. So the lawyer drew up an amended version of the will during that visit, and my grandpa signed it on the spot."

"And?"

"Three ways—but not an even split." Holly sets her phone down on the desk and folds her arms across her chest. "Do you think Buckhunter's opened the bar for happy hour yet? Because this feels like the longest day ever and I could really use a drink."

"He might be there," Bonnie says. "But let's back up to the uneven split—how did Frank divvy things up? If you don't mind my asking."

"33% each to Buckhunter and Coco, and 34 for me." A chill runs up her spine. Her grandfather had selected her to officially be in charge of Christmas Key.

"That's gonna go over like a ton of bricks, sugar," Bonnie says, dropping her glasses on the desk with a clatter. "Coco is going to lose it when she hears that."

"I know. I need to talk to Buckhunter more when my brain and my mouth decide to work together again. But assuming that we're on the same page, we can easily out-vote Coco on this."

"And on pretty much anything else that comes up," Bonnie points out.

"True."

"But you might have to be a smidge less contrary with the old goat now to make sure he stays on your side." Bonnie winks at her and slides her reading glasses back on.

"I'm not contrary with him," Holly says, "I just like to give him grief."

"Exactly my point."

"You know what? I think I'm going to run a couple of errands." Holly pulls her hair into a loose ponytail and grabs her purse and sunglasses. "Can you get back to our bride and work out some dates with her?"

"Sure thing, boss. I'm on it." Bonnie plucks a sharpened pencil from the cup on her desk. "Go get some fresh air, you hear?"

Holly sets her Yankees cap on her head and smiles. "Be back in a jiffy."

31

It's real and it's in writing: Coco can't simply show up and snatch the island away from her, even if she wants to. Holly feels like skipping down Main Street, her purse swinging from one shoulder as she grabs lampposts and spins around them, stepping jauntily over storm drains and singing to her own reflection in shop windows. Everything that had gone gray in her life with Buckhunter's revelation has turned Technicolor again, and she feels like kissing the front of the buildings along Main Street and jumping onto the back of a moving golf cart like it's a streetcar in a musical. In her mind, she's an extra in a Fred Astaire and Ginger Rogers flick, stopping in the middle of the road to sing to the heavens with every ounce of her being, arms thrown to the sky.

But in reality, she's taking Main Street in giant strides, the happiest smile she's worn in ages plastered across her face, thrilled that she's just—in an instant—gained the upper hand with her mother in the battle for the island.

She looks up from the sidewalk and slams straight into Jake.

"Holly, watch out!" He frowns, holding out his coffee cup from Mistletoe Morning Brew so that the hot drink won't slosh through the opening and land all over them.

"Sorry." She steps back to avoid the coffee as it slops onto the pavement. "I'm in a hurry."

"I can see that." He wipes his coffee-splattered arm on the side of his black shorts. "Where's the fire?"

"No fire. Everything is fine. Everything's good. We've got a bridal party looking to throw a wedding here next month, and I've got some other things in the works," she says, unable to stop her nervous chattering.

"Your first wedding. Nice job. And how are things with you? Now that, you know, all of our visitors have gone, and your mom is off the island..."

She smiles, refusing to take the bait. There's no way she's going to talk about either River or her mother and ruin her good mood. "Like I said, things are fine."

Jake sips his coffee, eyebrows raised. "I've been meaning to stop by and say hi."

They're right in front of Tinsel & Tidings Gifts, and the triplets are visible through the front window as they bustle around, stocking shelves and laughing together. Holly watches them for a minute before looking back at Jake. "Listen, I've got a lot of irons in the fire right now, Jake. Maybe we can talk later?"

He shifts his weight, one hand resting on his hip just above his holster. His mirrored aviators are folded and tucked into the collar of his shirt. "Yeah, sure. Okay."

"Anyway, see you at the next village council meeting?" Holly is ready to keep moving.

"I'll be there," he says quietly.

Holly gives a tight-lipped smile and steps around him on the sidewalk.

"Holly Baxter! You aren't leaving much to the imagination with that short skirt!" Maria Agnelli shouts at her from across the street. "I can see all the way to next Tuesday, missy!"

"Hi, Mrs. Agnelli," she yells back. "You're looking chipper today. And it's a skort, so it has shorts sewn into it!"

"It's short on something: *fabric!*" Maria hollers back. She holds the door of Poinsettia Plaza open with one arthritic hand, ready to head into Fiona's office for another round of questions and answers to determine the source of her aches and pains. Holly jokingly told her one afternoon that the source of her pain was old age; Maria had huffed at her in disbelief.

"Have a nice day, Mrs. Agnelli!" Holly glances over her shoulder. Sure enough, Jake is standing next to his police golf cart, chuckling at the exchange between her and Mrs. Agnelli.

"I've seen handkerchiefs that would cover more than that skirt," Mrs. Agnelli says in a voice that's still louder than it needs to be.

Holly rolls her eyes and forges ahead, determined to stay focused on the discussion she's about to have with Buckhunter. As luck would have it, he's on the sidewalk opening the bar right then.

"Just the man I'm looking for," Holly says, jogging lightly to catch up with him. She grips the strap of her raffia purse, the other hand holding down the back of her pleated skort.

"Two visits in one day?" Buckhunter's mouth turns up at one corner. "Aren't I a lucky guy."

"It took me a while, but I finally found my tongue. I want to talk. Are you busy?"

"Just opening up. Want me to grill you up a burger or pour you a drink?" He bends down and unlocks the corrugated metal rolling door with a big key, releasing it and letting it slide back on its rails overhead. He does it again with the next door, which completely opens the restaurant to Main Street. It's muggy inside, and Buckhunter walks around, flipping switches to turn on the overhead fans.

She thinks about the drink she'd like to have, but decides that keeping her head straight is a better choice for this conversation. "An Arnold Palmer would be awesome." She follows him inside the bar. "Oh, and thank you for the coffee earlier. Sorry I bolted on you."

He nods, shooting her a sideways glance. "Just shock, I'm guessing."

Holly sits down at the bar, resting her purse on the shiny, polished wood of the counter as Buckhunter takes down chairs and turns on his twinkling Christmas lights above the bar. At the back of the restaurant, he rolls up the other two doors, letting in more light.

"How would you have reacted if you were in my shoes?" she asks him.

"Same, probably." Buckhunter lifts the plank of wood that serves as a gate to get behind the bar, setting it down behind him once he's in position. "But I might have punched someone."

"I was tempted," she admits.

"Yeah, I could tell." He smirks at her. "So, one burger. Medium-well, with onions and cheese?"

"No, I'm good. Just the Arnold Palmer, please."

"You got it. Too early for a beer?" he offers, nodding at the tap.

"I'm still on duty."

"As you wish, Mayor," Buckhunter says, firing up the grill behind him. It fills the air with the scent of charred meat and grilled vegetables. Holly wanders over to the jukebox and picks out a Springsteen song to break the silence.

Buckhunter turns his back on her and throws a meat patty on the grill for himself. "So." He lays the opening out there for her, then busies his hands so that she can talk when she's ready.

"So, number one, I'm not calling you Uncle Buck," she says, sticking a straw into the iced tea/lemonade combo he's set on the bar for her.

Buckhunter throws his head back, laughing heartily. "Oh, Uncle Buck—don't I wish!" He flips the hamburger patty on the grill.

Holly stares at the back of his head. "Anyway, I figured we should talk about Coco's plan to sell the island, and I wanted to make sure you know the same things I know about the way things are divided up."

Buckhunter flips his burger neatly in the air, catching it on the edge of his metal spatula and setting it back on the grill. "I know enough," he says, reaching for an onion that he's already cut into spirals. He tosses it on the hot surface next to the burger.

"I called our attorney in Miami."

"Okay." He keeps his back to her.

"She says that after my grandmother passed, Frank made a trip to Miami to see her so that he could split everything three ways."

"Huh." Buckhunter turns his head so that she can see his profile; his face is thoughtful. "That's a doozy, innit?"

"Yeah, it is." Holly picks up her drink; the melting ice cubes clink against the glass. The heat of the late afternoon fills the open bar, and the overhead fans push the warm air around just enough to keep the beads of sweat from rolling out of her damp hairline.

"So you're thinking you and me against Coco means she's got no chance of selling us off and making us a corporate-owned slice of vacation paradise?" He flips the switch on the grill to turn it off, and shovels the perfectly done burger onto a bun, dumping the fragrant onions on top of the pile and then squirting ketchup over the whole mess.

"I'm thinking—" But suddenly the words are caught in her throat. The magnitude of everything that's happened so far that day hits her like a wall of humidity; it actually takes her breath away. "I'm thinking —" she starts again, tears welling up without warning. "I'm thinking that I don't actually know my family at all," she finally whispers.

Buckhunter keeps the counter between them, chewing the first bite of his burger. He leans his weight against the polished wood countertop, a clean dish towel tossed over one shoulder. "Hey, girl," he says softly, setting his burger on a plate and leaning toward her ever so slightly. "I know it's a lot to take in. It came at you out of left field," he says, voice laced with a calm sympathy that she's never heard from Buckhunter. "But just because you found out something you didn't know about your family doesn't make them strangers. We all have things we keep under wraps."

Holly sniffles, trying to smile through the tears that she can't hold back. "Yeah," she says, wiping under her eyes with the pads of her fingers. "I guess."

"I'm not lying. Just because people do things they aren't proud of doesn't mean they're terrible people. Your grandparents loved you enough to let you grow up without their baggage. Maybe they figured having Coco for a mother was bad enough."

Holly snorts at this.

"Here." Buckhunter tosses her the towel from his shoulder. "Now wipe that snot off your face, kid—we've got plans to make."

Holly's laugh turns into a hiccup. She uses the towel to wipe her cheeks. "Thanks, Leo," she says quietly. He fills her glass up with ice again and dumps tea and lemonade in from two different pitchers.

"Anytime, kid. Now drink up, and let's talk strategy."

32

WAYNE COATES IS INSISTENT ABOUT FLYING OUT TO THE ISLAND WITH
the NBC crew and being on hand for the village council meeting in
August. Holly isn't convinced that this is the best way to spring the
idea of a reality show on her neighbors, but she's worked hard to keep
Coco's talk of selling the island under wraps, and she'd like to present
the islanders with what she sees as a positive opportunity before any
gossip about mega-resorts and mass relocation gets out.

Holly has avoided talking to Coco directly since their email
exchange, but she and Buckhunter have been in cahoots, building the
case that they'll make to everyone else to convince them that a reality
show is an excellent way to showcase the island to the rest of the
world. Holly half expected Buckhunter to shoot down the whole idea
himself, but he seemed intrigued when she pitched it to him, and
even more so when he realized that it might catapult them into the
stratosphere in terms of making the island financially solvent. Their
hope is that the reality show—if it comes to fruition—will help
Christmas Key to become profitable enough that Coco won't *want* to
sell, but if she still does, they'll certainly be able to make a stronger
argument against it.

In the meantime, Holly and Bonnie have entertained requests for a possible family reunion on Christmas Key over Thanksgiving weekend, and they're talking to a gourmet cooking magazine about putting together a food and wine festival retreat on the island in January. With all that's going on, it's been easy to avoid Jake almost entirely, but Holly's managed to squeeze in a phone call or a text here and there with River, and he knows all about the reality show.

In the past week, Holly has spent most of her waking hours eating bar food on her lanai with Fiona and Buckhunter, creating flowcharts and covering posters with sticky notes of ideas and plans for the island. Instead of sleeping at night, she's mostly lain awake, listening to the hum of the air conditioner in the dark, and thinking about what will happen if Wayne Coates and the NBC crew like Christmas Key.

Holly processed the new twist in her life as quickly as possible, adjusting to the fact that she's been living next door to her uncle without even knowing it, but so far she's only told Bonnie and Fiona the news. She and Buckhunter agreed right away that Fiona should be in on their planning, not least of all because it would seem strange if the man Fiona was seeing suddenly started spending all of his waking hours with his next door neighbor—who just happened to be her best friend. So they sat her down and gave her the background on their family tree, answering as many questions as they could and watching her face while she went through the levels of shock and surprise herself.

There is grief for Holly to work through, but she mostly does that during the long, sleepless nights that she spends working on her shell wall. She has to say good-bye to her grandfather again—has to let go of who she thought he was—and learn to love and accept him for who he really was: just a man—a flawed, imperfect man like any other. After Buckhunter's initial revelation, she poured over the prospectus for the better part of forty-eight hours, searching for hidden meanings and clues. She let herself wonder if he'd felt guilt, keeping all that he had from her. In the end, she had to accept that he probably didn't think much about it at all. And if his own wife had forgiven him (and from the relationship Holly had observed all of her life, it appeared that she had), then who was she to let this one secret taint his memory?

Holly, Fiona, and Buckhunter are finishing off a pizza, three sets of bare feet up on her table as the sun sets over the ocean in the distance. It throws off rays of blinding light through the mangrove trees, and a gentle breeze moves the wind chimes on Holly's lanai. They've been talking about the reality show and planning for the NBC bigwigs to come and check out the island when Buckhunter leans back in his chair and looks right at Holly.

"They broke the mold after they made your grandmother, you know. But I do see a lot of her in you," he says.

"What do you mean?"

"Frank may have waited until Jeanie passed before he asked me to move out here, and maybe she didn't agree about him wanting to split the island three ways, but she did have a big heart. She cared about people, and I see that in you." It's the most Holly has ever heard Buckhunter say about her grandparents. "When my mom was sick, Jeanie was the one who called me to see what they could do."

"My grandma called you?" The idea that her grandmother could not only forgive Frank, but also accept his son with another woman is almost inconceivable. "What happened to your mom?"

"Breast cancer. About twenty years ago." Buckhunter's voice goes soft. "I wanted her to try every treatment she could." He stops speaking then, tapping the brown glass of the bottle in his hands with the silver ring on his middle finger.

"I'm sorry, Buckhunter," Holly whispers. "I didn't know."

"It's fine, kid. Of course you didn't. But your grandma—she was a real lady. A class act. When she found out how sick my mom was, she insisted that your grandpa pay all of the doctor's bills, and he did."

"Are you serious?"

"Every couple of months, Jeanie would call me in Miami—because we'd moved down there from Savannah by then—and tell me which bank to go to. I'd pick up the cash and pay for her chemo. She wouldn't have lived as long as she did if it hadn't been for Frank and Jeanie."

"Wait," Holly says, setting her glass of water down on the table. "Five thousand dollars to a First Union bank in Miami?" She stands up. "Hold on." Inside, she picks up the prospectus from her night-stand and flips through the pages to find the slip of paper.

"Here—look at this," she says, out on the lanai again. She thrusts the scrap of paper with her grandpa's familiar handwriting on it at Buckhunter. *January 13, 1994—Call L.B. today...$5,000 First Union Bank, Miami.* "Was this you? 'L.B.' for Leo Buckhunter?"

Buckhunter holds the scrap of paper in his hand, examining it. "January 1994—that would be about right, yeah."

"It's been driving me crazy!" Holly says, taking the note back from him. "I couldn't figure out what it meant."

Buckhunter shrugs. "It means that your grandparents were good people."

The idea that they would pay for Frank's mistress's medical care blows her away. Holly stares at the slip of paper. Another wave of longing for her grandparents washes over her.

Fiona reaches out and takes her hand.

"They were *great* people," Holly says quietly, pressing the slip of paper to her heart.

33

HOLLY AND BUCKHUNTER STAND ON THE SHORE OF CANDY CANE Beach. There's a stretch of undeveloped land on the north side of the island, and Holly chose this spot—with its empty stretch of sand and sea grass—as a perfect landing spot for the NBC helicopter. They would have preferred an actual helipad, but Holly assured them that the spot she's chosen is far enough from the water that the tides won't touch their helo as they visit the island.

For the past three days she's been making lists of things to change or fix: she's put new lightbulbs in all of the lamp posts on Main Street; cleaned up the foliage down by the dock; and added a fresh coat of paint to the front door of Mistletoe Morning Brew, the shop closest to the waterfront. She talked to Cap again about setting up a website for North Star Cigars, and tried to convince Joe Sacamano to do the same for his homemade rum. Getting all of their ducks in a row to maximize visibility for the island and its businesses has kept her totally occupied.

Holly and Bonnie have spent the morning making last minute tweaks to her speech for the village council meeting, and she's already mentally set up the day. It's easy to envision the producers of *Wild Tropics* touring the island and admiring the colorful holiday lights on all of the cottages and bungalows, and she's having Iris and Jimmy cater a huge dinner for the crew—fresh seafood and Key Lime pie, of course—and they'll toast the end of a great day with salty margaritas at Jack Frosty's. Buckhunter will man the bar, and she's already set up the playlist so that a steady stream of reggae and calypso will pour out of the jukebox.

Fiona, Buckhunter, Bonnie, and the triplets (who Holly let in on the reality show plans) have been eagerly pitching in to get the island looking its best, and consequently, Holly was able to climb into bed the night before the NBC execs' arrival with a feeling of calm preparedness. She slid between the sheets in the darkness, thinking of the way she'd felt the night before she left the island for college. She'd lain awake that night, too, but with a stomach filled with creaky pipes, her brain too busy to wind down and give her any peace. And even though she knew she was on the verge of another big event in her life on this night, there was the sensation of being on the edge of a different kind of cliff, and of turning a corner that she wouldn't be able to un-turn. With college, Holly had known that she could just pack up and go home if she hated it. But with this, she has to fully accept that she'll be taking herself, her neighbors, and her entire island on a trip that she can't easily change her mind about. There won't be any boxing up of posters and books, no sailing back home to Grandma and Grandpa this time if things don't work out.

In the distance, they hear the chop of the blades and see the black dot approaching in the sky. Holly shields her eyes with one hand as the helicopter comes into sharp view.

"They're about three minutes from touching down," Buckhunter says, leaning into her. Holly nods in response, trying to smile even though she's anxious and excited.

The copter approaches, hovering just overhead. As the pilot looks for a good place to land, the force of the blades whips their hair around.

Holly reaches up to put her hand on top of her Yankees cap so that it won't get ripped away, but then she remembers that Bonnie made her leave it in the office. "Doesn't go with the outfit, sugar," Bonnie had declared.

The gauzy dress Holly's wearing over her short leggings blows around wildly, and she wraps her arms around her waist to keep everything covered. It's so loud that when she tries to yell something to Buckhunter, her words get lost in the wind.

The blades spin to a stop. Three men and a woman climb out of the helicopter and step onto the sand. The woman is wearing an emerald green silk shirt dress with gladiator sandals and piles of gold bracelets; the men all wear plaid Bermuda shorts, collared golf shirts under blazers, and brown boat shoes. They look like they stopped in at Saks Fifth Avenue on their way to the airport and had a personal shopper dress them for a day of yachting or island-hopping.

"Wayne Coates," the shortest man of the group says, stepping forward and offering a hand. "I recognized you from your Instagram page," he says, shaking her hand enthusiastically.

"It's nice to meet you," Holly says, shaking everyone's hands in turn. "Thank you for coming."

"Beats the hell out of a day of meetings with the suits in the city," Wayne says. The other NBC producers laugh politely. Wayne has stubby, muscular legs and a five o'clock shadow. He smells of expensive cologne and gives the impression that he's used to being in charge.

Buckhunter introduces himself to everyone, and they lead their visitors across the beach and onto December Drive, where they've parked their golf carts. Wayne and the woman, Leanna Poudry, hop into Holly's cart. Buckhunter takes the other two men. In a mini-caravan, they cut through Turtle Dove estates, showing off the cute bungalows with pink flamingos staked in the lawns. The palm trees are wrapped in colorful Christmas lights that have been checked and re-checked for burned out bulbs, and giant, shiny ornaments dangle from the branches.

On Main Street, Holly points out the various businesses to her passengers. "This is Mistletoe Morning Brew, and that's North Star Cigars," she says, slowing as they pass the clean windows of the shops. At Tinsel & Tidings Gifts, the triplets are out front working in tandem to hang a new garland over the front door of the store.

"Whoa!" Wayne Coates says. "Triplets?"

"Yep. Gwen, Gen, and Glen are our unofficial welcoming crew. They own the gift shop with their husbands, and they always know what's happening on the island. If you want to know who just arrived by boat, or who has company visiting for the weekend, come by the gift shop. Three of the funniest, friendliest women you'll ever meet—guaranteed," she says, slowing to a stop and waving at the ladies.

"So do they already know who we are?" Leanna Poudry asks from next to Holly.

"Not everyone on the island knows that you're here or why, but the triplets do."

Gwen, Gen, and Glen leave the garland dangling over the doorway and approach the cart with their identical grins. "Welcome to Christmas Key!" Gen says, waving at them. "Did you all fly in from New York today?"

Wayne Coates leans forward in the back seat so that he can see the triplets. "We got to Miami yesterday and met with our affiliate station there. We're only on the island for the day."

"Oh, you can't even stay for one night?" Gwen asks hopefully.

"We have one other island we need to see before we head back to New York for a meeting, so we've only got today," Wayne apologizes. "But I'm hoping we can see it all, and we want to meet as many locals as possible."

"Oh, you will!" Glen promises, standing behind both of her sisters. "Enjoy your visit!"

The women wave them off and go back to hanging their garland.

"This is Jack Frosty Mugs, our Main Street open-air bar," Holly continues, giving the cart some gas and rolling forward. "Leo Buck-hunter is the owner and bartender here," she says, hooking a thumb over her shoulder at Buckhunter's golf cart just behind hers. "It's open for lunch and dinner, and Buckhunter mixes a mean margari-ta." They pull up to the B&B. "And this is the only place to stay on the island—"

"The Christmas Key B&B!" Wayne says, pointing at it. "I love it—it looks exactly like the pictures you've posted."

Holly smiles and pulls into the lot behind the building to park. She loves seeing Wayne recognize things from her photos on Instagram and Facebook, and so far the group seems impressed with the island. "Let's head in, and I can show you the accommodations we have for your crew if you decide to come to Christmas Key."

They take a quick tour of the B&B. Holly shows them the dining room and goes over some of the logistics for dining and ordering specific foods to be delivered to the island, and then they spend an hour driving through the wooded areas, admiring the scenery. The crew has a run-in with Marco on the steps of Christmas Key Chapel when he takes a strong liking to Leanna, but she laughs it off, stepping into the entryway of the church so that the bird ends up landing on Holly's shoulder instead of her own.

"Marco is totally domesticated," Holly promises, reaching out a hand for him to climb onto so that he'll vacate his perch on her shoulder. "Here you go, buddy," she says to him, resting his talons on the railing outside the church. "We'll be right back."

"So he's like the island pet?" Leanna asks, eyeing Marco.

"More like the island boss," Holly says.

They duck into the tiny chapel with its steeply-pitched roof. The stained glass windows throw prisms of color around the small room, and the tall trees outside keep the building shady and cool inside.

"This is a nice spot," Wayne says, examining the pews. "Who oversees your ministry?"

"Our last full-time pastor was Alfie Agnelli, but he passed away a few years ago. His widow, Maria, is still with us on Christmas Key," Holly explains, her hands clasped in front of her. "Since then it's been a quiet spot for reflection. Some of us come on Sundays pretty regularly to observe and to have a quiet moment, but it's been a long time since we had anyone here to give a sermon."

"Hmm," Wayne says, running a hand over his scratchy facial hair. He looks at Leanna and the other men, eyebrows raised. "Okay, good to know. And you said there was another bar, another restaurant, and a couple of different beach locations, right?"

"Yes, we've still got more to see," she promises. They head back out to the carts, twigs and dried leaves crunching under their feet. "We'll just follow Holly Lane here around the bend, and we can hit the Jingle Bell Bistro."

"Now what's the history of the Christmas theme? I'm curious about this street sharing a name with you," Leanna says, sliding back into the front passenger seat. "Is that purely coincidence?"

Holly gives them the broad strokes of the island's background, describing her grandparents, the way Frank had purchased the island and created a holiday-themed paradise for his granddaughter and for his wife as she battled cancer, and how she now presides over the island as mayor and shares the property with her mom and her uncle. The word "uncle" catches in her throat for a second, its sound still foreign in her head. She's never had an uncle before. Holly glances in her rearview mirror and sees Buckhunter in his cart behind her. They've been so busy planning for the NBC visit that she hasn't let the word properly sink into her skull: *uncle, uncle, uncle...* Buckhunter is actually family. And it feels good to have family with her on the island again. The notion that she alone is responsible for the success or failure of Christmas Key can be overwhelming, and knowing that there's someone else who has a vested interest in making the island into something great is comforting.

The sun touches her skin as it breaks through the tall trees, and the beauty of her island fills her with so much joy and pride that for a moment she doesn't even care whether or not they ultimately decide to come to Christmas Key to make the reality show, because the word *family* warms her from within.

So much has happened since July's village council meeting that it seems like six months have passed instead of one. Holly takes her place behind the podium for the August meeting, her sapphire blue bikini hidden under a lightweight black dress and short black leggings. She'd wanted to dress nicely enough to both greet the NBC execs and lead the village council meeting, and she flushes now, remembering the purple-bikini-under-a-white-dress incident from the last meeting. At least that didn't happen while five NBC execs were sitting in the crowd. She takes a sip of water from the glass on the podium and prepares her thoughts.

Heddie Lang-Mueller is at the desk next to Holly—as she is at every village council meeting—narrow shoulders squared, face authoritative and attentive as always. Bonnie is at the front of the crowd in the B&B's dining room, and Jake is seated on the side of the room this time, staring at the meeting agenda with such intense focus that he looks like he's reading a mystery novel. Wayne Coates, Leanna Poudry, and the other two men from NBC are lined up against the wall in dining room chairs, their clothes and posture standing out like beacons of light on a dark sea. Each and every villager eyes them with suspicion and curiosity as they enter the room.

The islanders file in, waving across the room at friends and neighbors. Holly waits. Buckhunter has a spot in the front row next to Fiona, and he winks at Holly encouragingly. Cap stumbles over to a chair and settles in a seat at the back, a flask in one hand, his long hair and beard unkempt. Like a ripple of wind through the trees, everyone cranes their necks to cast glances at him, making meaningful eye-contact with one another as they turn back around to face the front. Cap belches loudly and the sound echoes through the B&B's dining room. Holly and Bonnie widen their eyes at one another.

"I'd like to call to order the village council meeting for August twentieth," Holly says quickly, hoping to pull everyone's attention away from Cap. She waits as Heddie jots down notes for the meeting minutes. "May I have a show of hands of the registered voters in attendance, please?" Haltingly, hands go up to half-mast. Faces are placid and unyielding; from looking out into the crowd, Holly knows that there's been talk. They are obviously anticipating being called to vote on something important, and in an instant, Holly realizes that it might have been a mistake to spring the idea of a reality show and the news that Coco wants to sell the island on them while the NBC producers are in the room. She pushes on.

"Thank you," Holly says, nodding to indicate that they can put their hands down after Heddie has counted everyone. "I want to re-cap last month's exciting events, and to let you know that while our visit from the fishermen was—ahem—*eventful*," she says with a smile, "it was also successful. I can't even tell you how proud I am to live on Christmas Key anyway, but to see you all come together in a pinch means the world to me. I couldn't have pulled that off without every single one of you."

She pauses, letting her eyes drift around and take in the faces of her neighbors. It occurs to her as she stands before them that she is looking at a group of incredibly complex and wise human beings, a group whose total life experience surpasses and exceeds hers in ways that she can't even imagine. Having to tell them that she's going to do something that they may not agree with is suddenly something that she doesn't want to do. But she's here, and the NBC execs are here, and it's time to open up—about everything.

"Because I know you're all as invested in our home as I am, I'm hoping that this piece of news will be reassuring instead of upset-ting," she says, holding onto the edges of her small podium for balance. "But I think everyone deserves to know that my mother has expressed a desire to sell Christmas Key. She's secured the interest of a corporate entity that would like to turn it into a five-star resort with the capacity to hold eight hundred guests." She stops there, letting the news sink in.

The triplets turn to one another instantly, gripping each other's hands. A rush of chatter ripples through the small crowd. Faces fall, eyebrows fly up, and shocked expressions pass from one person to the next like a collection plate in a church. People turn to the NBC producers with angry faces, assuming that they're associated with the evil corporate entity in question.

"I'd like to be heard, Mayor," Maria Agnelli says unnecessarily, standing up from her usual spot in the front. "This is a goddamned travesty," she says, pointing a bony finger in the air. A few of the villagers gasp at her language, already preparing for the worst. "Your mother has no heart for this island, Holly. She knows nothing about what we do here, and she doesn't give a rat's ass about any of us." Maria's eyes well up. "She can't do this to us."

Iris Cafferkey gets up and walks over to Maria. She puts one arm around Mrs. Agnelli's frail waist, another under her shaking hand. Iris leads her back to her seat and sits her down gently.

Holly takes a deep breath, glancing again at Buckhunter for reassurance. "Well, I don't plan on letting her do it."

"How do you suppose you'll stop her?" Cap bellows from the back of the room. He's up and unsteady on his feet. "I'm not trying to piss you off again, Holly, because Lord knows I got your goat that day when I called you a little girl," he says. "But how in the name of Moses do you plan on stopping a hurricane like your mother?"

Holly ignores his reference to their spat in his cigar shop. "Coco and I have always labored under the impression that we share this island's interests fifty-fifty," Holly explains, smoothing her hair back from her face. "But it has recently come to light that we actually do not share Christmas Key evenly, or just between the two of us."

The villagers turn to one another, exchanging silent, questioning looks.

"As luck would have it, there is a third party who holds an interest in the island." Holly waits for everyone to turn their attention back to her. "It came as a complete surprise to me to find out—though it may not be a surprise to some of you—that Leo Buckhunter and my mother are actually half siblings." She stops and waits. All around the room, the back-and-forth flutter of meeting agendas being used as paper fans ceases. Sagging biceps flap as people reach out hands to hold on to their neighbors. Maria Agnelli leans back in her chair, eyes rolled heavenward like the Holy Spirit has entered her and taken over her very faculties. From the looks on the faces in the crowd, Holly gathers that she's not the only one who didn't know about Frank Baxter's big secret, though a part of her assumed that perhaps a few of Frank's cronies had known the truth and had agreed to keep it from her.

"I know, I know," Holly says, arms outstretched, palms facing the carpeted floor. "This is quite a shock for some of you, but certainly no more of a shock than it was for me to find out that my grandpa Frank was Buckhunter's father."

The voices in the room ratchet up another notch, filling the room with loud conversation. Heddie looks up at her from her chair, thin eyebrows raised questioningly.

"There's not much to write down at the moment, Heddie," she says as an aside, nodding at Heddie's meeting minutes, "except maybe *and the crowd goes wild.*"

In the front row, Fiona reaches over and pats Buckhunter on the knee. He rises slowly, gathering himself as he prepares to approach the podium. There is sincere hesitation on his face; it's clear that he isn't relishing this moment in the spotlight. Holly moves aside, giving him a nod as she cedes the floor to him.

Buckhunter steps behind the podium. He looks as uncomfortable as a man who's shown up at an event to give a speech in his underwear.

"As you all know," Buckhunter begins. The volume in the room drops to almost nothing. "I make a mean drink. What I *don't* make is interesting fodder for gossip. So I'm going to put this out there once and only once, then we're going to get on with what needs to be done here. Frank Baxter was my biological father. He supported me my whole life, and he moved me here when he fell ill with the sole intention of making sure that Holly had family on the island, whether she knew it or not." Buckhunter casts her a sideways glance. "Fortunately for her, I forgive her for her sassy attitude, and for her unneighborly habit of hanging her unmentionables out on the line to dry." The crowd chuckles, though their faces still bear the shock of the news. "I'm also not forcing her to call me Uncle Buck, though it does have a nice ring to it." More nervous laughter from the villagers.

Holly takes the first deep breath she's taken in days. It's working—

Buckhunter is telling their story. He's charming and straightforward in his delivery, and people are eagerly taking it in. She exhales.

"Anyhow, let's get down to business. Holly, Coco, and I all share this island. Coco wants to sell; Holly and I do not. Right now we hold the majority vote, and we're not interested in any fancy resort with elevators or waterparks taking over here. What we are interested in is keeping Christmas Key pretty much the way it is." A smattering of applause breaks out in the crowd. "But I'll let Holly tell you the rest." Buckhunter slides to the side, holding out a hand as if to invite her back to the podium. He's obviously glad to be done sharing his private life with the entire island, and he's going to let Holly take the heat on the next bit of news.

"So there you have it," Holly says, smiling at everyone with as much confidence as she can muster. "Who needs afternoon soap operas, right?"

"All right, mayor—let's hear it," Cap calls out, tipping his silver flask back as he puts the mouth of it to his cracked lips.

"Okay, this next bit of news might feel a little surreal to some of you, but the guests we have here in our midst today are actually the production team for a new reality show on NBC called *Wild Tropics*."

Another ripple goes through the crowd and heads turn to face the five visitors. Wayne Coates raises a hand in greeting as over a hundred sets of eyes bore into him and the other execs.

"*Wild Tropics* is looking for a location just like ours to use as a setting for their new show, and I've been in talks with them to see if we might be a good match."

"What exactly does that mean, Holly?" Joe Sacamano asks, arms folded across his chest.

"It means that if they select us, they'll spend a set amount of time on the island with the stars of the show, and they'll live among us and film the series. They would be guests on our island just like the fishermen were, and it would give us national exposure and the opportunity for Christmas Key to be come a household name."

People lean into their neighbors to discuss this possibility, and Holly sees a mixture of interest and opposition on their faces.

"How long?" Jimmy Cafferkey asks.

Holly turns to the NBC producers and nods at Wayne Coates. He stands.

"It will take us approximately two months to complete the actual filming and any post-filming re-shoots that we need to do. I can assure you," he says, turning so that he faces the whole crowd, "we would do our best to fit ourselves into your way of life, and that we would showcase the island in the most flattering light possible."

"So let's vote on it," Cap growls, sipping from his flask again.

"Actually, Cap, I'm not calling for a vote," Holly says, holding her breath. "I've spoken to our lawyer, and I've also been in talks with NBC, so all we need to know is who *doesn't* want to participate in any way. Those who don't mind being filmed will simply sign a release and then go about your business as usual—"

"Oh, so the rest of us have to hide out? We'll be made to live like prisoners on our own island?" Cap demands, standing up again. He hikes up his cargo shorts with one hand, still holding his booze in the other. "Who are you to say that we all have to be exposed, young lady? Don't you think some of us came here to live out our lives anonymously?"

Everyone in the room turns to Cap. His outburst and behavior are so out of the norm for him that everyone looks as surprised as Holly feels. Men hold their arms across their meaty midsections, jowls resting on their shoulders as they watch him. Women hold crinkled Kleenex to their mouths, patting their neat curls expectantly.

"We've all had lives that you can't even imagine," Cap says, swaying as he moves down the aisle towards Holly. "There are things in all of our pasts that we'd prefer to keep there, and having some uppity band of cameramen and network execs roaming our island isn't going to help us do that." He reaches the front of the room and stops on the other side of Holly's podium, his face just inches from hers. The smell of whiskey and sweat fill her nostrils as he places a hand on the edge of the podium.

"Cap," she says, trying to come up with something that will placate him. "My intention is not to *expose* anyone. I'm looking into this opportunity that we have to become more visible and profitable, and I'm also looking for ways to avoid becoming a cookie cutter resort. And that does mean that we'll have to broaden our horizons, but it could also mean that great things will come our way."

"You see," Cap says, staggering backwards as he holds out his empty hand expansively, the other fist still clutching his silver flask. "Our good mayor wants nothing more than to bring people *to* us, whether we want them here or not. Her own grandfather came here with secrets to hide," Cap says, looking pointedly at Buckhunter, "and she's choosing to air her family's dirty laundry for all the world to see. But that doesn't mean we have to let her air ours."

Maria Agnelli stands up, but keeps a noticeable distance from Cap's inebriated swaggering. "It's that Placebook," she says knowingly. "Ever since that damned thing started, everybody's got to know everyone else's business."

"It's 'Facebook', Maria," Bonnie says knowingly, reaching out a hand to touch Mrs. Agnelli on the elbow.

"Well, whatever it is, all of these damn young people want their face plastered everywhere. I saw it on the nightly news—they'll tell you everything you want to know, and even some stuff you don't, as long as you read the nonsense they write about their lives."

"Look," Holly says over the discussion that erupts at the mention of Facebook. "My intention is not to—"

"I'll tell you what, young lady," Cap says as he walks back down the aisle toward the back door of the B&B. He pauses in the doorway of the dining room, the hand holding his flask stretched out in her direction. "Your intentions do not match up with my intentions on this one." Cap walks out of the room, leaving a stunned crowd in his wake.

In the silence that follows, Joe Sacamano stands from his seat. "Clearly our good friend Cap isn't feeling quite like himself today," Joe says, nodding at the NBC producers in apology. "And to you, my friends and neighbors, I think what you need to consider is that our young mayor always has the best interest of the island at heart. We might not know what we're in for with a reality show, but I think we can all agree that no one loves this place more than Holly, and that she wouldn't do anything to jeopardize Christmas Key."

"That's true," Maria Agnelli says loudly.

"I'll support that," comes a voice from the side of the room. Jake stands. "I know Holly well enough to know that if this is something she's willing to do, then there's a real benefit to the island to be had." He looks at Holly directly. "I'll support it."

"Thank you," she mouths to him over the voices in the crowd. She clears her throat and goes on. "Anyway, I'll be glad to entertain individual discussions, and to talk through your concerns with you. Just drop by my office or give me a call anytime." A bead of sweat runs down her back as she speaks, and the desire to wrap things up without further ado pushes her to close things out. "This adjourns the village council meeting for August twentieth. Thank you."

Without waiting for Heddie to finish writing, or for her neighbors to approach her with comment, Holly makes a beeline for the peace and quiet of her own office.

"What in the hell got into Cap?" Bonnie asks, following her into the office and dropping a stack of papers on her half of the desk. "That man is three sheets to the wind, and I've never seen him drink more than one beer on any given night."

"I have no idea," Holly says, putting her head in her hands. "But he could have picked a better time to turn into the town drunk."

"It's okay, honey. He's gone now and he'll probably go sleep it off at his place. We'll deal with him and his secret past later. Right now you need to put on some lipgloss and go visit with those television people."

Holly looks up at Bonnie forlornly. "I should have told everyone before NBC came out here, shouldn't I?"

"Oh, sugar..." Bonnie puts a hand on top of Holly's shiny brown hair and smooths it lovingly. "I think you're doing things the best way you know how. You've got some tough customers out there, but you've also got a lot of adventurous old-timers who don't mind going along for the ride. It'll work out."

Holly rubs her face with both hands. "Thanks, Bon. I guess we'd better finish showing our guests around. We've got dinner at the Jingle Bell and then drinks at Jack Frosty's, and I hope at least a few islanders will drop by to be friendly."

When they arrive at the bistro, Jimmy and Iris have everything set up on the patio overlooking the water. About twenty people are waiting outside, sipping Joe Sacamano's rum and talking excitedly about the possibility of a reality show coming to their island.

"Holly!" Gen calls, handing her drink to Gwen. "There's our girl!" Gen rushes over and pulls Holly into a tight embrace. "We're really proud of you," she says, holding Holly's face between her hands. "You're so gung-ho about this progress business. And what a wonderful opportunity this show could be!"

"Thank you. That means a lot." The tension Holly felt at the village council meeting melts a little. There are bound to be some islanders who don't love the idea of a reality show, but those who support her are mingling at the Jingle Bell Bistro, beaming at her and holding up glasses of rum in a toast. Holly takes the glass that Iris hands to her and raises it in the air before drinking.

Over a lobster boil and dessert, the crew from NBC gets to mingle with more than half of the locals. It's a good turnout. Holly sits back in her seat, pleased to see everyone laughing and talking with one another. She feels a pang of guilt as she watches her neighbors interacting with their visitors, knowing that she purposely left them in the dark about the reality show. But frankly, it had been easier to prepare without the naysayers banging on her office door while she tried to make the arrangements. Holly knows that some of her neighbors will think she was being secretive, and they don't like being left out of the decision-making process. But perhaps knowing that she's been going through a lot—with Coco wanting to sell the island, and finding out that Buckhunter is her uncle—will buy her some leeway.

Wayne Coates pulls out the chair next to hers and sits down, a glass of rum in one hand. "What a place you have here," he says, resting one ankle on his bare knee. He leans back and watches everyone. "I don't want you to worry too much about the people who aren't on board yet, okay? I think they'll come around."

Holly isn't sure that they will, but she gives Wayne a look that is all polite agreement.

"And if they don't, then we can work around them. It happens," he says, tapping the bottom of his rum glass on the table cloth and leaving a wet ring there. "Anyway, cheers to a great day." Wayne lifts his glass and Holly meets it with her own.

Whether or not they'll actually choose Christmas Key for the show is out of her control. She's done everything in her power to make a good impression, and even if the network goes a different direction in the end, having such high-powered guests here for a day has given her yet another chance to showcase the island and to practice whipping it into shape for guests.

Holly's phone buzzes on the table at her elbow. It's River. She covers the phone with one hand and excuses herself, wandering down the steps and onto the sand to take the call.

"So, how did it go?" he asks immediately. He sounds just as anxious as she'd felt when the helicopter landed earlier in the day.

Holly walks to the edge of the water. "Cap got drunk and made a scene at the village council meeting, and I forgot that I'd have to spill the beans about Coco wanting to sell the island in front of the people from NBC. But other than that, it went great. We're having dinner at the Jingle Bell right now."

"When will they decide?"

"Soon, I think. They have one other island to visit on this trip, so I guess we just wait and see."

"Sounds like it could be wrapped up here pretty soon," he says encouragingly. "I'm rooting for you guys. I mean it."

"Hey," she says softly, standing at the edge of the water as a wave washes over her ankles. "I wish you were still here. It's a beautiful night, and the water is still warm." Her heart jumps into her throat as she says the words, hoping that it's the right time to remind River where they left things.

"Yeah, me too," he says, his voice husky. "I'd love to see you in all your glory, showing off the island. Then I'd take you for a walk under the stars to celebrate."

They're both quiet. Holly looks up at the moon. They're on opposite sides of the country, but it might as well be opposite sides of the world.

"I should get back to the NBC crew. They're flying to Miami after dinner, so we need to wrap things up here." Holly turns toward the bistro, watching everyone on the patio from her spot at the water's edge. A string of Edison bulbs hangs from the railing around the patio, casting a soft light on the people gathered at the tables. "Can I call you later?"

"Mayor, *you* can call me any time."

Holly giggles. "Then I'll have my people call your people."

"And I'll make sure they put you right through."

"You do that, slugger."

34

"I'll be damned, but almost everyone I talk to seems to have come around, Holly Jean Baxter." Bonnie is out of breath and wearing her Hawaiian print sun visor over her red hair. She's joined Holly, Mrs. Agnelli, and the triplets for their weekly morning walk the following Thursday, and she spares no opportunity to remind them that this is a completely uncivilized thing to be doing at such an early hour.

"Oh?" Holly reaches down to pat Pucci as they power walk across the sand. She's trying not to get her hopes up about the reality show. It's been a week since the NBC producers visited and Wayne Coates still hasn't given her a definite answer yet.

"Yep. Everyone except Cap is acting like it might fun to have a camera around filming our ugly mugs as we go about our daily business."

"That was quite a scene Cap put on at the meeting," Gwen says. "I've never seen him like that."

"He's just worried that some of the ladies he's been avoiding will track him down and put the screws to him," Maria Agnelli says, pumping her arms furiously like she always does on their beach walks.

"For what?" Holly asks.

"Child support," Mrs. Agnelli says.

Bonnie hoots, slapping her thigh. "You don't say!"

"Oh, Mrs. Agnelli, I don't know about that. I don't think Cap's ever even had a girlfriend." Holly is mildly scandalized at the thought of Cap with scads of abandoned kids floating around out there.

"You never know. It could be that." Mrs. Agnelli makes a face.

"I think he was a pirate," Glen offers. "I'm pretty sure he's wanted for robbing yachts at gunpoint—"

"Sword point," Gen interjects, holding up a finger.

"Probably," Glen says.

"Come on, y'all. It's nothing like that," Bonnie insists. "Cap was never a pirate—he just likes to let people think he was. The real reason he doesn't want to be on camera can't be all that exciting. It's just Cap."

"Humph." Mrs. Agnelli watches Pucci in the distance as he chases after a tennis ball that Holly's thrown for him.

"It might not even matter," Holly reminds them. "I still haven't heard back from NBC. They could just as easily go a totally different direction and then none of us will end up on camera."

The women end their walk with coffee at Mistletoe Morning Brew, where Pucci lays on the pavement outside so he can watch the slow-moving traffic go by. Several islanders stop by the table to chat and ask Holly if she's heard anything about *Wild Tropics,* and she promises to spread the word as soon as it comes her way.

"Hey, sugar," Bonnie says that afternoon as they fill out an estimate for the wedding party that includes lodging, flowers, a catered dinner, cake, an open bar, decorations on the beach, and Joe Sacamano playing his guitar at the reception. They're listening to Garth Brooks on the CD player (Bonnie's choice), and both women have kicked off their shoes.

"Yeah?" Holly doesn't look up from the form she's filling out.

"Might wanna check your email." Bonnie tosses a dog biscuit at Pucci.

Holly tosses her sharpened pencil onto a pile of printer paper on the corner of her desk. She clicks on her inbox: *mail from Wayne Coates.* Holly squeals, stamping her bare feet on the rough sisal rug under her desk chair. "Oh my God, Bon—this is it. I'm scared to open it."

"We're going to be living in suspense forever if you don't. Just read it."

Holly,

Super excited to extend the offer to you...we'd really like to come to Christmas Key this fall and film Wild Tropics. *Your island is the perfect backdrop for the show, and we're looking forward to working with all of the locals. Please let me know at your earliest convenience if you're still on board and we'll start talking details.*

Best,

Wayne

This is it. Opportunity. Visibility. Tourism. Salvation. Holly isn't even sure who she wants to call first. Definitely not Coco. She'll talk to River later that night to share the good news. Jake can hear about it right along with everyone else. She hurries over to Pucci's dog bed to find the flip-flops that she kicked off there, and grabs her Yankees hat from the hook by the door.

It's only as she's nearly sprinting down Main Street that she realizes where her legs are taking her: to Jack Frosty's, because the first person she wants to tell is Buckhunter.

35

THE WAY IT'S MAPPED OUT NOW, THE CREW WILL ARRIVE ON Halloween, and they'll prep for a week before the reality show competitors arrive. Shooting will go on right up until Christmas, and then they'll clear out to do their editing and behind-the-scenes work, with a window in early February to come back and do any re-shoots they might need. Holly's already informally calculated the possible revenue the island might see from the show, from the chunk of cash that the network is paying for their time at the B&B, to the meals and incidentals that the crew will need to pay for during their stay. And that doesn't even take into consideration the long-term positive exposure the island will get. Even if her neighbors don't fully see the whole picture when it comes to *Wild Tropics*, Holly does. And she likes what she sees.

As it turns out, most of the islanders are willing to humor Holly on this one—and several are even excited about their star turns in a major network production. It's been fun hearing everyone talk about how their friends and family off the island will get to see them on national television, and it's been good to have help as Holly starts planning the things they'll need to do to get the island looking sharp for the show. Bonnie likes to joke that Mrs. Agnelli is ready to give the reality show competitors a run for their money in an effort to get camera time, and Holly isn't sure that she's wrong.

Joe Sacamano is having a jam session at the Ho Ho that Saturday evening, and from her lanai, Holly can see the headlamps of golf carts as they pass by her property in the darkness on their way to the bar. She told Bonnie and Fiona that she wasn't sure she was up for a night out, but it's really because she doesn't feel like squaring off with Cap again in public. She's been chasing her tail for days wondering what he could possibly have in his past that would make him so violently opposed to the reality show, but she's come up with nothing. His drunken dressing-down at the meeting had humiliated her, sure, but more than that it left her wondering who he really was. The funny, jovial, faux-pirate she's known all her life feels like a totally different person from this new Cap, and he'd lashed out at her as a reminder that spending a few years off the island as a college student didn't amount to a real-world education. She got his message loud and clear, and now there's been nothing but radio silence from him since the village council meeting.

Holly is sitting on her lanai, lights off, a sweaty glass of iced tea at her elbow. She runs her finger through the little pool of water it leaves on her glass table top, scooting the iced tea to the side. In the distance, the music from the Ho Ho fills the night air, the sound of laughter rolling down the beach like waves. No doubt Joe is mixing drinks with his special Christmas Key rum, her neighbors loosening up as the sultry summer night settles in around them. It feels strange to be purposely avoiding a gathering of the people she's always seen as her family. Holly picks up the glass and sips her watered-down tea.

With the island prospectus on her nightstand, she's been falling asleep at night with her grandfather's words echoing in her head: *From far and wide come people who want to share in this paradise. With them, they bring their histories, their passions, their gifts. They also bring agendas and desires that may or may not align with your own. Find ways to harness what works with your vision for development, and ignore what doesn't. You have no other choice.*

The screen of her phone lights up in the dark as a message appears.

Did you get the package?

It's River. She frowns at the phone.

No...what package?

I sent you something in the mail last week. I was sure you'd have it by now. You got big Saturday night plans?

No big plans tonight. Just sitting on my lanai. How about you?

Ahh, the lanai. I have fond memories of the lanai. I've got nothing tonight. I bet you could scare up a drink at the Ho Ho or something...

You're right, she responds. *I can and I probably should. I did get an invite...okay, you convinced me—I'll go. Can I text you tomorrow?*

Absolutely. Have fun.

Holly carries her glass into the kitchen. She has a Coldplay CD on the stereo, and Pucci is sprawled out on his side on the cool tile floor, his eyes shut as Holly steps over his body.

"Hey, Pooch," she says, tickling his golden fur with her toes. "What are you doing there, old man?" Pucci opens one eye lazily, glances at her, shuts it again. Holly's canvas bag is on the couch where she left it when she got home from the B&B the day before. She'd hurriedly stuffed a few things from her desk into the bag—including her mail—and headed home for a Friday night jog on the beach to clear her head.

"Pooch, I totally forgot about my mail," she says, running a hand over his silky ear. "I've been a little preoccupied, don't you think?" Pucci opens his eye again and stares at her in silent confirmation. He's spent so much time on Buckhunter's porch lately that she feels like she's sharing custody of her dog. "I'm sorry I've been so busy, dude," she says soothingly.

Holly turns her bag upside down and dumps out the contents on the overstuffed, canvas-covered couch. Bills from various vendors flutter onto the rug under her feet, and a thick packet from her lawyer lands on her bare knee. She'll deal with that later. At the bottom of the bag is a lumpy manila envelope with her name and address written in block letters; it falls on the coffee table, nearly knocking over a fat candle in a hurricane lamp. There it is: the package from River.

She stares at the words he's written with a blue Sharpie pen. It makes her happy to think that just days before, he'd bent over this same envelope and carefully addressed it to her. She rips into the package, pulling out a folded note.

For you, Mayor. A small gift that I hope you will take with humor, and wear with love—now that you know we're not really sworn enemies. —R.

She puts her hand into the envelope, already knowing what she'll find. Sure enough, she slides a perfectly-worn Mets cap from the package. A goofy smile spreads across her face. Fastened to the bill of the hat with a paperclip is a picture of a younger River in the same cap, squinting into the sun in full uniform as he poses on a baseball field, ball in one hand, the other hand hidden inside a battered mitt.

Holly runs her fingers over the intertwined "NY" embroidered on its front. It's a meaningful gift in so many ways. Obviously it's something special to River, and his giving it to her symbolizes a letting go of the past—and shows her that he's truly inviting her in. And her accepting it is a sign that she, too, is ready to say good-bye to some long-held truths, to finally embrace a future that isn't rooted in the security she's always believed that it would be. Holly puts her fist inside the hat, unfolding it so that it's head-shaped.

With the Mets cap in one hand, she steps over Pucci again and grabs her oversized purse from the counter. She digs out her Yankees hat and holds them side-by-side. Past and future. Certainty and the unknown. Security and adventure. With a deep breath, she walks over to her bookshelf and stands before a framed photo of her grandparents. It was taken on the porch of the Jingle Bell Bistro. Behind them is the ocean, stretching out to meet the horizon. On either side of their smiling faces are the pillars of the building, wrapped from deck to roof in twinkling strands of holiday lights, even though the photo was taken one year in June, just after her grandma's birthday. She stares at them, thinking of all that she knew and loved about them, and all that she thought she knew but really didn't.

Looking at the hats in her hands one more time, she sets her

Yankees cap on the shelf next to the photograph. She finds her own reflection in the glass of the picture frame as she set the Mets cap on her head, adjusting the brim so that it comes down just over her eyebrows. Her long, light brown hair spills over both shoulders.

Chris Martin wails in the background as Coldplay's *Parachutes* spins over the laser in her cd player. She moves away from her reflection until her grandparents' faces come back into focus, her own image a blur in the glass once again.

"Hey, Pooch—wanna go to the Ho Ho?" she calls. In an instant, Pucci is up on all four paws, ears at full attention. Holly slips her feet into a pair of flip-flops and runs a tube of Chapstick over her lips. "Let's do this."

She isn't sure whether she and Jake will ever find a happy place where they can coexist on the island, and she has no idea whether the three thousand miles between them will snuff out the flame between her and River. She doesn't know whether *Wild Tropics* will bring excitement and opportunity to Christmas Key, or the unflinching gaze of a faceless audience who might judge the island without ever setting foot there. The future itself is somewhat uncertain. Will all of her efforts to turn the island into a self-sustaining travel destination come to fruition, or will she just end up alienating everyone in the process? It feels kind of like going off the grid without a map, and for the first time in her life, that thought isn't completely terrifying.

For now, she's choosing adventure, she's choosing possibility. For now, she's choosing a shot of Joe's Christmas Key rum and a night of live music with her neighbors, and she'll worry about Cap if and when she sees him.

Holly pulls the brim of the hat down further on her brow, getting used to the feel of it. She whistles once for Pucci, but he's already at her heels. In the darkness, she crunches over rocks and shells as she seeks the light of the moon. The sound of Coldplay fills the bright house behind her, and the creaking of the night creatures surrounds her as she makes her way to the bar.

· · ·

YOU JUST FINISHED BOOK ONE OF THE CHRISTMAS KEY SERIES! FIND OUT WHAT HAPPENS NEXT ON THE ISLAND IN BOOK TWO, *WILD TROPICS!*

READY FOR THE NEXT BOOK IN THE CHRISTMAS KEY SERIES?

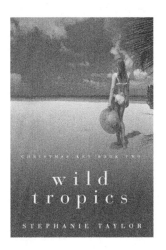

With the crew of 'Wild Tropics' arriving to film their reality show, Holly Baxter has her hands full and not everyone is thrilled to have cameras on Christmas Key. Before she knows it, Holly is defending her choices for progress and development in front of the whole island...

ABOUT THE AUTHOR

Stephanie Taylor is a high-school teacher who loves sushi, "The Golden Girls," Depeche Mode, orchids, and coffee. Together with her teenage daughter she writes the *American Dream* series—books for young girls about other young girls who move to America. On her own, Stephanie is the author of the *Christmas Key* books, a romantic comedy series about a fictional island off the coast of Florida.

https://redbirdsandrabbits.com
redbirdsandrabbits@gmail.com

ALSO BY STEPHANIE TAYLOR

To see a complete list of the Christmas Key series along with all of Stephanie's other books, please visit:

Stephanie Taylor's Books

To hear about any new releases, sign up here and you'll be the first to know!